The Birth

Sarah Ward is a critically acc_____ ___ ___ g___
thriller writer. Her book, *A Patient Fury*, was an Observer
book of the month and *The Quickening*, written as
Rhiannon Ward, was a Radio Times book of the year.
Sarah is on the Board of the Crime Writers Association,
Derby Book Festival and Friends of Buxton International
Festival. She is an RLF Fellow at Sheffield University.

THE
BIRTHDAY
GIRL

SARAH WARD

CANELO CRIME

First published in the United Kingdom in 2023 by

Canelo
Unit 9, 5th Floor
Cargo Works, 1–2 Hatfields
London SE1 9PG
United Kingdom

A CIP catalogue record for this book is available from the British Library.

Print ISBN 978 1 80436 316 4
Ebook ISBN 978 1 80436 315 7

This book is a work of fiction. Names, characters, businesses, organizations, places and events are either the product of the author's imagination or are used fictitiously. Any resemblance to actual persons, living or dead, events or locales is entirely coincidental.

Cover design by Andrew Davis

Cover images © Trevillion, Unsplash

Look for more great books at www.canelo.co

Printed and bound in Great Britain by Clays Ltd, Elcograf S.p.A.

1

For Gareth Evans

THE CLOISTER HOTEL

GUEST LIST

Room 1

Scott Gregory
Beth Gregory
Edith Gregory (minor)

Room 2

(empty)

Room 3

Noah Vass
Charlotte Vass

Room 4

(empty)

Room 5

Michael Hutton

Room 6

(empty)

PROLOGUE

BRYONY: THE BIRTHDAY GIRL

September was a perfect month for dying. The drop of parched leaves from the sycamore outside Bryony's kitchen window matched the shrivelling of her heart. Circumstance had made her choose this time of year. There was a limited window for getting everyone together and now was the time to act. While the last drama had taken place in the July heat, this time she would revel in the autumn sting. Already, plans were falling into place. Invites accepted and bait taken.

She checked for the final time that she had everything for the poisonings. Her luggage was already stuffed to bursting and she'd had to repack it once to fit everything in. She'd divided the carefully prepared potions between her shoulder bag and case. She was paranoid that one of her belongings might get lost on the island boat, which looked worryingly primitive. Once she was on Eldey, the opportunities for replacing her supplies would be limited so she was hedging her bets. If one piece of luggage went missing, she'd have reserves as backup.

She'd spent the previous week scrutinising her doses. It was vitally important that her calculations were as accurate as possible. A single error, where the drug failed to work its warped magic, would throw everything into disarray.

Concoctions would need to be made on Eldey, but that could only happen if she had the right ingredients. There was just one chance for her to target each of her victims, although she might have a little fun too. That was what she'd really missed. The enjoyment of being at the centre of things. She was now desperate to get to the island, eager to initiate the plan that had been fermenting in her mind for a very long time. The years of incarceration culminating in this.

She was going to Eldey, the magical island of saints and sinners, if the stories were to be believed. The place that had captured her imagination as a child. Eldey, in her beloved Wales that had induced a desperate yearning while she'd languished in the secure centre. Eldey, where she would finally get her revenge.

As soon as Mallory saw Eldey, she knew she wanted the job. After an early start and a wearying train journey from London, she was finally in the open air, a persistent breeze tugging at her hair. It had taken her a moment to get her bearings. The harbour at Tenby was busy with fishing boats bringing in their haul and lines of people waiting for pleasure cruisers offering trips around the bay. The town was considered the jewel in Pembrokeshire's crown and Mallory could see why. Georgian buildings painted in primary colours overlooked the bay and the place gave off an air of cheery affluence.

The summer season was finishing and she'd struggled to find a boat that would take her across to the Cloister Hotel. Finally, a man in his fifties, his face lined from the sun, said he'd make the trip although he wasn't supposed to be going for another half an hour. Mallory stood on the harbour wall gazing across the water while the skipper fussed with his boat. Eldey, undulating from jagged cliffs to dipping coves, rose from the waves, which gave it a faintly mystical air.

She'd researched the Cloister before her interview, of course, but the website had focused on the comforts contained within the walls of the former convent. A lavender sauna, hot tub and long narrow pool in the spa suite, luxurious bedrooms, and Michelin-standard meals.

The text was aimed at attracting the wealthy and respectable to Eldey. Here, however, Mallory could see the sweep of the island in its forbidding beauty. Beside the big house, there were a cluster of smaller buildings encircled by trees to provide shelter from the weather. Outside this enclosure, visitors would be confronted with an expanse of nothingness punctuated by stunted trees. It was only at the other point of the island that a smaller, squat building stood. The former chapel, perhaps.

In response to a gesture from the tugboat's captain, Mallory moved forward. She stepped onboard the boat, wrinkling her nose as diesel fumes pumped into the cold air, and felt the swell beneath her feet.

'You staying at the Cloister?' The weather-beaten man who was to be her pilot was looking at her rucksack. Not the usual luggage for the hotel's guests, she assumed.

'Yes, but not as a guest. I have a job interview.'

'Ah, the new night manager. You're the third I've carried over today.'

'Really?' Mallory's mood sank. 'I hadn't realised there would be many applicants.'

'Don't worry about any of them. The first one I brought back told me he wouldn't fancy being stuck on the island after dark. A hard man he was, too, looked like a bouncer. But the island does that to some people. The legend around here is the island likes to choose its guests.'

It must be busy with a hotel, she thought, enjoying the man's words. Mallory had to wait a moment as he steered the boat from the shore before they began chugging towards their destination.

'And the other applicant?' Mallory asked, when they were in deeper water.

'A woman like you. I can't see Alex, the new owner, going for her.' The pilot was in his element. 'High maintenance. She asked me if the town had a John Lewis.' The man gave a throaty laugh.

'If it's a boutique hotel, maybe it's high maintenance that Alex is looking for.'

'Take it from me, it's not. Alex has got a good reputation around here. He employs locals, pays them a fair wage and he's an eye for a solid worker. You're as good a prospect as any and, anyway, the island wants you.'

'What do you mean?' asked Mallory.

'The swell's gone down, can't you tell? There was a wind blowing when you arrived. The sea's making sure you're being delivered safe and sound to your interview.'

Deciding to humour him, Mallory went along with it. 'A good omen then. I'm a shoe-in.'

'You will be if you can hide that gammy leg.'

Mallory swore under her breath. 'Is it that obvious?' She'd spent the previous week practising to walk without her cane. She thought she'd made good progress but there was clearly still improvement to be made. If this boatman had noticed it then it would be difficult to hide her injury from a potential employer. Damn.

'Obvious to me and, as I said, there's no flies on Alex either. Tell him the truth. It's usually the best way.'

The pilot turned and winked at her. It was at that moment Mallory got her first close-up view of the Cloister. The boat motored around the headland and suddenly the hotel was above them looking less like a former convent than a conventional family home. The building wasn't white as she'd initially thought but rendered in a pale grey shade, giving the 1920s building a more contemporary look. The most distinctive aspect of the house was its roof, the lime green tiles giving the place a jaunty air.

'Interesting roof,' shouted Mallory.

'Us locals call it Greentiles and I think the sisters who lived here called it that too amongst themselves. Naming it the Cloister was Alex's idea.'

Greentiles was a good name, although again it reinforced the building's suburban air. The Cloister would definitely attract more guests. In fact, the only clue to the house's former use was a small bell tower perched on the edge of the cliff, the type you might find at a medieval monastery. Through the screech of the seagulls, Mallory watched fascinated as the bell swung in the wind.

'I can't hear it ringing,' she shouted.

'They've stoppered it. It'll still ring if someone had a mind to have a go. You just need to know how to release the catch. In the old days, we could hear it all over Tenby. Now, it's to be used only for emergencies and even then, the telephone is more reliable.'

'Is there a satellite connection?'

The boatman nodded to the sea. 'Underwater cable. You won't get no mobile signal on Eldey.'

Mallory nodded, staring transfixed at the bell tower as they passed under it. The old chapel must be nearby. It made no sense having a bell tower if the call to worship was at the other end of the island.

'What's the building to the far west?' Mallory asked. 'I could see it from the mainland.'

The skipper kept his eyes in front of him. 'It's the mausoleum, although some call it the crypt, which is the wrong word. Crypts are underground, but the ground's too rocky for burials. They had to find somewhere to put the dead nuns.'

Mallory pulled her jacket tighter. 'Right. Do the tourists go there?'

'Some do. It's more popular than you'd think, but the actual vault is obviously kept sealed. Anyway—' he turned to look at her again '—don't worry about that. As I said, the island likes you.'

He steered the boat towards a concrete landing stage built with skill on an outcrop of rocks. As she gathered her rucksack, Mallory spotted her first obstacle. The path to the hotel had been chiselled into the cliff face and a sign at the base warned that many of the steps were uneven. A railing had been installed to ensure the safety of those going up and down but it would still be a tiring climb. A short queue of day-trippers was waiting to take the boat back and even the thought of pushing past them to begin her ascent was exhausting. The boatman noticed her indecision.

'Take that road there.' He pointed to a wide path snaking down the hill, its route disappearing into rocky boulders near the harbour. 'The entrance is behind the white gate. It's not locked. There's a cart to ferry passengers and their luggage to the hotel. You won't be wanting to use that. Not a good first impression, but the climb's gentler on the path.'

Mallory followed the man's gaze. It was a strange place to put a tall ornate gate that wouldn't look out of place in a London street. The convent would have needed an access road to ferry provisions from the boats, but why install a gate at the bottom? Aware her leg was throbbing after the battering she'd given it, first in the confined seats on the harbour train and then on the boat, Mallory regarded the steep steps and nodded. If challenged by

Alex, she'd say she wanted to see the approach to the hotel. It's what any decent security guard would do.

'Thanks, um…'

'It's Owen. Everyone knows me around here. Ta-ra.'

Pushing open the gate, Mallory began the climb to the top of the cliff. Owen, she saw, wasn't wasting much time as he signalled for the queue of people to get onto the boat. There was an air of jollity about the crowd, sand-covered children screaming in delight as adults marshalled them onto the tug. A couple of the kids were holding ice-creams so there must be a shop nearby. Mallory thought of Toby, her son, at that age before it had all gone wrong with her and Joe. He'd been a cheerful child, tow haired with a perpetual smile. Where had that boy disappeared to?

She turned her back to the crowd, the memories too painful, and concentrated on her surroundings. All she could see of the hotel building was the green roof. Most of the façade was obscured by trees designed to give residents protection from the wind and sea. As she climbed higher, the hotel dipped in and out of view. It gave off an air of enclosure and self-sufficiency, from the shuttered windows designed to keep out the roar of the sea to the well-ordered beds planted with herbs rather than flowers.

At the top of the path was an ice-cream booth, a small cabin painted in blue and white stripes. It sold milkshakes and hot drinks, probably the only source of food unless you ate in the hotel restaurant. Mallory checked her watch and saw she was a little early. She ignored the hotel. She'd surely be shown around the building as part of the interview, and she wanted to see what else the island had to offer. Opposite the entrance to the former cloister was a gift shop. A quick browse in the window made Mallory wince at the prices. The gifts weren't aimed at the day-tripper but the wealthy hotel residents who were after locally made leather handbags or artisan silver jewellery.

Ignoring the spasms of pain radiating from her leg, Mallory ploughed on. It wasn't a large place – just the hotel, a gift shop, some outbuildings with large barn doors and a wooden lodge. The building caught her attention. She peered through the window, taking in the empty room with its mismatched fittings. As she leant in closer, she started as she caught sight of a face in the glass's reflection. She spun around and came face to face with a woman of around fifty, her grey hair scraped back into a bun.

'Mallory Dawson?'

'How did you guess?' Mallory kept her tone light, aware of the thumping of her heart.

The woman looked over her shoulder, as jumpy as Mallory. 'Owen's called from the boat to say you'd arrived. Sorry, but everyone knows everyone's business here. I came out to look for you. *Croeso.* Welcome to Eldey.'

Mallory picked up her rucksack. 'You're…'

'Alys. I live on site so, if you get the job, you'll be seeing plenty of me.' Alys looked again behind her.

'Is anything the matter?' asked Mallory.

Alys frowned, smoothing down her dress. 'Not at all. Why do you ask?'

Mallory shrugged. Once a cop, you get to read the signs. Alys was worried and not doing a very good job of hiding it.

'Do you want to come with me?'

The woman would have made a good nun, thought Mallory as she followed her across the lawn. Small and compact, she gave an air of competence despite her anxiety. Perhaps it was the recruitment process. A new member of staff could make all the difference in a small place like this.

Mallory, finding the silence oppressive, cast around for something to say. 'Fingers crossed I make a good impression. I heard from the boatman he brought two other candidates today.'

Alys frowned. 'Trust Owen to be indiscreet. I don't think either is who Alex is looking for. You look more like it. Respectable but tough.'

'I'll take that as a compliment.'

'You do that. It was meant as one.'

'You need a night manager, then?'

They were both distracted for a moment by the sound of a child crying, its mother was trying to hush it by jiggling it up and down. Alys frowned at the interruption. 'Why do people bring such small children to the island? There's nothing here for them. But yes, to answer your question, we do need another manager, preferably someone with a bit of experience with difficult people. We had trouble last week. A stressed male guest decided he was going to take over the old housekeeper's lodge, the one you were looking at, and live here permanently. Never mind the place isn't for rent.'

'Did it turn nasty?'

'Alex called the police in the end so it was fine but he'd rather concentrate on welcoming the residents than dealing with a guest petrified at having to return to work the next day.' The woman stopped. 'You ever dealt with difficult people?'

Mallory thought of the violent felons she'd dealt with over the years. 'Oh yes. I've got the scars to prove it.'

'Excellent,' said Alys. 'Excellent.'

2

The interior of the hotel took Mallory's breath away. The architect had combined the luxury of an upmarket city hotel with a simplicity of design echoing the building's former use. Mallory had already checked the price of a night's stay. Cheaper than a central London hotel but only just. People would want more than a place with an interesting history for that kind of money. The lobby would be guests' first impression of the hotel. Pale oak-framed armchairs overstuffed for comfort sat around glass-topped tables. There were flowers everywhere – Alex had eschewed orchids and lilies for more rustic hollyhocks and alliums – and Mallory could see why the place had been the darling of fashion magazines when it had first opened.

'Alex is a little tied up. Would you like me to show you around the hotel while you're waiting?' Alys flicked her eyes towards a woman wearing round orange glasses who was tapping the reception desk with a pen.

'Don't worry. See to the guest. I'll have a wander around the ground floor.'

'Great.' Alys made an effort to relax. 'I'll find you as soon as Alex is ready. It won't be long.'

Mallory pushed open the door to the room adjoining the lobby. Linen-topped tables were laid for dinner and Mallory saw each held a vase of fresh flowers, echoing the theme in the lobby. The blooms must be brought fresh over from Tenby each day – a nice touch but hugely expensive. To the right, away from the diners, was a set of double doors, presumably leading to the kitchen. In the distance, she could hear a radio playing Beyoncé. Alex might be a strict taskmaster, but the music suggested he was happy to let his staff get on with the job.

A small, pale-green sitting room further along the corridor offered more clues to Alex's taste. One wall was covered in books and not the buy-by-the-weight titles usually displayed in hotels. A selection of contemporary novels sat alongside political biographies and books on Welsh history. The wall opposite the window was dominated by a picture frame, its heavy mahogany wood in contrast to the Nordic-style restraint of the rest of the decor.

Mallory crossed to the photograph and saw it featured a group of twelve women, all in religious dress. It was difficult to date the picture from the women's clothes but, if the house had been built in the 1920s for the first of the sisters, then this must have been a decade or so later. Most of the women were in their thirties and Greentiles, looming behind the group, had a weathered, lived-in look. Mallory leant forward and tried to decipher the expression on the women's faces but each face presented a unified look to the world.

'Interesting, aren't they?'

A woman with flame-coloured hair was standing at the entrance, her arms resting on each doorpost.

Mallory stepped back. 'They are. I wonder what it must have been like for them living here, cut off from the rest of the world.'

The woman crossed to stand next to Mallory, who was enveloped in the scent of gardenia perfume. 'This place was luxurious even then. The order's founder, Margaret Taylor, liked her comforts, which she saw no reason to give up when she entered holy orders.' The woman paused. 'They were all her friends, you know?'

Mallory turned. 'You mean the nuns?'

'Exactly. She recruited from within her social circle for the Companions of the Good Shepherd. Don't forget it was 1922 when the order was founded. For some women after the losses of the First World War, spinsterhood was guaranteed.'

'Which is why they all look the same age.'

'Exactly, although there was about ten years' difference between the oldest and youngest sister. Still, the same generation.'

'You work here?' Mallory wondered if she should mention she was here for an interview.

'Goodness, no. I'm a guest but, as I've booked in for a whole month, I've kind of immersed myself in the island's history. It's interesting.' She stuck out her hand. 'I'm Mona Rubin.'

Mallory grasped the woman's cool fingers. 'Mallory Dawson. Is there enough here to occupy you for that long?'

'No, which is why I chose the hotel. I'm an illustrator with a commission to complete. I needed a place I could be completely within my head and I discovered here. I've only been here a week, but I can see I've made the right choice.'

'You paint in your room?'

'Why not? The hotel doesn't have a problem with it and, besides, it's only watercolours. I'm not making a mess.'

Mallory smiled. 'I hope all the guests are as well-behaved as you. I'm here for a job interview.'

'How wonderful. I'm almost jealous. Fancy getting to stay here permanently.'

'It's just until Christmas when the hotel closes.'

'I'm still jealous. There is the most wonderful flora and fauna on the island.' A shadow crossed the woman's face.

'You're interested in nature?'

Mallory felt Mona withdraw at the innocuous question. 'No more than the ordinary person.'

'Anywhere else I should see while I'm here for the interview?'

Mona shrugged. Mallory saw she was wearing a green dress chosen to complement her deep red hair. On one side of the bodice, she'd pinned a small amber brooch that looked expensive. 'It's a small hotel. There's a little spa suite with a sauna, hot tub, and pool. All exquisitely done.'

'I'll take a look.'

'There's also a gift shop outside and the mausoleum at the other end of the island if you like that sort of thing. You get plenty of goths coming over just to pose at the door of the crypt. It's an interesting building, though. Definitely worth taking a look.'

'Some other time, perhaps.' They both turned at the sound of a male voice. In the doorway, stood a man in his forties wearing a suit that could only have come from a Savile Row tailor. He gave Mallory the once over and she straightened, making sure her painful leg was firmly on the floor.

'I'm Alex.' Unlike Mona, he didn't hold out his hand. 'It's Mallory, isn't it? I see our guest is keeping you abreast of the island's history.'

Mona kept her smile but Mallory picked up an undercurrent of tension between the pair. Perhaps Mona didn't like her immaculately dressed host.

'It's a fascinating place. I can't wait to hear more about the Cloister.'

Mollified, Alex nodded and inclined his head towards the door. 'Let's go, shall we?'

3

CHARLOTTE

The island was already testing her resolve. Charlotte watched as Noah threw the brass key into the crystal bowl on the mirror-topped table. Like everything else in the hotel, the ornament looked expensive and new. It'd be chipped before the weekend was out if Noah continued to treat it with the same disdain he showed towards anything he hadn't paid for. He was in a filthy mood. She made sure her face was expressionless as she dropped her bag onto the bed.

'You're not going to leave me here alone, are you?'

Noah froze. 'What the hell does that mean?'

Charlotte experienced the exquisite thrill of fear which always accompanied her interactions with her husband. She swallowed, determined that this man, after everything, wouldn't cower her. 'It's been a long day getting here. I've asked room service to bring up a bottle of fizz to have before dinner. I thought we could spend some time together before we eat.'

'I won't have time for that. I've a few calls to make. I'll use one of the downstairs rooms so I don't disturb you and then I'll have a sauna.'

Charlotte felt her mood turn sour. On the long drive from London, he'd disappeared to make a call out of

16

earshot when they'd stopped at the service station, which meant only one thing: he was playing around, and not for the first time either. The thought was infuriating, especially as she was stuck in this place with her stepdaughter. She'd be playing happy families while he continued his intrigues and secrets. Well, two could play that game. As Noah vanished into the bathroom, she opened her handbag and moved its contents to the bedside drawer. A knock on the door made her jump. Shit, she was jittery. It was room service with the prosecco she'd planned to share with Noah. After tipping the girl, she opened the bottle and poured some of the liquid into a flute glass, listening to the sound of the shower coming from their en-suite. Noah emerged from the steam with a towel wrapped around his waist.

'Do you want me to check on Julia while you're making your calls?'

He frowned. 'Let her be. You know what teenagers are like. She'll be in a filthy mood at dinner if you get on the wrong side of her.'

'Suits me.' Charlotte took a sip of the fizz and turned away as her husband rummaged around in his case. He'd initially sold this trip to her as a romantic getaway but she'd suspected the presence of Julia had always been on the cards. Trouble at school, which was nothing new but the older her stepdaughter grew, the greater the problems. Soon, Charlotte suspected, there would be no school to return to. 'I think I'll have a wander around the shops.'

Noah was in his underwear, pulling a new t-shirt from the top of his case. 'Use the joint credit card, won't you? I'd like to see what you're spending. I don't like surprises.'

Charlotte froze, but as Noah had his back to her, she couldn't read his expression. 'Of course,' she said lightly, looking at the bottle of prosecco. She'd like to smash it over his head. Didn't like surprises, did he? That, really, was a terrible shame.

4

'What would you do if reception informed you one of the guests was attempting to leave without paying?'

Mallory frowned and looked down at her jeans. She'd had plenty of excruciating interviews over the years, but this was the dumbest question yet and an indication of the type of job she'd be taking on. She'd be paid to stop guests pilfering from their hotel room, advise them against swimming in the sea after drinking alcohol and to keep an eye out for disgruntled employees. The day-trippers weren't the hotel's responsibility because the family of Margaret Taylor still owned the island. Alex had bought the former convent and its buildings. The gift shop belonged to the hotel but not the ice-cream booth. Mallory would be working evening shifts, seven in the evening until one a.m. followed by a two-hour break when she would still be on call, and then three a.m. until seven when Alys would take over reception to check out guests. She was unlikely to get the hooligans as you'd expect in other security jobs. The hotel didn't take group bookings. Maximum four to a party and no hen or stag dos. It sounded easy enough. She caught Alex's eye and saw he was waiting for an answer.

'I'd suggest to them they'd accidentally forgotten to pay and perhaps they'd like to make their way to reception. In the meantime, I'd radio the boat at the harbour and ask them to delay a few minutes until payment had gone through. Just in case.'

Mallory could see Alex hadn't thought of doing that. He smiled, his mouth a thin line.

'In any case, we have their credit card details with the charge pre-authorised.'

'Then no need to get the boat involved,' Mallory conceded, which won her another narrow smile.

From the window, she could see the sea, which had taken on a darker hue. The changing colour of the water fascinated her, as did the boom of the waves hitting the cliff beneath them. You could spend all day just watching and listening to the sea, which was perhaps what the city escapees who booked rooms at the Cloister did.

Alex put down the paper he'd been reading his questions from and regarded her. It gave Mallory a moment of fleeting panic. On cue, her leg wound began to seep through her jeans. She'd worn black on purpose, of course. The utilitarian clothing and dark colours were what any boss would expect from a security guard, and she'd done a pretty good job of hiding her limp as Alex had shown her around the resort.

'I appreciate this job is below what you're capable of.'

She forced a smile. 'As you know from my CV, I've now left the police. While I readjust to civilian life, I think the Cloister is the perfect place to consider my next steps in my career.'

Alex nodded. It was a good ploy on Mallory's part, one she'd rehearsed on the boat coming over to the island. If the hotel was drawing clientele by advertising itself as a place for reflection, then she would appeal to its unique selling point.

'What exactly happened? You mention in your application that you were injured in the course of your work.'

The image of her assailant's knife ripping through her thigh flashed into Mallory's head. 'I was with my partner, Shen, returning a former prisoner back to jail for breaching his licence conditions. He attacked me with a knife and I sustained damage to my leg and shoulder.'

Again, the memory of lying on the pavement while the paramedic performed CPR came back to haunt her. Ever since the incident, she'd sought to downplay her injuries, first to the occupational health consultant and then to her bosses. Feeling Alex's eyes on her, she forced a smile.

'And you're able to undertake the duties I've set out for you?'

'Of course,' said Mallory, ignoring the spasm in her leg.

'OK. Well, I see you have a medical statement saying you're fit to work. There's the issue of accommodation,' said Alex, massaging his forehead. 'There are three rooms set aside for live-in staff at the back of the building. Most of our employees, however, are local and come over by boat each day. I can let you have one of those rooms.'

'What about the lodge I saw earlier? Alys mentioned a guest had wanted to rent it. Would it be suitable for me to use?'

He screwed his eyes in incomprehension. 'Lodge? Oh, I see what you mean. I call it the cabin. Lodge is a little grand sounding until we get it renovated. Won't you need to be onsite in case of an emergency?'

'It's a five-minute walk at most. I'd expect to be working with a two-way radio anyway. The thing is, if you're looking for a night manager, the lodge will be somewhere quiet to sleep in the day. It doesn't stop me being contacted if any problems arise.'

She saw Alex consider the proposal. 'The island is hardly noisy, but I take your point. Perhaps you'd like to take a look first. It's a little spartan. There's no smoking in there or anywhere on the island. Do you have a problem with that?'

'Not at all,' said Mallory.

The phone rang and she saw him frown. 'I'm sorry, I need to deal with this.' He swung round to open the door of his small office. 'Alys, can someone show Mallory inside the cabin?'

'I'm not sure there's anyone here who's free,' said Alys, standing with a phone in her hand.

'I can show her if you like.' A thin girl with pale hair was pulling on a puffa jacket that was slightly too large for her.

Mallory rose, wincing as she put pressure on her leg.

'You sure you've got the time, Elsa *fach*?' Alys's eyebrows were raised in surprise. 'I know it's time for you to go, the boat leaves in five minutes.'

'I'll give you an extra hour overtime,' shouted Alex, and pushed the door shut.

The girl looked across at Mallory, her eyes huge pools of brown under the hood. 'I'll take you to the cabin.'

'And you're...?'

'Elsa. I'm one of the room attendants. I've just finished my shift but I don't mind showing you round.'

'You clean the hotel?' asked Mallory.

Elsa zipped up her coat. 'Basically, yes, although Alex often asks me to help out in other areas.'

'You like it?'

'It's OK.'

Alys went into the room behind reception and emerged with a key, which she handed to Mallory, not Elsa. 'Make sure you lock up after you.'

'So you don't live on the island?' asked Mallory as Elsa led her across the lawn.

'Oh no, my mam wouldn't let me do that. She likes me back home at night.'

'Who exactly lives in?' asked Mallory. 'I forgot to ask.'

'Just Alex, Alys on reception and Tom the chef. The rest of us live on the mainland and come over each morning.'

'What if the weather's bad?'

'Owen usually knows the forecast and it's not far even if the sea is rough. There's a room for us to stay overnight if we think there'll be a problem, but the island is closed from Christmas week until Easter so we avoid the worst of the weather.'

'It sounds like Alex has it all worked out.'

'The shift rota works like clockwork. It's an OK job until I go to college next year.'

As they neared the lodge, Mallory saw the wood had recently been stained deep mahogany.

'It's not as nice inside,' said Elsa, 'but it'll make a nice *cwtch*. Somewhere for you to relax. I come in here once a week to give the place a dust.'

The door opened easily. It was a large room and her first impressions from when she had peered through the glass were confirmed. The place was tidy but drab – a room that hadn't yet been subject to the design makeover Alex had given the rest of the resort. A single bed was pushed against a wall, its mattress at least clean. The sofa, however, had seen better days.

'There's a bathroom here.' Elsa opened a door and Mallory looked in. It was decent enough with a turquoise suite probably fitted in the 1970s. The girl paused, pursing her lips. 'Do you like it?'

'It seems OK.' Mallory glanced around the space.

'You don't want to stay in the hotel?' asked the girl.

'I'd like a bit of distance when I'm off duty. Do you understand?'

'Oh, I understand.'

Mallory decided to ignore the cryptic emphasis of the girl's words. 'What was the place used for?'

'When the Cloister was a convent, the housekeeper lived here. The religious sisters liked the main house to themselves.' The girl made a face. 'My Auntie Joanne was a housekeeper for a while. She has stories about living here.'

'You'll have to tell me about them sometime.'

The girl shrugged.

'You think I'd be better off in the room inside the hotel?' Mallory asked the girl, picking up on her mood.

'Oh, no.'

Mallory frowned. 'Why not?'

'This cabin's separate from the convent. You won't come to any harm here.'

'But I might at the hotel?'

Aware she was being enigmatic the girl smiled. 'Never mind me. You'll be all right in here. I'll add you to my cleaning rota. When I'm on duty, I'll do the room for you.'

'All right. Thank you.' It was a relief to get back into the open air. Mallory, conscious that her wound was now sticking to her jeans, was feeling queasy and needed a lie down. They turned to see Alex walking towards them.

'Sorry about the interruption. If you're keen, I'm happy to offer you the position. The two previous applicants weren't at all suitable.'

He didn't look happy. Alex, for all his quiff and old-fashioned charm, could spot when something was off. He glanced at her leg. 'How soon can you start?'

'This week. I just need to return to London to tell my son about the job and collect some clothes.'

He stared at her. 'This week?'

'If it's all right with you. I can make sure my referees are on standby to reply to you by my return.'

Astonished, Alex looked at Elsa who kept her eyes lowered. 'Why not?' he said finally.

5

MONA

The island was already testing her resolve. Frowning, Mona watched from the upstairs window as the woman she'd met in the sitting room took a tour of the grounds. She noticed Mallory walked with a limp that she was trying hard to disguise and felt a dart of sympathy towards her. She was young and attractive with natural curls clipped short. She must be desperate for work if she was coming for an interview while still clearly ill. Despite appearances to the contrary, a position in this hotel wouldn't be easy. Most of the guests, outwardly self-reliant, were wealthy and therefore demanding in that restrained insistent kind of way. The stream of gripes seemed never ending. *The white wine isn't chilled enough, the red wine is too chilled, the omelette is runny, the fish dish is too salty*. It was a shame because the chef clearly knew what he was doing. Not perhaps Michelin standard, as the hotel liked to claim, but near enough. In fact, the food was too appetising, and Mona was only having a light breakfast and a main course evening meal to ensure she didn't gain any weight. She rubbed her hand over her stomach, enjoying the concave contour that came through self-deprivation and iron control.

Mona picked up the watercolour paper on her desk – she'd not got any further than pencilling in the outline of what she intended to fill in with colour. Her latest commission was a children's book where the main character, a little girl, was from a Traveller family. She liked both the story and the message behind it but was struggling to connect with the words. The gulf between the lives she was illustrating and the people who swilled around her was just too great. Just as well she had another enterprise to keep her preoccupied.

She turned her attention back to the pair outside who had reached the wooden structure in the garden. She recognised the girl showing Mallory around as one of the chambermaids or whatever title they gave themselves now. She watched as the pair disappeared inside the rectangular building and out of her view.

Looking at the time, she saw it was nearly three o'clock. She couldn't resist a glance out of the window again. The couple had reappeared and were making their way back towards the hotel. At the doorway, Alex appeared and spoke to them both. A handshake and he was gone. The relief on both Mallory and the chambermaid was evident. Alex, she suspected, had that effect on most people. His intensity wasn't for everyone.

She put her paints back into their case and carefully lifted the sketch onto the top of the wardrobe. With the tools of her work out of the way, the space looked like any ordinary, if luxurious, hotel bedroom.

A knock on the door and she went to open it. Alex stood on the threshold, and she stepped back to let him in.

'I saw you with Mallory outside. I liked her. Did you make a decision?'

Alex made a face. 'She's not perfect, but she'll do as long as that leg copes with the work.'

'There isn't exactly far to go here, though, is there?'

'Possibly not.' Alex began to take off his tie. 'The other two weren't suitable at all. We'll see how she gets on.' He sat down on the bed. 'Perhaps you could keep an eye on her for me.'

Mona put the chain on the door. 'No, thanks. You can do your dirty work yourself. As I said, I liked her. When does she start?'

'This week.' He made a face. 'Don't look at me like that. She wants to begin immediately and I'm desperate. She's ex-London Met and has been medically retired. Her references should be fine.'

Mona made a quick calculation, wondering how much the presence of Mallory would affect her plans.

'I'm sure you know what you're doing.'

'Sure do. Anyway,' he smiled at Mona. 'Enough of that.' He looked at his watch. 'I've got about half an hour.'

6

BETH

The island was already testing her resolve. The problem was the weather, which was totally shit, and the island was not geared for kids at all. She couldn't understand why a hotel would advertise itself as welcoming children and then make no effort to entertain them. The only games Beth had been able to find were Monopoly and Scrabble, so she'd had to rely on the small bag of toys she'd brought with her. The plan had been to leave her husband, Scott, to his writing, but Edith was having none of it – she'd screamed for her father, and Scott, to be fair, had agreed to devote the day to them. They'd spent the morning down by a cove until the wind had begun to billow through their clothes. They'd then taken the boat to Tenby and found a recreation centre with a soft play area. Scott's cheer had begun to wear thin – he'd been itching to get back to his manuscript, and they'd had an argument on the boat back.

He was ignoring her now as he stared into his laptop but at least Edith was asleep, which gave Beth a respite from the pair of them.

'I'm going to take a sauna,' she told him. 'I'll be back before dinner.'

'Hmm.'

She wasn't sure if he was engrossed in his story or whether he was making the point he was working and didn't want to be spoken to. Beth gathered her towel and toiletry bag and shut the door quietly. Before she'd reached the end of the corridor, she heard Edith's cry.

'Beth,' Scott called, but she ignored him and carried on down the stairs towards the spa suite. She had her swimming costume on under her clothes and after a shower, she opened the door to the sauna.

The advertised lavender sauna was nothing more than an ordinary room with a range of essential oils you could add to the coals. The person before her had used lily of the valley, a sickly cloying smell. Beth made a face. She thought it was probably that red-headed woman who wafted about the place trailing flowery perfume. Putting her towel over the slats, she lay back and contemplated the ceiling. Eldey might not have been exactly what she was expecting, but she mustn't allow her disappointment to distract her from the wider benefits of the place.

After five minutes, the door opened and a huge man, well over six foot and built like a Viking, walked in.

'Oh, do you mind if I join you?'

'Not at all.' She turned over onto her stomach, conscious of the stretch marks on her breasts from when she was pregnant. 'I won't be long. I'll need to get back to my little girl before she screams the place down.'

'That's children for you.' The man took off his towel and sat on a bench opposite her. He gave her a quick glance – he looked like a man who sized up every woman – and then averted his eyes. 'I've brought my own too.'

'You have a child with you?' Beth's heart leapt at a possible playmate for Edith.

'My daughter, Julia. She's the only teenager in the place, I think.'

'Oh. Not much for a girl of her age to do here.'

'I don't know about that. Julia's fascinated about the history of Eldey. She's discovered a relative on her mother's side was one of the original nuns who lived here. It was her idea we come and soak up the atmosphere. Not that I'm complaining. I could do with a break.' He closed his eyes, a clear message he was tired of talking.

'Great she's interested in keeping in touch with the past,' said Beth.

She heard him grunt. 'At least someone is.'

7

'You enjoying Eldey?'

Mallory watched Tom skin one of the rabbits brought over by the morning's boat. He wasn't what she'd expected. Yesterday, Alex had suggested she eat in the dining room that evening so she could see the quality of food on offer. It had been offered with a note of pride – Alex had selected an up-and-coming culinary star to run the hotel's kitchen. Given the exquisite food – she'd dined on Devon oysters and Carmarthenshire rump steak – Mallory had expected a neurotic French-trained chef, precocious about his food. Instead, Tom was ex-military and had used his discharge payment to subsidise his training in one of London's top hotels. He was a natural. His fingers expertly wielded the knife as he slit the animal's stomach.

'It's different.' She wasn't yet sure of her allegiances. Any comments she made, good or bad, might make it back to Alex.

'Liking it?'

Mallory shrugged. 'More than I expected.'

Tom smiled as he ripped off the animal's fur. 'You don't sound sure.'

'What about you?' she asked, moving away as the skinned body emerged from the fur.

'Me? I like it here. Alex expects a high standard of food but other than that, I'm left to myself. If I get bored, I can take a boat to Tenby and see a bit of the mainland. Otherwise, when I'm not working, I read or listen to the radio. What's not to like?'

'What will you do in the winter season?'

'Find another post. Hotels are always on the lookout for chefs but I'll be back here at Easter for the reopening.' He paused, looking at her. 'Think you'll come back?'

'Doubt it, to be honest. This is a stop gap for me.'

'Nothing wrong with that. The hotel trade's full of people like you looking to bring in a few extra quid.'

They were interrupted by Alys, who pushed open the double doors into the kitchen. She was nestling a mug of coffee in her hands. '*P'nawn da*. Tom, do you have the menu for tonight? I need to get it typed up for the tables.'

Tom passed to her a handwritten note and she squinted down at his spidery handwriting. 'Rabbit pie? We didn't have many take ups of that last time it was on the menu. Are you hoping our weekend guests are more game loving?'

'I've had a request for the dish. Owen brought over a brace of them for me.'

'Fair enough.' Alys hesitated, looking around the kitchen. 'Do you have anything in the fridge I could have for my lunch? Late lunch I should say. I haven't eaten anything yet. It's been one of those days.'

Tom, his hands bloodied, indicated with his head. 'There's cold chicken and hummus on the top shelf. Will that do?'

'Fine.' Alys placed her mug on the counter. Mallory saw it was nearly empty.

'Can I get you another brew?'

'Don't worry, I help myself from the jug in reception. The way I drink it, I might as well set up a drip.'

Mallory watched Alys heap a small portion of hummus plus a chicken wing on a plate before retreating to reception.

'Does she always eat so little?' she asked Tom once she was sure her colleague was out of earshot. 'She says that's the first meal she's had today.'

'She survives on black coffee during the day, gin in the evening. She'll outlive us all.'

Mallory smirked, stifling a yawn.

'Keeping you up?' asked Tom.

'Still coming to.'

'Don't let Alex see you like that.'

Mallory grimaced. She hadn't yet settled into night working and was finding it impossible to sleep. The weather was the main issue. A cold wind blew across the bay, its gusts keeping her awake at night. She worried about the boats on the sea and the safety of the guests. Now it was promising to be what Elsa called a sticky night. A gale was coming across the Irish Sea. It would miss the island but Eldey was likely to feel the tail of the storm. Even across the noise of the kitchen, Mallory could hear the thump of the sea hitting rocks.

'Give me something to do, Tom.'

'You could chop the carrots.' He handed her a carving knife. 'Uh oh. Trouble.'

Mallory frowned as raised voices, one defensive, the other shrill, drowned out the boom of the waves.

'What's going on?'

Tom raised his eyes. 'Sounds like Alys and Elsa are squabbling again.'

Mallory put down the knife and headed towards the noise. Alex surely wouldn't be happy with staff arguing within hearing distance of guests. As she came out into the main lobby, she saw Elsa backed into a corner, pleading with Alys.

'Could you keep your voices down?' Mallory was conscious of the curious gaze of a teenage girl making her way upstairs.

Alys turned to Mallory, her face full of wrath. 'Elsa's been talking to one of the guests about that dead nun again. I've told her time and time again it's a load of old rubbish.'

'What dead nun?' Mallory asked Elsa.

The girl's words came out in a rush. 'The sister from the 1930s who died a terrible death.'

Jesus, thought Mallory.

'It's a really interesting tale, honestly. Julia, the girl who's gone upstairs, thought there was a tour taking place this weekend and she's really disappointed it's not happening. So, I told her the whole story myself.' Elsa's eyes were shining.

'What story?' asked Mallory.

'I don't want to hear about it,' said Alys trying to control her temper.

'It's about the nun who died because she didn't want to leave the island. She's in the photo in the sitting room. I can even show you which one if you want.' Elsa wasn't going to be put off.

'I told Alex we should put that photo out of sight,' said Alys.

'But listen.' Elsa grasped Mallory's sleeve. 'It's interesting.'

Mallory was once again aware of the power of the emotions that ran off Elsa. She was only a little older than Toby but had an intensity that was hard to resist. Mallory sighed. 'OK. Why don't you tell me the story and I'll see if it's suitable for the guests, OK?'

'Well, you know the order was founded by Margaret Taylor. It grew slowly and one of the last sisters to arrive – Bridget Marsh – was from an old, landed family who were furious she'd become a religious sister. Because she was under twenty-one, the family went to court and got a ruling that Bridget had to return home as a minor. But...' Elsa paused for dramatic effect. 'Before they could come to collect her, she ate berries from a bush on the island and died.'

Mallory glanced at Alys who put her hands up in despair. 'That part is true but it'd be long forgotten if madam here stopped going around frightening everyone with the tale. But, oh no, she tells it to everyone who's prepared to listen to her and adds in murder for extra effect.'

'Extra effect?' Elsa's face turned pink. 'I'm not saying anything that isn't true. There's plenty who think it was murder. One of the sisters didn't want Bridget to leave so poisoned her.'

'That's enough,' said Alys sharply. 'Aren't you supposed to be helping Tom in the kitchen?'

'I'm going now,' Elsa huffed.

Mallory followed Elsa as she stalked away. 'You can't go around telling stories without Alex's permission. I know you're encouraged to be friendly with guests but it might put them off staying here.'

'Mallory, they *love* it. Alex has told me to lay it on thick.'

'He has? Why didn't you say that to Alys?'

'I did but it just annoyed her further. Thinks she rules the roost just because she's been here the longest of us all. She was the last housekeeper to the nuns and when the final one died in 2009, the family asked her to stay on as caretaker.'

'So what tour was the girl you spoke to expecting? I didn't realise there were organised events.'

'There aren't. I'm not sure what she was talking about, to be honest. She said she had an email giving the time and date.'

'Strange. Maybe Alex will know what she was talking about. I'll ask him when I see him next.'

Mallory turned to see Alys settle herself behind the reception desk, two bright spots in her cheeks. What, she wondered, was making the woman so upset? It was, after all, just an old story.

8

Mallory had about an hour to kill before her evening shift officially started. To pass the time, she helped herself to coffee from the jug provided for guests in the lobby and took the mug down to the cliff edge, the heat from the brew warming her chilled hands. It was a gusty evening and the white crests of the waves suggested the final guest boat of the day would have a rough crossing. Below her, waiting at the harbour, there would be a group of day visitors waiting to be picked up. Once November arrived, even these trippers would be banned, the island only open to guests who had booked a room. Alex had told her the weather was more unpredictable from November onwards and boats less likely to leave the harbour. Mallory didn't think she'd be sorry. She preferred it when she felt she had the island to herself.

She was conscious of that sense of containment she'd noticed on her first day here. They could be marooned far from civilisation rather than merely a mile offshore. The increasing wind added to her sense of dislocation. As she stood next to the bell tower, she could see the lights of the town glittering across the waves, but it felt like another world. She looked up at the huge brass bell, its stopper leaving it mute. She was seized by a desire to ring it and see what the reaction was. A spurt of rebellion making Mallory smile into her mug. She watched as the little tugboat touched the landing stage and deposited a couple with a child whose shrieks could be heard across the wind. Like Alys had mentioned on her first day, she wondered what on earth had possessed the parents to choose the Cloister for their break. There was nothing for the little girl to do on the island. At least the small town had an amusement arcade and some shops to loiter in. They climbed into the waiting cart, driven by Alex, which sped them up the cliff path. The boat had another passenger, a single guest arriving for the weekend, judging by the size of suitcase she pulled behind her. Even from this distance, Mallory could see she was wearing heels. Owen, bless him, was pointing towards the gated path but she was shaking her head. She was clearly going to wait for the cart ferrying the family to reception to come back for her.

Mallory turned to go back to reception, throwing the remaining coffee onto the grass. It was over-brewed, sitting around all afternoon in the jug, and she should make up a fresh pot. Across the grass, she could see a man walking slowly with a wooden cane, taking each step carefully. She frowned, wondering why the image jarred until she realised it wasn't an elderly man as she'd first assumed but someone around her own age, a slim figure in jeans and black zip-up cardigan. She cursed herself for her own prejudices. The gash in her leg should have made it perfectly obvious it wasn't just the ageing who needed help walking. Trying not to stare at his slow progress, she wondered how he'd managed on Owen's boat. To Alex's credit, the hotel had been made accessible for a range of mobility issues but the tug over to the island was twentieth century. As she got closer, she saw the guest's face had a puckered look, the result of a laceration, which crawled from his temple to the top of his cheek. Without thinking, Mallory touched the scar above her ribcage.

'Is there anything I can do to help?' she called over to him.

Her impulsive offer was a mistake. The guest frowned and turned his face away, annoyed at her query. She could feel the displeasure radiating across the grass. I've put my foot in it, thought Mallory as she walked towards him to make amends.

'I'm Mallory, the night manager.' She held out her arm. 'Sorry if I was too direct. It's my job to check up on guests and I ask everyone the same question.'

He hesitated before taking her hand, leaning on his cane. 'Michael Hutton. And I'm managing fine, thanks. I always do, despite what people think.'

'No offence intended.'

'Right.' He gave her a sharp glance. 'It never is.'

His attitude towards her gaucheness made her stiff with embarrassment. 'Have you just arrived?'

Michael resumed his slow walk towards reception. 'I've been here since Monday. I had a busy summer at the practice, and this is the first chance I've had at a break.'

'Practice?'

'I'm a doctor.'

Mallory felt some of her assumptions slide away. Perhaps people would express the same surprise when they saw her injury and she told them she was an ex-cop. Mallory walked by his side, the reduced pace doing her own leg no favours. The cobbled path across the front lawn was lethal in this weather and she had to concentrate to make sure her legs didn't slide from underneath her. Michael glanced at her briefly and made to say something. Perhaps the expression on her face made him stay silent.

As they turned the bend, another of the weekend guests came along the track. She was the same woman with cropped, grey hair and round orange glasses who'd been impatiently tapping on the desk the other day. Mallory thought she might be a relative of Michael's as she appeared put out at the pair of them being together. Mallory prepared to introduce herself but the woman sped away, acknowledging them with a tilt of her head.

'Hi Stella,' said Michael, his voice relaxed.

'Evening, both,' she said, giving Mallory a sharp glance before hurrying away.

'Strange,' said Michael. 'She was very friendly over afternoon tea.'

Inside, the couple were wrestling their child up the stairs, her shrieks filling the cavernous interior. Michael headed to the glass coffee table and began to flick through the day's paper while Mallory picked up the coffee jug from the machine and poured herself another mug. Alys was checking in the female guest from the boat – Alex had made quick work of ferrying guests up the path. Mallory had been right about the girl's footwear. She was wearing high-heeled boots to accompany her long tight skirt and short jacket. The visitor had chocolate brown hair sculpted helmet-like into a sharp bob. It was both effortlessly chic and unflattering to her slightly broad face. When she'd tottered off to her room, Mallory went over to Alys.

'You know, Elsa's only young. I wouldn't worry too much about her chatting about Eldey's past. It's a great story about the nun, for example. Visitors like a bit of local flavour and, besides, she's been told by Alex to entertain guests with the story.'

A grimace of pain crossed Alys's face. 'I don't like people playing fast and loose with the island's history. Us locals feel protective over the place.'

'But Elsa is local, isn't she? She told me her aunt used to be a housekeeper when it was still a convent.'

'Yes, but she has the resilience of the young. Eldey isn't an island to be laughed at.'

She was just like Owen, referring to the place as if it were a living being.

'I think Elsa takes this place more seriously than that.' Mallory saw Alys flinch. 'Are you OK?'

Alys's face was the colour of ash. Her lavender shirt clung to her chest, a ring of sweat spreading from her armpits.

'I've got stomach pains, that's all. I must have eaten too much hummus.'

Alys winced and tried to prise her blouse from her skin. 'I look a state.'

'Look,' said Mallory. 'I'm hanging around with nothing to do. Go and lie down, I'll take over from here.'

'You sure?' Alys's relief was unmistakable. 'I feel terrible leaving the shift early.'

'It's nothing. Anything I need to know?'

Alys hesitated, twisting her torso to try to relieve the gripe. 'I'm not sure.'

'Sure about what?'

'I don't know. Nothing I can put my finger on. It's just a strange set-up of guests this week.'

'You mean the couple with the child?'

'Well, yes, it's partly them. Children are allowed, of course, but we don't really get many here. The price of rooms more than anything puts off families. It just seems an odd choice of destination for such an energetic child. Wouldn't Center Parcs have been better?'

'They must have their reasons for choosing Eldey. Have they said anything to you?'

'Nothing at all to explain why they chose us. Keep an eye on them, would you, Mallory? Beth and Scott Gregory. They have a little girl – Edith.'

Mallory touched Alys's arm. 'Of course. Don't worry about it.'

'Then we have another couple with a teenage daughter. Hold on.' Mallory waited while Alys bent over to catch her breath. 'The husband's a bully, I'm sure. He looked the type.'

'Look, Alys, don't worry about it. Leave the guests to me.'

'They're Noah and Charlotte Vass and their daughter's Julia. She… she was the girl Elsa was telling about Bridget, the dead nun.'

'OK. I'll keep an eye out for them.'

Alys clutched her stomach. 'I'm going to have to get to a bathroom quickly. The other thing is we have a lot of single guests. Take Grace Pagonakis who just arrived. What's a girl like her doing here?'

Mallory shrugged, taking in Alys's sweat-drenched face. Perhaps her gripe was making her paranoid. 'It's a hotel. You get all sorts.'

'We don't.' Alys stood and then bent double. A stream of vomit sprayed the desk, covering the computer keyboard.

'Jesus, Alys.' Mallory went behind reception and put her arms around the shaking woman. 'Let me get you to your room.'

'I don't think… I mean, I can't stay on my feet. I—'
Alys collapsed onto her chair.

Conscious of a movement behind her, Mallory glanced
over her shoulder and saw Michael had joined them. 'Let
me look at her.'

Mallory moved back as Michael knelt opposite Alys.
'When did you start feeling like this?' he asked.

'Um, about an hour ago.' Alys's face was contorted in
pain. 'I think… I think I'm going to be sick again.'

Mallory tipped the paper out of the bin under the desk
and pushed it under Alys's face. 'Use that. I'll clean up the
mess.'

'You need to go to hospital.' Michael had a finger on
Alys's wrist. 'Your pulse is very fast. An island isn't a place
for you in this condition.'

'It's just food poisoning,' said Alys. 'Take me back to
my room, I'll lie in bed until it passes.'

'I don't think that's a good idea. I think you're right
about food poisoning and you can become very ill with
it.' Michael's voice was insistent. He met Mallory's gaze
and inclined his head towards the telephone.

'I'll call the boat,' said Mallory.

Owen answered on the first ring as seagulls screeched
in the background. 'It's Mallory. Alys is sick. I know
you've finished for the night, but could you come over
and pick her up? I'm going to ask for an ambulance to
come down to the quayside on the mainland.'

Owen didn't hesitate. 'I've just moored. I'll get rid
of the passengers and come back. The wind's a bit ripe
tonight. Can you hear it? I'll have to be quick.'

'I think the main thing is to get Alys off the island.'

'I'll be with you in twenty minutes. Once we're back
in Tenby, I'll wait with her until the ambulance arrives.'

Mallory's next call was to III who insisted on speaking to Alys. When she was overcome with another bout of vomiting, Michael took over the phone and spoke to the operator, his voice low and firm.

'It's on its way,' he said to Mallory. 'I think you should take her down to the launch now. I don't like her pallor.'

'I'm not sure if I feel up to even that.' Alys's eyes were glazed and her breathing laboured. 'I feel terrible. It's... it's painful to breathe.'

Mallory glanced at Michael and saw the gash on his face didn't end at his neck but opened out into his shirt where his skin was covered in a network of fine scars. He noticed her stare, stiffening in fury. Mallory stood and, out of the corner of her eye, was conscious of just missing a figure retreating up the stairs. A flash of someone's presence, nothing more. Mallory was glad whichever guest it was had a bit of discretion, although it was odd they hadn't come down and offered to help. That's what usually happened in a crisis. A gathering circle whose actions ranged from hand wringing to taking charge as Michael had just done. This guest, however, had decided to watch in the shadows and leave. Oh, well. It took all sorts.

Michael was lowering Alys to the floor. 'How long will the boatman be?'

'He's coming as soon as he can. Around twenty minutes, I think. Isn't that quick enough?'

'She's stopped breathing. I need to perform CPR.'

Michael began to push down on her ribcage with the heel of his palms. Mallory watched in horror, wondering if she should leave Michael to find Alex or stay for support.

'Is there anything I can do? We have a defibrillator in the back office.'

Michael shook his head, his face pale. 'It's not her heart. She's gone into some kind of respiratory arrest. I don't understand it.'

Mallory nodded, her eyes on Alys. She'd administered CPR many times in her career and it was always traumatic, especially if the resuscitation wasn't successful. After a minute, he stopped and shook his head.

'You can't carry on?'

'She's gone.'

Mallory knelt next to Alys who she'd only met a few days earlier. She'd seen death hundreds of times in her former job but it seemed an affront in this peaceful place.

'Does food poisoning usually cause death as quickly as this?'

'Of course not. Sorry, what I mean is that it's not usual at all. Alys must have had underlying conditions if eating something bad has made her this ill. The post-mortem will give us a clue. I'm sorry for the loss of your colleague. Did you know her well?'

'I've only recently arrived.' Mallory shook her head in disbelief. 'I need to find Alex. Can we move her into the back office? I don't want any guests seeing her like this.'

Together, they pulled Alys into the small space behind the reception desk and Mallory reached for her radio.

9

BRYONY: THE BIRTHDAY GIRL

The commotion downstairs was initially a good thing. It had been her intention to have a little fun before the main event. Play around with her stash of poisons before she went in for the kill. From her brief look at the scene taking place in the reception area, however, it looked as if she might have overplayed her hand. She hadn't been able to see the face of the woman on the floor being resuscitated but, whoever it was, her death hadn't been part of her scheme at all. She wondered what had gone wrong and how much it would affect her plans. A police investigation would take place, but only after the presence of the drug had been found in the woman's bloodstream. That would be days away and it would be all over by then.

The weather, she realised, was likely to be her ally. The wind was beginning to wail through the hotel compound, upending planters and destroying trees. They'd be lucky to get the dead woman off the island and, if that was the case, then possibly her plans could be stretched a little. She could take a little time between each victim, a previously untested scenario for her.

It appeared that for once in her life, good fortune was blowing her way. She was sure it was down to Eldey. The place and its lurid history had fascinated her since she was a child. Soon, she would be part of its story.

10

Despite reeling from the shock of Alys's death, Mallory's training kicked in. As she'd done so many times in the past, she worked to contain the trauma. There was no need to keep Alys's body in situ. Once police permission was sought, Alys could be moved to the hospital on behalf of the coroner until a post-mortem took place. Interviews would come later. The non-emergency number was answered by a duty officer in Carmarthen who took down the details and arranged for a police car to arrive alongside the ambulance to meet Owen's boat. A team would be sent over in the morning to take statements. In the meantime, he would let DI Harri Evans – that's Harri with an 'i' – know about the death.

'Harri will want to come over. Likes to see things for himself.'

Mallory made a face. Good for Harri. She'd had enough of CID to last a lifetime and wasn't looking forward to being a witness rather than investigator. She replaced the phone and went to look for Alex who wasn't answering her urgent messages on the two-way radio. She tracked him down outside, securing the garden furniture for the blowy night ahead.

'My God.' He pushed past her and sprinted into the office, staring down at Alys on the floor. Michael had put a coat over Alys's face and, as if to confirm Mallory's news, Alex pulled it up, swiftly replacing it after catching a glimpse of his dead colleague's face. 'This is terrible.' He turned to Michael. 'You think it was food poisoning?'

'I... I'm not sure.' Michael's eyes sought Mallory's, trying to convey some of the confusion he felt. 'The vomiting is consistent with poisoning, but I wouldn't expect someone to die so quickly. I'm wondering if she had a heart condition.'

'What did she eat?'

'A chicken leg and about two tablespoons of hummus, both of which were in the fridge,' said Mallory. She was exhausted and conscious she smelt of her colleague's vomit.

'Is there any of it left?'

The thought hadn't even occurred to her in the panic. 'I'll check,' said Mallory.

'Put it in a Tupperware bowl and bring it to me. I'll have to hand it over to the police although God knows what message that will send. No one else has been ill so let's hope it's contained to leftovers.'

'Are you going with the boat?'

'Of course. This is a nightmare for the hotel. If I do the damage limitation on the mainland, can you try to keep a lid on things here?'

'I'll have to tell the staff.' Poor Alys being shunted off the island as if she were an embarrassment.

'Later, please, Mallory. Can we just have a quiet evening here first? We know Alys hadn't eaten anything else other than yesterday's leftovers. We're not even sure it's food poisoning. Please.'

Mallory considered his plea. Alex was behaving as she'd expected but there was some sense in his proposal. It was evening and boats to and from the island, except for the late-night staff boat, had stopped running. For the moment, news of the death needed to be contained.

'I can see the sense in it. What will we do about a replacement for Alys in the morning?' she asked.

'I'll have to get someone over from the temp agency. I just hope they can find someone. Not everyone wants to take the boat to work. The wind is picking up, which is a worry. I thought we were only supposed to get the tail end of the storm.'

Alex was surprisingly strong as he lifted Alys's body out of reception, through the back corridor and onto the electric cart that was charging by the garage. Mallory grimaced as a gust of wind tipped the buggy, which righted itself violently. 'Isn't there something else we can use?'

'I have a quad bike in the garage but I need you with me, Mallory, in case I run into problems on the way down. This will have to do. Where's the guest who was with you?'

'Gone to his room, I assume.' Michael had disappeared without a word when he realised he couldn't physically help carry Alys. 'I'll check on him once Alys is off the island. I just need to speak to Tom.'

In the hot and steamy kitchen, Tom bristled under her questioning. 'It's not anything I've cooked. It can't be the chicken as I had the other leg myself for lunch.' Poor Tom, his reaction would be different if he knew Alys was now lying dead outside.

'Is there any left?'

'A chicken's only got two legs.' He gave her a smirk, his tone changing when he saw the expression on her face. 'Look, take it easy, I'd be ill by now. It's not the chicken.'

'What about the hummus?'

'I only made it this morning to go with the Moroccan flatbreads. It wasn't as smooth as I wanted so I didn't serve it at lunch. I left it in the fridge so the staff could help themselves.'

'No guest ate it? You're sure.'

'Definitely no guest. Only Alys, I think, has had the hummus.'

Mallory opened the fridge but the covered bowl that Alys had scooped the dip from was gone. 'It's not here.'

'Then someone must have finished it and as no one has been sick then it can't be the hummus either. It's probably a stomach bug.'

'We have a doctor staying as a guest. He thought it was food poisoning.'

She saw she'd lost his attention as he concentrated on the evening's food. She couldn't blame him. An ill person, after all, was a distraction not a tragedy and she was sure he'd be devastated when he heard of Alys's death. Crossing over to the industrial dishwasher, Mallory pulled open its door where the empty bowl sat upturned on the top tray. She inspected it and saw the glass surface had been rinsed.

'The hummus has completely gone.'

'It was me.' Elsa came into the kitchen wearing a black dress. Out of her usual jeans she looked older and more assured.

'Are you feeling OK?' Mallory asked her.

'I'm all right, *diolch*. What's the matter?'

Shit, then it probably wasn't the hummus either. 'Let me know if you start feeling under the weather. Alex says we're to chuck uneaten food out.'

This did get Tom's attention. 'What? Just because Alys has been sick?'

'It's a health and safety issue.'

Tom opened his mouth to reply but, in the distance, she heard a crack and boom as a heavy object hit the ground. The house shook slightly and settled again with only a glass rolling on the counter showing the strength of the crash.

'What the hell was that?' asked Mallory.

'Sounds like a tree falling,' said Tom. 'I'm not surprised in this wind.'

'I need to make sure the path is clear to the harbour.'

Mallory left the kitchen and grabbed a torch from her office behind reception, pulling on her padded jacket. Aware her leg was beginning to pound, she slid down her trousers and changed the dressing on her wound, wrapping the used plaster and throwing it into the bin. She pulled up a thigh bandage to give her leg more support, uncomfortably aware it was digging into her skin. The ointment she needed was in her cabin so this temporary fix would have to do. As she was leaving, she saw the mess left on reception and used a wad of paper towels to clean it as best she could, shoving the waste into her office to deal with afterwards. As she emerged from the room, she bumped into Mona, dressed not in her usual elegant pre-Raphaelite style, but in walking trousers and a thick jumper. She'd tied her curly red hair into a knot on top of her head.

'What was that noise?' Mona asked. She was carrying a little bag with her, a small travelling case, its leather a beautiful burnished brown.

'I think a tree's come down. You weren't planning to go outside, were you?'

'Just a brisk walk before dinner. I've brought my paints in case I can find a sheltered spot.'

Mallory frowned, looking at the bag. 'In this weather? I wouldn't advise it.'

Mona frowned. 'Seriously?'

'Have you heard the wind out there? My advice would be to stay in. If a gust can fell a tree, it'll create havoc with debris out there.'

'Fair enough, you're the boss.' Mona kept her tone light but there was an edge to her words. As Mallory stepped outside and turned on the torch, she saw Mona hadn't gone back to her room but was standing watching her progress.

Outside, Alex was sitting in the cart next to Alys who was slumped against the window. 'I think a tree's gone down. Hop in and I'll get us as close to the harbour as we can.'

The afternoon had darkened to a slate grey murk. It was a night for branches falling and she didn't much fancy being out amongst the elms and unstable conifers, especially near the cliff edge. At the top of the slope down to the harbour, a tangle of branches barred their way.

Alex wiped his hands on his trousers. 'It's one of the old firs. I just need to move it out of the way.'

'I can help you.'

'Are you sure you can manage?' asked Alex looking at her leg.

'Of course. It's getting better by the day.' On cue, Mallory's thigh went into spasm. Grimacing, she turned her face away from Alex's sight.

Piece by piece, they carried the fallen branches of the desiccated tree into the clearing next to the path. The swollen sea hit the rocks, spraying foam at them and the wind whistled through fissures and foliage.

'You will keep the hotel running in my absence, won't you? None of the guests know Alys well, they'll just assume she's not on duty.'

'I'll do my best. When will you tell the staff?'

'I'll come back in the morning and let everyone know. It's just Tom and Elsa on duty tonight. The evening server didn't turn up. Probably looked at the weather and decided to stay indoors.'

'Will the evening boat make it over to pick up Elsa?'

'I certainly hope so. Just keep a lid on what's happened to Alys and I'll deal with everything in the morning.'

As the final branch was cleared, Alex was struggling to contain his anxiety. 'The boat's in the harbour. Let's get the hell off here.'

Owen took one look at Alys and no explanations were needed. He helped Alex carry Alys onto the vessel and began to disengage the ropes. The deck rose and fell with nauseating regularity as Mallory ran back to the cart and inexpertly turned it back towards the hotel. Towards the top, she could see a light flickering near the cherry laurel hedge. One of the guests must be having a pre-dinner stroll. It was probably Mona who hadn't looked pleased when Mallory had asked her to stay indoors. The weird thing about holidays was that people left their inhibitions behind along with their mobile phone reception. They wouldn't wander around their gardens in a strong wind but guests thought nothing of entering a clump of trees outside their hotel bedrooms. There was nothing she could do to stop them, of course, but she hoped she wouldn't be accompanying Mona to the emergency room later.

With a sigh, Mallory decided to leave the cart under a tree and speak to the guest. The light had an uneven intensity to it and it was only when she got closer she realised the guest wasn't carrying a torch but a home-made lamp. They were one of Alex's affectations, glass storm-lanterns containing nothing more than domestic candles. Whoever was carrying it would soon come to harm if they used that as their only navigation in this wind.

'Hello,' she hollered, hearing her words double back to her.

The light sped away, its yellow orb bobbing as it receded into the distance. Perhaps she'd frightened the lamp bearer. At least they were heading towards the hotel building. It surely couldn't be Mona, who had no reason to run from Mallory's call. Mallory had asked her not to go out but she couldn't actually enforce it. Confused, Mallory looked around. What was the point of being out in such inclement weather? She could see nothing beyond the cherry laurel and there was surely no attraction there.

11

'How do you feel about staying the night?' Mallory caught Elsa on the stairs carrying a tall glass of fizzy clear liquid on a tray.

Elsa frowned. 'My mum wouldn't like it. She told me to make sure I always get the last boat home in the evening. I can walk home from the harbour.'

'With Alys ill, we'll be short of staff tomorrow.'

'Tomorrow? What do you think I'm doing here now? I was cleaning this morning and Alex has me waiting tables this evening. Now you want me to check out the guests in the morning too?'

'Listen to the wind, Elsa. I'm not sure the evening boat's coming to pick you up tonight. There's a staff room at the back of the hotel. You might need to stay here.'

'If the boat comes, I'm going on it.'

'Fine.' Mallory was in no mood for an argument. 'Who's asked for room service?'

'Guest in room seven called Grace has a headache. She's asked for a drink of lemonade.'

'Let me take it. I'll check if she's OK.' A headache sounded a relatively minor ailment but you never knew. Elsa willingly gave up the tray and smoothed down her dress ready to return to the kitchen.

Grace Pagonakis answered on the first knock wearing the hotel's monogrammed dressing gown. Her hair was damp and had gone slightly frizzy. She gave the appearance of having recently emerged from the shower, but Mallory's first thought was the figure by the laurel hedge. Perhaps it had been Grace she'd seen, trying to shake off the headache.

'I've brought your lemonade. How are you feeling?'

'Could you put it on the table over there? I feel awful, to be honest. My head is thumping. It's all my fault. I rushed down here in the car without thinking what toll it'd take on my eyes.'

'Perhaps you're dehydrated from the journey.' Mallory put the tray on the glass table.

'It can't be that. I drank loads of water in the car.' Grace made a face. 'Might be the coffee I drank. Caffeine's not brilliant for me so I only had a sip. Oh well, don't worry, I'll hopefully be OK in the morning.'

'Did you come far?'

'From Hastings. It was ridiculous coming all this way just for the weekend, but I just couldn't resist it when I discovered I'd won the prize.'

'A prize?'

'Didn't you know? I subscribe to a beauty box company called Gum Candy. I won this weekend trip away.'

'Must have been a nice surprise. I don't think I've ever won anything, let alone a break in a place like this.' Mallory switched on the floor lamp and pulled the curtains to shut out some of the noise from the roar of the wind.

'Me neither. I thought it was a scam when I first got the card telling me I'd won. I couldn't actually remember entering the competition, but when I called to make sure it was real the lady on reception told me the room had been booked and paid for.'

'You must have entered somehow.'

'I know. They do some great giveaways and I always click on the links in their emails and then forget about them. I was so excited I'd won but I hadn't realised it'd be such a long way.' Grace made a face. 'In fact, I bunked off school this afternoon.'

'You're a teacher?'

Grace reddened. 'I know it's not on. Now I feel so guilty. I made an excuse that I had a doctor's appointment, so they got cover for me. As it was, it still took five hours to get here because of the traffic. Perhaps my headache is divine retribution.'

'I don't believe in that.'

'I do. No good deed goes unpunished.'

Mallory turned at the girl's tone but her face was hidden by the towels she was using to rub her hair dry.

'Were you outside just now?'

'In this weather? Not a chance. Why do you ask?'

'I saw someone near the hotel with a lamp.'

'Crazy. Thanks for bringing my lemonade.'

'My pleasure. Let me know if you need anything. Dinner is in an hour.'

–

In her office, Mallory kicked off her soaked shoes and, using the hotel's wi-fi, sent Toby a message on WhatsApp.

Missing you. I'll call tomorrow. Hope all is OK xx.

58

Alys's death had shaken her and she needed to check in with her son. Although two blue ticks indicated the message had been read, there was no reply. He must still be angry with her after she told him she'd be taking the job on Eldey. She could understand he might resent her getting a job so far away from him, but he had been adamant he wanted to live with his father when she and Joe separated. At fifteen, his preferences had carried a lot of weight with the judge. Perhaps she had misread the signals and should have pushed for more access. Still worrying about her son, Mallory jumped at a knock on her door. The woman she had seen earlier in the garden stood at the threshold.

'I'm Stella Atkinson in room nine. Are you the person to complain to?'

Mallory frowned. 'I can certainly help with any complaints. What's the problem?'

'The coffee this afternoon was disgusting. It wasn't like this yesterday.'

'What was the matter with it?'

'It was very bitter, almost herby. Are you sure you didn't serve me chicory?'

Mallory bit her lip. Did the woman think they were on rations here? 'I'm pretty sure we don't offer chicory on the menu. Did you say anything to your server?'

'Server? I'm talking about the jug of coffee in reception. I'm not one to be made a fool of, you know.'

Mallory looked closely at the woman. It was an odd choice of words. Her expression was a mix of defiance and unease. Mallory remembered throwing away most of the mug she'd been sipping earlier, its taste over brewed. She also recalled Tom's comment that Alys lived on coffee during the day and gin at night.

'It's not made you ill, has it?'

'Why do you say that?'

Mallory was shocked at the woman's aggression. 'I'm just checking you're feeling OK.'

'I have a headache but it's probably the stress of everything. Nevertheless, I'd like to know exactly what I've drunk.' She left Mallory, who stared after her puzzled.

—

In the kitchen, Tom was checking his individual rabbit pies. He barely glanced at her through the steam as Mallory hunted around next to the coffee machine.

'Where's the jar of coffee we use for the machine?'

'There.' Tom pointed at the glass pot.

'Give it to me.' Mallory wet her finger and put some of the grains in her mouth. It tasted like ordinary coffee, bitterly pungent. 'One of the guests has complained about the taste.'

'Nothing wrong with the beans.' Tom folded his arms. 'Perhaps the water is a bit salty, I know we've had complaints about it before. People don't realise it's not like getting your water from a reservoir. The well we use has freshwater sitting on top of seawater, which does you no harm to you.'

She saw she'd offended him. 'That's probably it. I'm going to make a brew out of these grounds myself so I can reassure the guests that all is OK.'

Mallory pulled out a cafetière and poured hot water on the grains. It wasn't making any sense. Coffee didn't go off and certainly didn't cause food poisoning. Mallory poured the brew into a mug and took a gulp. It tasted all right to her.

'Can you grind a new batch in any case?' she asked Tom. 'I'm putting the rest to one side.' At least she'd have something to hand over to the police, although she was pretty sure the coffee was fine.

Tom nodded, his mind clearly elsewhere. Outside room nine, Mallory rapped on the door. Stella took her time to answer.

'Who is it?'

'It's Mallory, the night manager.'

Mallory heard the chain being removed and the door opened a crack. Stella's face remained in shadow.

'What is it?'

'I'm sorry about the coffee,' said Mallory. 'I've just had a taste of it and it seems fine but I've asked for some new beans to be ground.'

'You've tried it?' Stella opened the door an inch or two. She'd taken off her glasses and Mallory saw her eyes were rimmed in red.

'I made myself a drink from the same grains used in the jug on reception. Let me know if there's a problem this evening.'

'I think I'll pass on the coffee full stop,' said Stella, shutting the door in Mallory's face.

12

At seven p.m. the night boat for returning staff was officially cancelled and the forecast was promising gale-force
winds for the following twenty-four hours. The storm
that had been due to dissipate over the Irish Sea would
now hit the Pembrokeshire coast. The island was cut
off. Mallory was left horribly aware that she was solely
responsible for the safety of everyone on Eldey. Alex,
naturally, was frantic.

'I'm stuck in this bloody town. I've had to book a room
somewhere.'

'What's it like over there?' asked Mallory. 'It's wild
here.'

'The rain is coming down non-stop and they're saying
some of the houses near the estuary might flood. I've left
you all up shit creek.'

'How did it go with Alys?'

'The ambulance was waiting for us as promised. My
statement to the police took an hour. Is that normal?'

'It can take that long. What did they say?'

'They want to speak to you and the guest. Also the
kitchen staff but it'll all have to wait until this storm passes.
Thank God you're there. That's the problem with using
contractors for everything. No one's on site. You're lucky
you've got Tom. At least you won't go hungry.'

'What shall we do about dinner?' asked Mallory. A headache was building pressure behind her eyes and the roof of her mouth was parched. She hoped she wasn't coming down with a cold.

'I've sent an email to all residents to say there'll be one sitting at seven thirty p.m. I can't have guests ambling down at nine p.m. in the circumstances. You don't have enough staff. So far no one's complained. Elsa can serve if you don't mind helping out with the drinks orders.'

'That's fine. Do we know how long the storm's going to last?'

'The forecast is a nightmare. The wind's picking up between midnight and five. Yes that's right, picking up, so you're in for a stormy night and into tomorrow. The lull's due the day after next in the early hours. By daylight on Sunday morning we should be able to get to you.'

'You think you'll be able to come then?'

'If I can get a boat, as soon as it's safe, I'll pilot it myself.'

After the call finished, Mallory considered the situation of the guests on Eldey. Most of the adults should be able to look after themselves but she had to ensure the vulnerable came to no harm. She would pay a visit to the two families with children before dinner to check they were coping as the weather closed in.

The Gregory family were in a room at the end of the upstairs passageway. Alys had been right to give the family a bedroom away from other guests, but Edith's shrieks could still be heard as Mallory approached. She rapped on the door and the man she'd seen at dinner the previous night answered it. Scott Gregory was made from the same mould as Alex, down to the cream chinos and preppy jumper. Unlike Alex, however, his gaze was slightly out of focus as if he'd been drinking.

'I'm Mallory, the night manager.'

'Oh.' He was at a loss for words, pushing his hands deep into his pockets.

'I'm sorry about the storm. I'm afraid it's taken us all by surprise. I wanted to check everyone's all right and I'm starting with the guests with children.'

'Edith!'

Mallory felt rather than saw a shape rush past her and Scott brushed her aside to race after his daughter. He returned carrying a squirming child in his arms.

'This is Edith.'

Mallory was again reminded of Toby at that age, a pent-up ball of energy. She smiled at the girl who turned her head. 'Do you need anything while we get through the next day or so? I don't think it's a good idea for you to go outside.'

'We'll be fine. Do you want to come in?' He still had that unfocused look but Mallory realised her first assumptions had been wrong. She watched as he hunted around for his glasses until his hand brushed over a pair on the bed. He put them on, the heavy black frames giving him a geeky look. 'That's better. I've got the Met Office page open on the internet. Storm Ettie is headline news. The calm weather's coming on Sunday. We'll be able to look after ourselves until then. The enforced rest might even help me work.'

Beth Gregory came out of the bathroom, wiping her hands with a towel. 'I don't share my husband's confidence. I don't like to feel we're trapped. Suppose Edith has an accident?' She was pale skinned with washed-out dyed-blonde hair with the brown coming through at the roots. Under her blue eyes were smudges of grey and Mallory remembered the absolute exhaustion of having a young toddler.

'It can make things feel claustrophobic, but try to see it as nothing worse than a bad storm. As soon as the wind stops, the boats will start again. As your husband says, it's just for a day or so.'

Beth nodded.

'Dinner is in the dining room at seven thirty. If it's easier I can get something sent up for you all.'

'Oh no, I need to get out of this room.' Beth looked at her husband. 'Edith will like the change of scene too.'

Mallory hesitated. 'Was there a reason you chose the Cloister? It's quite remote.'

'My idea.' Beth Gregory put her hands up in apology. 'My husband's trying to write a book in his spare time. I thought Edith and I could play in the rock pools and pop over to Tenby while he got on with his manuscript, but she's been quite clingy and insisting her father accompanies us everywhere.'

Mallory glanced at the pile of papers spread out on the table near the window. 'Perhaps the weather will give him a chance to write,' she said doubtfully. 'I'll see you at half past seven.' Mallory shut the door behind her.

Noah and Charlotte Vass were in room three, while their daughter Julia had a single chamber at the other end of the corridor. Unlike the Gregory family, Noah Vass didn't let her into the room but stood at the threshold with his arms folded. Furious at herself, Mallory felt the stirrings of attraction despite his antipathy towards her. She remembered Alys hadn't liked him and had pegged him for a bully. *Plus ca change*, she thought. Noah listened to her with a bored expression.

'We're fine but it's a bit bloody inconvenient. What's the point of paying three hundred quid a night if we're stuck in the hotel? I mean, we can't exactly go out for a walk, can we?'

'I think there's something on the website which says the hotel on occasion does get cut off. For some, it'll be part of the place's charm.'

Noah let out a snort. 'Then I clearly didn't read the small print.'

Over his shoulders, Mallory saw a woman move away from a glass table covered in beauty products. She stepped towards the door but her face remained in shadow.

'What about your daughter? Would you like me to check on her?'

Noah frowned. 'Julia? Don't be ridiculous. She'll be fine. She's at the age where everything we say annoys her, so we've given her a room as far away from us as possible. She'll have to find a way to occupy herself, won't she?'

Noah turned to his wife who finally came out of the shadow. She was a striking woman with light brown hair pulled back into a ponytail. Unlike Beth Gregory who had been free of make-up, Charlotte Vass had spent time on her face even though she'd not be able to leave the confines of the hotel. She was at least dressed for the countryside in navy cords and a Scandi-style sweater.

'OK. But any problem just dial 12. I'm putting reception through to my mobile. I'll pick up any messages.'

Noah shut the door and Mallory stayed for a moment looking at the door. Something had struck her as off but she couldn't immediately put her finger on it. It was probably nothing. It was only as she was returning to reception that it struck her what had been the problem. The two of them standing in the room had the feel of an oil painting.

Vermeer perhaps. A portrait of a couple. Only now, as she thought about it, it also had the studiedness of a stage set. That was it. The poses had looked staged.

13

Mallory stationed herself at the entrance to the dining room and ticked off each guest as they came down the stairs. She'd only just had time to go to her cabin, wash quickly, and change into the only black dress she'd brought with her. In the cabin, she smeared some of the ointment on her leg wound and changed the dressing. It would have to do until she could shower later in the evening. On the way back into the hotel, she'd grabbed the cleaning rota from Elsa's clipboard, panicking that guests she hadn't managed to get in touch with might be strewn around the island as the weather closed in.

The Vass family were the first to arrive, the parents an attractive couple who radiated affluence. Charlotte Vass carried a magazine under her arm, something Mallory associated with women dining alone, not with a partner. She had the same understated elegance. Her fair skin was alabaster smooth, clearly helped along by makeup, and her hair swept into a chignon. Mallory got a closer look at their daughter, Julia, who she'd seen climbing the stairs after Elsa's story of the dead nun. She was a pretty girl, tall for her age with some of Noah's solidity. She sat down with the martyred air of someone forced to dine with her parents.

Beth and Scott Gregory were next in, their daughter, Edith, twirling alongside her mother. The adults looked tired with Beth Gregory keeping her eyes downcast. Watching the child dance, Mallory thought again of Toby. She would have to try to call him this evening if she could get everyone out of the dining room by ten p.m. Any later and she'd incur the wrath of Joe.

The first of the single guests came in a minute or so later and Mallory put into action the plan she'd been forming in her head. Stella Atkinson, the woman who'd given her an odd glance earlier that day, hovered at the door, frowning at Mallory's clipboard.

'*Noswaith dda.* Good evening.' Mallory had asked Elsa on her first day to give her a few words of Welsh to welcome guests. The unfamiliar words tripped over her tongue, her embarrassment not helped by Stella's scornful expression. 'How are you feeling now?'

'Terrible. My head has been banging all afternoon.'

'If you want to sit on your own, you're very welcome but we've also laid a group table. I thought it might be more relaxing to have some people to talk to, given the weather. It's nothing to worry about but I thought it might be more welcoming to offer the option.'

The woman glanced around, her eyes falling on Edith who was being wrestled into a highchair. 'I'm not sure. I suppose it'll be OK, although I usually have no issue with dining alone. Are there other single guests here?'

'A few.'

'Well, OK.'

Stella pulled a seat at the round table and poured water into her glass. Mallory turned and saw Mona tying back her hair as she approached the room with a breathless air.

'How are you doing?'

Mona grinned at her. 'Fine. Everything's brilliant.' An odd choice of words. She listened as Mallory repeated the offer.

'I'd rather sit by myself if that's OK. I'm not feeling lonely and don't need company.' She had her eyes on Edith as if the little girl's presence wasn't making the offer appealing. She took one of the single tables without embarrassment as Mallory ticked Mona off the list of names.

Michael, who'd been waiting behind Mona, surveyed the room, frowning. Mallory got a whiff of the hotel's shower gel. He too must have wanted to remove the smell of Alys's vomit. She wondered again why someone with mobility issues would choose to come to an island poorly accessible except on foot. There was a story behind his disability, probably connected to the scar on his face. He looked like he was torn between a desire to sit by himself and the need to be sociable.

'It's completely up to you. There are plenty of free tables.'

He smiled for the first time, softening his features. 'Sorry. Is it obvious I'm dithering? Don't worry, I'll sit with Stella.'

Mallory watched as he crossed the room. He was slightly built but not with the leanness that came from fitness. Instead, his body told a story of pain and deprivation. However, his severe good looks had their own charm. The older woman looked pleased as he took the chair opposite her. Mallory surveyed her list. Just one guest still to arrive. Grace Pagonakis must still be dressing. She was probably running late after feeling under the weather. To pass the time, Mallory handed a drinks menu to each guest and pushed open the doors to the kitchen where Tom was standing over a deep fat fryer.

'All OK? Don't burn yourself as we'll never get you off the island in this storm.'

'Tempura fish on the menu. Can't cook it any other way.'

Mallory watched as he shook the basket. 'Do you need me to do anything?'

Tom gave her a distracted glance. 'Everything's under control. I'll make sure they're fed if you ensure they're watered.'

Mallory left him to his preparations and took the drinks orders from the guests. Noah Vass was clicking his fingers to attract her attention.

'What can I get you?'

He didn't look up from his menu. 'A bottle of Burgundy.'

'I'd like a glass of sauvignon blanc,' said Charlotte. 'It'll go well with the chateaubriand.'

Noah flashed a look of irritation at his wife. 'I've told you before, you can't have a white wine with steak.'

'She can if she wants,' said Mallory. That caught his attention. She saw his skin flush a purple.

'I beg your pardon.'

'It's perfectly acceptable to have white wine with steak if that's what you fancy.'

'And you're the fucking expert, are you?'

So, the self-composure had been an act. Mallory's instincts had been right. 'I'm simply making the obser-vation that it's perfectly possible to drink white wine with steak. It's not a feat of impossibility.'

'What?'

'I tell you what,' said Mallory. 'Let me take another table's order while you decide.'

She forced herself to walk away. Men like Noah Vass always brought out the worst in her. They reminded her of Joe with their need to be in control. The desperation to be an expert in something they knew little about. She caught the eye of Mona and hurried across to the table.

'He was like that last night too,' she murmured. 'I don't like the feel of the dynamic between them.'

Mallory's wound was causing her leg to weep again and her tiredness made walking difficult. She took everyone's wine order, including that of the Vasses, who had clearly decided now wasn't the time for an argument. As she was heading for the wine fridge, she collided with Grace Pagonakis rushing towards the room.

'Sorry, I'm a bit late. I lost track of the time.'

The girl had made an effort with her clothes despite being under the weather. Her black dress with buttons down the front was paired with a pair of suede heels. 'Is everything OK?'

'I'll take you into the dining room. You have a choice of sitting with a group or on a table on your own. It's up to you.'

'I'm happy to sit with the group.'

The girl was relaxed as Mallory steered her towards the dining room. She caught the eye of Tom, who was standing at the door to the kitchen. She nodded to him that she was coming over but had to push past Grace who had stopped at the threshold of the room.

'Jesus. What the— Is… is that her?'

'What's the matter?' Mallory tried to follow Grace's gaze but she had turned her head and was staring at Mallory in shock.

72

'I don't believe it.' Grace looked as if she was about to faint. Mallory touched her lightly on the elbow but she flinched from the touch.

'Is something wrong?'

Grace was attempting to regain her composure. 'It's the birthday...' Grace checked herself.

'Who?'

'It doesn't matter.'

'You recognise someone here.'

'Yes, I mean, I don't know.' The girl forced a smile. 'Don't mind me. Mistaken identity, I'm sure.'

'You mentioned a birthday.'

Grace's left eye began to twitch. 'No one's birthday, I promise...'

Mallory frowned. Grace was doing a bad job of lying. Perhaps one of the men at the tables was an old flame. Grace wouldn't be the first girl to remember the birthday of an ex. She must mention it to Tom. It was usually the chef who guests contacted to let them know a diner had a birthday. It would be a good distraction if it was someone's birthday. Something to take the guests' mind off their confinement. She too could do with the diversion. Alys's death had cast a pall over the evening and Mallory could not shake off the sense of dread.

'Which guest—?'

But Grace had moved forward in a daze while Mallory hurried over to Tom who was signalling to her.

'What's the matter?'

'The lights are pulsating at the back. What's going on?'

'Probably due to surges on the electricity network,' said Mallory. 'The current is being affected by the wind.'

'I can't cook without electricity.'

'It'll be fine. I'm sure the generator will kick in if the power goes. Listen. I think it might be someone's birthday. Can you arrange a cake or something from the freezer? I'll just look through the guest list on the computer and tell you which table.'

Tom knew the drill. 'Will do.'

At reception, Mallory spent a few minutes going through each guest's booking information. The hotel only accepted direct bookings and asked for each guest's date of birth to fulfil the requirements of its licence. None of the people at the hotel, as far as she could see, had birthdays on that day. Stella Atkinson was the closest on 10 October but that was still two weeks away. Confused, Mallory hurried back to the dining room.

14

GRACE

Grace couldn't believe it; her head was spinning as she sat down at the table. She picked up the menu card and studied it to keep her face hidden from the rest of the diners. She'd noticed the flash of confusion on the night manager's face. Grace had offered to sit at the communal table and had changed her mind. No wonder Mallory was puzzled, but Grace had a bloody good reason for changing her seating arrangements. She needed time to think and settle her stomach. To calm herself, she studied the menu, which offered a decent choice, but her gaze was drawn to the person she hadn't seen for over twenty years.

Bryony had changed. That shouldn't be a surprise given the time that had elapsed. Her hair was a different style and, always a skinny child, she was even thinner than Grace remembered. Grace let out a puff of air, marvelling at the odds of her meeting Bryony at a random hotel in Wales. But then, weren't these coincidences the type of thing that happened all the time? She should not read too much into the fact that Bryony was here because she certainly wasn't paying any attention to her fellow guests. The main thing was, Grace was pretty sure she'd not been spotted because she'd changed too. She'd dyed her hair to a mocha-brown, which suited her skin tone better, and it'd been cut into a severe bob which was easy to maintain when she had to get ready for school. Grace pulled her reading glasses from her bag, which added another layer of protection. Bryony would not remember her with glasses.

A teenage girl came to take the order. Small with dyed blonde hair, she was slightly sullen, which was fine by Grace. Her mind was still churning and she doubted she'd be able to indulge in small talk. After she'd ordered her antipasti and rabbit pie, she took out her phone and used the hotel's wi-fi to do a Google search on Bryony. It was just the usual salacious fare and, in any case, she knew it off by heart.

She wished she hadn't mentioned birthdays to the night manager. Mallory looked the inquisitive type and Grace didn't want to draw attention to herself. It couldn't be Bryony's birthday – that had been in July – although there was always the horrible possibility that Bryony had been given a new birth date as well as a fresh identity. She saw her fingers were trembling. To steady her nerves, she took a slug of wine and opened the weather app installed on her phone. They were in for a rough night if the forecast was correct. High winds with gusts of up to seventy miles per hour. She took another gulp of her red wine and tried to relax.

Mallory tapped a fork on a glass to get their attention.

'OK, everyone. Many thanks for your flexibility regarding dinner tonight. We'll keep the arrangements for tomorrow evening too. A routine will help the kitchen and give some structure to your day.'

Grace watched the big man with blonde hair roll his eyes. He looked the type who wouldn't appreciate a woman telling him what to do.

'Do we have enough food?' The question came from a birdlike woman with orange glasses. Was it her imagination or did she look at Bryony when she asked the question? Grace wasn't sure. The question got a titter from the room and even the night manager relaxed.

'We have enough food to last us weeks, but I can assure you the storm will be over in twenty-four hours.'

Thank God. Grace could hear the thud of the waves against the cliffs and she didn't much like the thought of being stuck here. She snuck a peek at Bryony whose face was expressionless. Either the weather left her unmoved or she was determined not to show any weakness. Grace would have put bets on the latter being the case.

She took another gulp of her red wine and tried to relax. She'd used the sauna that afternoon and she intended to make full use of the other amenities in the spa suite. It would give her a chance to unwind. But, while she was making plans to enjoy her stay, the person in the room, the childhood friend she'd not seen for a very long time, continued to worry her. On reflection, perhaps she shouldn't even venture into the spa suite but watch Netflix in her room. In fact, now she thought about it, what a terrible, terrible coincidence. She could hardly believe it.

15

Mallory had forgotten what it was like to witness an act of violence. In the force, you kept an eye out for the sudden outbursts of ferocity when you were going about your work. It could catch you unawares and you'd find yourself drawn into the scuffles if you weren't careful. But after nearly a year out of her job, she'd let down her defences. Which was a mistake. Noah Vass had been drinking steadily and, as she collected the plates from the main course, Mallory had chosen to ignore the strained silence that settled over that part of the room.

'Will you just shut the fuck up?'

The accompanying glassful of red wine thrown at Charlotte Vass silenced the other guests. Stunned, Charlotte gave a gasp and got up, tugging ineffectually at the fire doors which led out onto the raging storm.

Mallory hurried over to her. 'Not there. This way.'

She pulled Charlotte by the arm out of the room. Despite her thinness, Charlotte was strong and towered over Mallory. In reception, the woman regained some of her composure. 'I don't suppose you have a cigarette on you?'

Mallory shook her head. 'It's a no smoking island.'

'Bloody typical. Soon you won't even be able to smoke in your own home.'

Mallory grinned. Charlotte Vass was a little tipsy but funny with it. Some of her aloof demeanour had dropped – alcohol and shock lowering the woman's defences. 'Given we're currently stuck on the island, we don't really want to have to deal with a fire alongside everything else. The smoking ban is a sensible idea.'

The woman shrugged, her expression glum. 'What must you think of us? The gentry are always the worst behaved, I'm sure.'

Mallory frowned. 'What do you mean?'

The woman caught sight of Mallory's confusion. 'Sorry. I'm not making myself clear. Noah is Viscount Noah Vass. His father is the industrialist, James Vass.'

Mallory remembered his father, who'd often been interviewed on TV when she was growing up. One of Lord Lucan's set, he was reputed to have helped Lucan escape the country after his attempted murder on his wife, which left the family nanny dead. His views could best be described as conservative. Mallory could think of a few other descriptions.

'Gentry? Is that what you call yourselves?'

Charlotte let out a laugh. 'Ridiculous, isn't it? Never mind. What do you think of my stepdaughter, Julia?'

'She seems a little bored. There's not much for a girl her age to do around here.'

'You'd think so, wouldn't you, but now I've discovered that we're here at Julia's suggestion. I thought it was her usual trouble at school but this island has piqued her interest. She was even expecting there to be some kind of tour this weekend, but the hotel knows nothing about it.'

Mallory frowned. 'There's been some misunderstanding about what we offer here.'

Charlotte swayed, swallowing hard. 'It's no bother to me but it was the tour that brought Julia here. Not that my husband's told me. He's been trying to blame me for being stuck on the island, but I wheedled it out of Julia. She'll have to take responsibility for this whole fiasco. Why's a fifteen-year-old girl suddenly getting excited about a group of nuns, even if they're family? Not mine, I hasten to add.'

'We all have our passions. None more so than teenagers.'

'Believe me no one was more surprised than me. Last year she was nearly expelled for being drunk in chapel, this term she's fascinated by a nunnery.'

'I see.' Mallory paused. 'You know that alcoholism runs in families?'

Charlotte looked closely at Mallory. 'You think nature more important than nurture?'

'I'm not sure but your husband's hardly setting a good example, is he?'

'Noah knows when to stop though. That's his superpower.'

'Is that before or after he's humiliated you?'

'After.' Charlotte moved away. 'I'm like the music at the end of the film. Once you hear the final chord, the show's over.'

Charlotte made towards the stairs, pulling at her ruined dress. Mallory wanted to go after her. Explain that she'd arrested drunken toffs for domestic abuse as well as the ordinary wife-beater. But she saw Julia Vass making her way across the lobby towards the restroom.

'I hope your stepmother's OK.'

'Of course she is.' The girl was distracted, fiddling with her hair.

Mallory frowned. 'Your father just threw a glass of wine over her.'

'It's an act.'

Mallory, who'd spent a year in the domestic violence team had to bite her lip. 'Excuse me, I have to get back to the guests.'

'Don't mind us,' the girl said over her shoulder. 'It's all for show. It doesn't work without an audience. That's what you need to remember.'

Across the room, Mallory saw that Stella and Michael were having a disagreement and Mona Rubin was sending them concerned glances. In the end, Mona picked up her wine glass and went over to join them for pudding.

'I'm feeling a bit lonely over there by myself, so I thought I'd join you. What are you discussing?'

The pair drew apart. Michael's expression was concerned, Stella's harder to read. Grace Pagonakis stayed at her own table, her head bent over her food, ignoring everyone including Charlotte who made a defiant reappearance in a pale blue dress. Ten years in the police force had shown Mallory the vagaries of all human nature. Very little surprised her, and she liked to think she could read people as well as anyone. But tonight, her radar was a little off. Grace, when she had come down the stairs, had been full of bounce. She had clearly thought she recognised someone whose birthday it might be. Perhaps, after sitting down, she'd realised that she'd been mistaken. Wouldn't that make her more rather than less likely to join the others to distract herself?

Mallory, helped by Elsa, began to serve the dessert. Jugs of coffee using freshly ground beans had been placed on a side table for guests to take through to the lounge or back to their rooms. It would take the three of them well past midnight to clear up the kitchen and lay the dining room for breakfast. For the rest of the evening, the guests would need to look after themselves. Mallory watched as Charlotte stumbled slightly as she left the table, her husband keeping his hand in the small of her back as he steered her out of the room. Julia raised her eyes as she passed Mallory. Sorry for the show, the gesture said.

Mallory checked her phone and sighed when she saw she'd missed a call from Alex. She could either ensure that the guests had a good experience during the storm or she could keep reassuring her boss. She'd take five minutes when she got a chance and call him back. She'd missed the chance to ring Toby and would have to make amends in the morning.

'So it wasn't anyone's birthday?' Tom was putting cling-film around a cake he'd taken from the freezer.

'The guest must have been mistaken. Leave it in the fridge and we'll use it for afternoon tea tomorrow. I think we'll offer it as a freebie for the guests to look forward to.'

'More work,' said Tom but his tone was light. His training in the navy meant he was unafraid of hard graft and happy to muck in with everyone. Elsa was quiet but had also gone about her work diligently. Mallory offered a prayer to the patron saint of hard workers. Thank God for Tom and Elsa.

As she passed through the hall to call Alex, she saw Beth Gregory standing in front of a large glass window, looking out at the storm.

'It's getting louder and louder.'

'We're on a promontory. The land juts out into the sea so we're exposed to the wind. Don't worry, the convent has been here for over a century.'

'I just worry that with global warming we're getting weather we've never seen before.'

'We're perfectly safe.'

The words reassured the woman who smiled at Mallory. 'I don't like to feel that I'm trapped.'

'I don't think anyone does. It'll hopefully settle down tomorrow.'

'Maybe.' Beth moved away and picked up a magazine left on the table.

'I think I'll go to my room. Do you think the phone lines will stay OK?'

'They should be fine.' Mallory wasn't as sure about this. Phone lines went down in floods and storms frequently. It was one thing to have a hotel full of guests with the phone and internet, quite another to be without any communications. Fingers crossed, she thought.

16

BETH

It was the night for fulfilling promises. Beth opened the door and glanced at her husband lying on the bed with Edith, both exhausted after the day's exertions. Her own mood couldn't be more different. She was a night owl, beginning the day sluggish and gradually waking up until she reached peak mental alertness about this time in the evening. She was desperate to get out of the room. Scott's book was a bloody nightmare, if truth be told. He'd been writing it for four years. A crime novel come comedy jape, he called it. Well, it wasn't a book she'd want to read and, having glanced at his flowery prose, it was not a novel he was likely to ever sell. The weird thing was, out of the two of them, she was the people watcher. The person who noticed things. She'd had plenty of practice.

Take tonight. There had been a strange atmosphere in the dining room and Scott hadn't noticed a thing. Perhaps it was just the wind and the sense of isolation but a few of the guests were unnerved and trying not to show it. Even the night manager, Mallory, had appeared worried and she'd given the impression when she knocked on their room earlier that nothing would faze her.

'I'm going out for a walk.'

Scott was dozing and woke with a start. She put a finger to her lips.

'Not *out* out. I'm going to walk around the hotel. There has to be something I can do to occupy myself even if it's having a coffee with a random stranger.'

'All right.' Scott rolled over, putting his arm around Edith.

In the corridor, the sound of the wind was louder, the noise seeping in through the row of windows looking out over the island. She preferred this view to the one over the front lawn. She liked watching the expanse of nothingness which led to the mausoleum at the far end of the island. When she reached the lobby, she saw the male guest who walked with a cane playing cards with the woman in orange glasses. They both looked up at her arrival.

'Fancy a game,' said the woman, shuffling the deck.

'It's whist and we're both equally bad.' Michael nodded at a spare seat.

Beth hesitated. She was useless at cards and it was unlikely to calm her racing brain. 'It's fine. Carry on. I'm just going for a wander before I turn in for the night.'

'We're here if you change your mind,' said the woman and began to deal the pack.

Beth walked behind the reception desk, which took her to the back of the building. To the right was the kitchen at the end of the corridor and at the opposite end, a spa suite she hadn't yet had time to explore. The feeling of disorientation persisted. It was a strange evening on an odd island. She hesitated. She merely had to decide which way to turn but she was left with the impression it made all the difference in the world. Shaking away her fears, she made her decision and began to walk.

17

Once the kitchen was cleared, before retreating to her cabin, Mallory made sure to secure the hotel. Alex was still frantic, but focusing on forecasting to the exact hour when he'd be able to pilot a tug back to the island. Elsa had been surprisingly philosophical that the boat hadn't come to collect her. The poor girl was probably exhausted and she readily took the key to the room next to Alys's. Michael had been playing cards with Stella in reception and only a slight smile from him hinted at the secret he shared with Mallory. She'd have liked to speak to him alone, check that he was OK, but he'd not given her any opportunity. Now, outside room five, she could hear the drone of the TV. She hesitated, wondering whether to knock, but was distracted by a trail of wet footprints on the parquet floor near the entrance to the spa suite.

Taking out her keys, she unlocked the door to the spa, which she'd shut at 10 p.m. in accordance with hotel rules. The room was in darkness and showed no sign of recently being occupied. Mallory flicked on the lights. The surface of the long, narrow pool glimmered as she pushed open the sauna but it was empty with the faint aroma of a floral-smelling oil. Locking the room, she checked the fire door that led out onto the garden. The door was rarely used. Guests were encouraged to enter either through reception or via the double doors of the sitting room leading out onto stone steps. Mallory pushed the handle and it opened easily. Easy to get out, harder to come back in. The whole point of a fire breaker. The night was blowy and wet. Whoever had used the door would have got a drenching.

Mallory followed the water trail back along the corridor to the lobby. Feeling a little like Sherlock Holmes, she decided the prints were that of a woman with long thin feet wearing soft soled shoes. The prints faded at the entrance to the kitchen but when Mallory pushed the doors, the room was still.

'Is anyone there?'

The usually busy kitchen was silent. Forever the cop, Mallory eyed the row of knives lined along the wall. Tom kept the blades sharp and oiled. Good for food safety but Mallory could recall her assailant's knife as it sliced into her thigh. As she walked around the room, the sensor lights came on one by one, illuminating the space. There was nowhere for anyone to hide. Shrugging off the mystery, Mallory escaped to her cabin.

Although the outside lights were still blazing, all she could see were grey sheets of rain dancing in front of the yellow orbs. The wind roared in unison with the sea and she pitied any boats out on the water that evening. The sensible thing for her would be to make up a bed in the room on the other side of Alys's so she could be on site if any of the guests needed her. She'd also be nearby to reassure Elsa. Only, she'd got a splash of the red wine Noah had thrown at his wife and she stunk of alcohol and the oil from the kitchen. A hot shower and clean clothes were a bigger draw.

As soon as she got a few metres from the building, she realised her mistake. It was almost impossible to stand in the ferocity of the wind. One misstep and she'd be lying out here on the sodden ground. At least she'd had the foresight to leave her front light on, which she could see shimmering in front of her. But distances were hard to judge in bad weather and, as a gust of wind nearly blew her off her feet, she wondered if it were easier to turn around or whether she was over halfway to the cabin and to safety. She picked up her walkie talkie and spoke into it.

'This is Mallory. I'm just walking back to my cabin. Is anyone there?'

There was no response. She'd left the other handset on the desk in her office where either Tom or Elsa could use it if they wanted to contact her. Feeling alone and aware of her heart thumping in her chest, Mallory put her head down and plunged on. Suddenly, her senses were on high alert. If Noah Vass's superpower was knowing when to stop, hers was to recognise danger when it was close by. Someone else was out here with her, she was sure of it. She could sense their presence. Her instinct was to take shelter amongst the trees but that would be fatal in this weather. She needed to stay in the open ground, which made her a clear target. She looked around for the source of danger and focused on a figure near her cottage. The sight released some of Mallory's tension. Perhaps someone had got stuck in the storm and was looking for shelter.

'Hello,' she shouted across the air, her voice swallowed up by the roar of the wind.

The figure moved, not towards her but away from the light and disappeared.

'Hello. Do you need help?' shouted Mallory.

'Are you OK, Mallory?' Tom's voice crackled over the walkie talkie. 'Where are you?'

Mallory fumbled for the handset. 'Walking back to my cabin.'

'Are you mad? You'll kill yourself. Turn back, for God's sake.'

'I'm nearly there. It'll be safer to get there than come back.'

'Then for crying out loud once you're in the cabin, stay there. I'm staying on the line until you arrive. How far have you got to go?'

'Another two minutes, I think. It depends on the wind.'

'Then keep going. Keep your eyes in front of you and shuffle as you move forward.'

'Shuffle.'

'Yes, keep your feet close together and shuffle. You're less likely to fall if you don't keep your feet too far apart. Walk on the flats of your feet too. Your centre of gravity needs to be over your shoes.'

Mallory did as she was told, battling another gust but seeing how the shuffling motion gave her more balance. The figure was now nowhere to be seen through the sharp needles of rain charging at her face. The light came towards her quickly and she fumbled for the door, kicking away with her legs the detritus that had accumulated over the evening. She briefly dropped the walkie talkie and stooped down to retrieve it. With a heave, she opened the door and fell into the cabin. It was chilly from the drop in temperature but away from the wind, it provided welcome shelter.

'Are you there?'

Mallory pulled off a glove and wiped the rain from the device.

'I'm in.'

'Thank God. I'm going to turn off the lights of the hotel and secure it for the night. You stay there.'

'Leave the light on over the front door. I think a guest is out in this weather.'

'You sure?'

'I definitely saw a person near my cabin.' Mallory rubbed her eyes. Why was she doubting herself. It was only the rain that had given the figure a hallucinatory appearance.

'Were they trying to get in?'

'I doubt it. I left the door unlocked.'

'Surely the guests wouldn't be out in this weather? You think it might be a day-tripper who's not made it home.'

'I don't think so. The weather's terrible. You couldn't stay out in it for long. Now I'm worried it might be a guest.'

'Shall I do a quick sweep of everyone?'

'I'd feel better if you did. There's a list in my office of all the guests. I printed off spares in case the electricity goes down.'

'Leave it with me.'

The walkie talkie went silent as Mallory, with shaking hands, lit the wood burner. She was still on duty and wouldn't sleep but Tom had been right. Battling her way back to the hotel would be as foolish as the initial decision to come here.

After half an hour, she heard Tom's voice. 'Everyone's in the hotel.'

'You're positive that everyone is accounted for?'

'I've just checked off the list. Even Elsa.'

Then who had she seen at her doorway?

In the shower, she closed her eyes as she recalled Alys's death. With any luck, the guests would never know the receptionist at the Cloister had died. For Tom and Elsa, the news would be hard to take and Alex might find Elsa unwilling to return to the island. She was full of stories and fears about the place as it was. Out of the shower, she applied her cream to the wound and pulled on her thick pyjamas.

It was only as she was in front of the stove ripping open an energy bar with her teeth that she remembered about the birthday cake. Watching the stove spit and hiss, she wondered what had been wrong with Grace Pagonakis. She'd looked into the room, recognised a fellow diner, and mentioned birthdays. But Grace's manner had been odd and she'd changed her mind about where she was going to sit. She'd gone from sociable to unfriendly in seconds. Mallory, never one for a conspiracy theory, was inclined to dismiss the whole incident. She sat back in her wicker chair, more comfortable than it looked, and put her aching leg up on a stool. Her headache was now a dull thud and she'd hopefully sleep it off. If her mind had been sharper, she'd have asked Grace when she was sitting down whose birthday she'd thought it was. The question would have answered the riddle and that would have been that.

She heard the hoot of an owl once, then twice — God knows where the bird was taking shelter. The sound reminded Mallory of the late hour. Her official title might be night manager but tomorrow she'd need to be on duty all day. She should get her rest now. The thought of the guests safely in their beds was enough for Mallory to crawl into bed and fall into a deep sleep.

18

MONA

It was the night for fulfilling promises. Mona pulled off
her hat and untied her messy ponytail. Frizz was a constant
problem for those with hair like hers, although few realised her curls, like their colour, came from a bottle. She'd
decided long ago that her natural hair didn't give her
enough distinction. No one ever forgot Mona of the red,
curly hair and she played up to her pre-Raphaelite image
with long dresses and cords of beads around her neck.
It weirdly allowed her to go about her days incognito.
People were so focused on your appearance they were
blind to other aspects of your life – namely work, your
acquaintances, what you did or didn't eat. The presence
of children on the island unnerved her. She hadn't anticipated that and it reminded her of all she had lost through
her obsession.

Mona threw the bunch of foliage on the table. She
wouldn't be able to keep it in her room as Alex had been
clear that he was only allowing her to use her room for
painting as long as it remained to the high standard of the
rest of the hotel. This was largely easy to comply with but,
on occasions, like now, she needed to bring the outside
in to study it closer. Mona placed the dark green leaves
between her thumb and finger, releasing its heady aroma

and put her hands to her nostrils. The plant smelled of witchy herbs, her nose twitching as she put the branch back on her desk.

Mona opened her paint bag and lifted off the false bottom. It was an old doctoring case, the compartment underneath where physicians would keep the tools of their trade outside the gaze of anxious patients – forceps, scissors and knives. From it, Mona retrieved a rack and glass beaker and began her painstaking work.

After twenty minutes, she massaged her sore neck and drew back the curtains for a moment. In the distance, between the needles of rain and swaying trees, she could see the light of Mallory's cabin. The woman had gone back to her room. That was odd. A night manager should surely remain on the premises and not retire to their accommodation. Mona frowned. She had a feeling of things going wrong, a train of events knocking into each other like a row of dominos. She shook her drying curls. Fancy, nothing more. She should concentrate on the task in hand. Here was where the danger lay.

19

Mallory slept deeply for an hour, the previous night's restlessness forgotten in her exhaustion. Into her dream came the sound of a bell ringing and Mallory jerked awake as the shrill sound engulfed the room. She still had a deep headache and found her sheets were drenched in sweat. She was used to restless nights but not this feverish sleep. She rolled out of bed clutching her head. The weather had clearly taken a turn for the worse. The blanket fell to the floor as she stumbled to the phone, aware that the wind was screaming around the cabin.

'Mallory here.'

There was silence at the other end followed by a groan. She peered down at the display and saw the call was coming from room seven.

'Hello. Can I help?'

Mallory scrabbled for her jeans and reached into the back pocket pulling out the guest list. Room seven was occupied by Grace Pagonakis.

'Grace, is that you?'

The sound the girl was making was terrible, choking and gurgling into the handset.

Mallory, with mounting dread, kept her voice calm. 'I'm sending help now. Just wait there.'

Cursing there was no mobile signal in the cabin, Mallory cut the phone and dialled Tom's room. He answered on the third ring, his voice hoarse. 'Hello?'

'It's Mallory. I've just been called by the girl in room seven, a Grace Pagonakis.'

'What's the matter?'

'I don't know. There's just a strange sound coming down the phone. I'm worried she might be sick.'

Mallory heard Tom get up and clear his throat. 'Want me to look?'

'Would you? I'm coming over too. I'll just have to brave the weather. How was she when you checked on her earlier?'

'She seemed fine. She had her hair wrapped in a towel and was doing her nails. Hold on a sec while I put on my trousers. What's it like outside?'

Mallory drew back the curtain and stared into the black night. 'The wind is much worse. Tom, will you go straight away to check on the guest?'

'Are you sure? Maybe a woman would reassure her.'

Mallory thought of the sound at the other end of the line. 'No, you go. Try to speak to the girl to get her to open the door. I'll catch you up.'

When she'd cut off Tom, she tried to call Grace back but got the monotone of the engaged signal. She dressed quickly, pulling on a fresh pair of jeans and a clean vest and jumper. Mallory pulled on her walking boots, ignoring the agony in her leg. She fumbled around in a drawer and found some of the strong painkillers the hospital had given her. She took three – that would at least ease some of the misery. When she realised she could hardly place her foot on the floor, she changed the dressing, slathering the pad again with her ointment. That, at least, gave her enough relief to step out into the night.

She pulled at the door but it refused to budge. Panic made her pull harder until finally the door gave. Mallory looked out into the darkened evening and stared at the trail of destruction in front of her. One of the huge iron bins used by the gardener had upended and had rolled around the lawn, distributing grass clippings and pruned foliage in a wide arc in front of her cabin. Aware that the painkillers were only just touching the edge of her headache, Mallory ploughed forward as the wind howled around her. The orange lights of the Cloister gave her something to aim for and she kept her gaze on the building, conscious she hadn't prepared herself adequately for the walk. She needed a head torch, her lace-up boots, and a whistle or some kind of alarm in case she fell. Her phone was useless. She began to count to ten as she concentrated on putting one foot in front of the other and felt her breathing even.

The owl continued to hoot in distress, its cries carried out to sea by the wind. Thank God Tom had left the hallway light on, she used it as a beacon to guide herself across the grass using the step motion he'd taught her earlier. There were two lights shining from the upper floor windows. The first was Grace's room, which gave her hope. Perhaps the girl had let in Tom and was, at this moment, apologising for the phone call. The other light came from a room along the corridor, but Mallory was too tired to count the windows. One of the guests was still awake, which was hardly surprising given the howl of the wind.

She fell into the silent lobby with just the ticking of the wall clock audible. The silence was not reassuring. A guest in distress should surely call out before picking up the phone. The lack of noise suggested the other guests had heard nothing. Mallory took the stairs in twos, ignoring the knot of pain in her thigh. As she reached the top of the stairs, she heard a muffled knock. Tom must be trying to wake Grace. From her pocket, Mallory took out the master key as she turned the corner. Tom, she saw, had pulled a pair of jeans and a jumper over his pyjamas, and put on a pair of boots. His face was still crumpled with the imprint of his pillow.

'I can't get any answer.'

They both turned as a door opened at the end of the corridor and Julia Vass stuck her head out. 'Is everything all right?' she asked. She looked more curious than concerned.

'Nothing to worry about,' said Mallory in a low voice. 'Go back to bed. A guest needs a little help, that's all.'

The girl obligingly withdrew but Mallory got the impression that she was continuing to listen behind the closed door. She put her fingers to her lips. 'I'll go in first,' she told Tom.

The doors to each room had individual manual locks. Alex had wanted to install software where each guest opened their door with their smartphone. It fitted in with his discreet, high-tech vision for the place but had been persuaded that, in weather like this when power might go down, an old-fashioned key was equally in keeping with the design of the place. It suited Mallory fine as a single master key was easy to manage. She slipped it into the lock and saw that Grace had put the safety latch on.

'Shit.' Mallory put her face in the crack of the door. 'Grace, are you there?' She was met by a silence she knew too well from her days on the force. The sound of a complete absence of life.

'What can we do?' asked Tom. 'I can put my shoulder to the door if you like.'

'I need to get the security latch opener. It's kept in the safe.'

'Do you know the combination?'

'Of course I do. Stay there and wait for me.'

Mallory looked longingly at the lift but, worried it would make too much of a noise, stumbled down the stairs instead. Alex's office still smelt of the aftershave he splashed on himself. The latch opener with its forked prongs sat where Alex had showed it to her and she grabbed it, locking the safe after her. Back at Grace's door, it took her a minute or so to work out how to use the bloody thing. She'd been promising herself that she'd practise opening a door but had forgotten all about it in the busyness of her first few days here. She was aware of Tom breathing heavily behind her. Finally, the clasp gave and the door swung open. Mallory fumbled for the light. Aware that Tom was close on her heels, she blinked as the room was illuminated and together they stared at the floor.

20

CHARLOTTE

It was the night for fulfilling promises. Charlotte lay in bed fuming. Stuck on an island for the next day with an indifferent husband and a stepdaughter who despised her. What, wondered Charlotte, have I done to upset God this time? At least Noah couldn't blame her for their predicament because it had been his idea to come to the island. He'd initially told her he'd read about the place in a business magazine. Charlotte had spotted the lie immediately as he'd gone red in the tips of his ears, which was what he always did when he was being economical with the truth. Like the time he told her he didn't like her friend Diane flirting with him despite the fact Charlotte knew they were sleeping together.

Anyway, Noah was at home on Eldey. He liked anything which stank of exclusivity and had had money thrown at it. And this place fitted the bill, although the guests were an odd bunch. The small child stuck out like a sore thumb for starters but that wasn't what was really bothering her. Behind the restrained décor and high-end service, there was a weird vibe about the place that neither her husband or his tin-eared daughter had noticed. But Charlotte had felt it the moment she'd set foot on the place. She'd shuddered and the boat man who'd helped her off the craft had noticed.

'You'll be fine,' he'd whispered and touched his nose.

Oh, I'll be all right, she'd wanted to tell him. She always was, even though she'd not been able to shake the feeling something was off about this island. Perhaps it was because it'd once been the home of nuns. These Anglican religious sisters had been an exclusive bunch. Only women from the best families could enter the order and even then, the community was created and then closed off almost immediately. The whole concept stank of privilege and conceit.

The only positive was that she'd decided to use Eldey and its history to her own advantage. Well, why not? Noah thought her obsession was all in the past, despite his barbed comments, but things like that never really went away. She would make the best use of her time here.

Charlotte, lying next to her husband, was desperate to get out of bed, but Noah always woke immediately if she moved bedside him. He'd been late coming to bed, deciding to have yet another drink, which at least had allowed her the freedom to escape from the room. The weather outside had been terrible – a night for secrets and dark temptations. The hotel hadn't offered up much in the way of interest for Charlotte. If she was going to make the most of this trip, she needed to explore outside.

She'd followed the night manager out of the hotel without her even noticing. The wind had drowned out any noise she might have made and, in any case, Mallory had been busy talking into her two-way radio. Towards the grass edge, as Mallory had headed towards her cabin, she'd taken a different direction towards her destination. At the final moment, she'd been interrupted, a job left undone, which was no matter as she had plenty of time especially now the weather had closed in. The only issue was someone else had been out there, she was sure. The question was, had she been spotted?

Noah hadn't missed her damp clothes when she came back into the room. He raised his eyebrows, an expression which spoke volumes.

'Up to your old tricks again, Charlotte?'

Now, as she lay worrying, she could hear hushed movements in the corridor near their bedroom. People going about their business trying not to disturb other guests. Only she knew it was far too late for that.

21

Mallory had seen plenty of dead bodies. Knew how they looked and how they smelled. Knew in her old job that the discovery of a dead person was the beginning for her even if it signalled their end. A hotel bedroom is a miserable place to die, even one as luxurious as the Cloister. She glanced at Tom who was doing a good impression of a man trying not to be sick. He'd boasted about his time serving on a navy frigate but never actually explained what he'd done. Not seen many dead, judging by his complexion as surely battle-scarred casualties would look worse than this horror.

Mallory knelt over the body.

'Should we try CPR?' Tom swallowed, the guilt of the living temporarily displacing his fear, thought Mallory.

'I'm afraid it wouldn't do much good.' Mallory lifted Grace's hair. 'Look at the pool of blood and vomit around her head, and the burns on her lips. She's ingested something caustic which has ruined her insides.'

The statement threw Tom off kilter. He stumbled towards the toilet and from the cubicle came the unmistakable sounds of retching. In her job, she'd have been furious. Bathrooms are a forensic goldmine when faced with unexpected death. It was too late to warn him now. They'd have to incur the wrath of police when they arrived here. They'd be coming to investigate the death of Alys and now would be looking at another passing. Mallory's instincts were on high alert. Something was very wrong.

Mallory looked out of the still-dark window. It wouldn't be light until eight a.m. but even in the black-ness, she could hear the roar of Storm Ettie crossing the island. She needed to make some phone calls and hope that the phone line held. They relied on the subsea cable for the phone, which was connected to the hotel via seven poles. If any of those connections went, it would take the phone and internet with it. The lack of mobile coverage was also a big problem. She tried to remember how strong the signal was down by the shoreline but was pretty sure it was non-existent.

Tom came out wiping his mouth. 'Sorry about that.'

'How are you feeling?'

'Like shit.'

Mallory moved closer to Grace and looked at the girl's face. She'd died a horrific death. It said a lot about her personality that she'd tried to call for help while her throat was aflame. Something shifted inside Mallory, a hardening of her resolve. God, I've missed this, she thought. Tom, meanwhile, was likely to be a hindrance as she tried to work out what had gone on.

'What did you do in the Gulf War?' she asked him.

'Royal Navy Catering Service. I've never actually seen a dead body.'

'Figures.'

'You think she's drunk something she shouldn't have? Maybe she's killed herself.'

Mallory shrank from the note of hope in his voice. 'It's not suicide. No one would willingly drink this unless they were in a state of psychosis. It's a bloody awful way to die.'

'Jesus.' Tom looked like he was going to be sick again.

Mallory looked around her. There was an empty wine glass, with a small pool of vinegary red liquid at the bottom sitting on the table. Mallory bent over the goblet without touching it. 'I served her a glass of merlot last night. It looks like she brought it up to her room to finish, although I'll have to check with Elsa she didn't call down for another glass.'

'How does it smell?'

'Like merlot.' Mallory placed her finger in the pool. No stinging pain. She cautiously put a drop of the liquid on her tongue. 'Tastes like it too.'

'There's a glass on the floor over there.'

Mallory followed Tom's gaze and saw a tumbler lying on its side. Its creamy contents had spilt onto the carpet, turning the nutmeg-colour a scorched brown. Mallory, taking care not to move the position of the glass, dipped her finger in the liquid around the rim. The skin on her fingertip fried in an instant.

'Shit.' She ran to the bathroom and held her finger under the cold-water tap. So much for worrying Tom was disturbing a crime scene. It was more painful than her leg and that was saying something.

'Are you all right?' Tom appeared behind her.

'No, I'm bloody not. Whatever's in that cup nearly took my fingerprint off. Can you imagine how it must have felt swallowing that?' Mallory's hand began to shake as she held it under the icy water.

'Will you be OK?'

'I'll try to find some ointment in the first aid kit. I'll be fine.' Reluctantly Mallory withdrew her finger from the stream of water. 'When you came to check on Grace, did you see the glass by her bed?'

'I don't remember. I was in a rush to get to each guest after you said you'd seen someone outside your cabin. She said she was fine and I moved on.'

'Did she say anything?'

'I… I dunno.'

'Come on, Tom, how did she act?'

'She was surprised to see me and looked over my shoulder as if to check if anyone else was there.'

'She thought someone was with you? She wasn't worried?'

'No, not worried.' Tom scratched his stubble. 'A little distracted maybe.'

And the distraction would have made her careless. A glass of milk was an odd choice of drink. Not everyone, in these days of dairy-free alternatives, was likely to welcome a bedtime drink of milk. The question was how the glass had arrived at the room? The first possibility was that Grace had asked for a glass of milk and Elsa had delivered it from the fridge. She could check that easily enough. There was no staff apart from Tom and Elsa to deliver the drink and Tom clearly had no knowledge of it. The second possibility was that Grace had gone down to the kitchen and poured herself a glass of milk which by accident had been mixed with a poisonous substance. The final possibility was that someone else had brought the glass to the room – either while Grace was here, or when she was down at dinner. It was this last option that made Mallory go cold.

'What do you think happened? How did the stuff get inside the glass?' asked Tom.

'That's what I intend to find out.'

Mallory rifled through the bathroom, which held a few scraps of tissue and the wads of cotton wool Grace had used to remove her makeup. She'd need to painstakingly check the room once Tom was out of the way. His sickly complexion was putting her off the tick box list she usually went through when faced with an unexplained death.

'She was calling you for help?' Tom grimaced at the blood splatter on the receiver.

'She'll have dialled reception and been transferred to me. It was an act of bravery in terrible circumstances. We might not have noticed anything until well after breakfast otherwise. We'll need to leave everything as it is while I call the police.'

'What will we do with the body?' asked Tom.

'We'll turn off all the heating to this room and lock the door. Within hours the temperature should drop to that of a domestic fridge given the weather conditions outside. Even colder, hopefully. I'll find a thermometer and keep an eye on it. It'll halt decomposition for a while.' And make things more complicated for the pathologist, no doubt, she thought.

'We leave her here?'

For a moment, Mallory felt sorry for him. 'It's the best I can do, Tom. It's a crime scene even if it's an accident. That substance shouldn't have been in the glass.'

'What about the other guests? Won't they notice she's not around?'

'If they ask, we'll say she wants to stay in her room. With any luck the storm will ease off later and the police can make their way over here tonight.'

'It won't happen today.'

'Probably not,' admitted Mallory. 'In any case, it's forecast to pass by tomorrow. It's only just over twenty-four hours. Just carry on as usual, starting with breakfast.'

'Breakfast?' Tom made a face.

'Listen, Tom.' Mallory crossed the room and grasped his arm. She could sense his fear, his desperation to be anywhere but this room. 'You have to try to act as normal. I'll speak to Elsa so she doesn't come in here to clean, but we keep it between us three. We don't want guests panicking because they're sharing the space with a dead body.'

'No. You're right. I'll manage.'

'The first thing you do is check the milk. Wear gloves and put anything opened to one side. Use only unopened milk and check it first by pouring a little into a glass and testing it with your finger. If it gets too much for you, give me a call and I'll help. But I want to be in the dining room reassuring guests when they start to wake.'

'Do you think it's connected to what happened to Alys?'

Good question. 'I don't know. Look, we'll talk about this later.'

Before leaving the room, Mallory squatted once more over Grace and looked again at the trail of blood and vomit. The girl had been acting strangely at dinner admittedly but she was positive the girl hadn't died this way by her own hand. She would need to talk to Elsa as to the whereabouts of the cleaning fluids. Any accident involving caustic substances would be disastrous for the hotel, but the alternative was much, much worse. Because only she knew that Alys had also died the evening before. If the two were connected, she was on the island with a killer.

22

Mallory hesitated outside room five. The correct thing to do would be to ring the police immediately. The investigating officer, when they managed to get here, would check the precise moment Mallory and Tom discovered the body and how it fitted with the timing of the emergency call. A gap between the discovery and reporting of a victim hinted at prevarication and guilt. Mallory, however, was prepared to wait. She was conscious of the safety of the guests and the first thing she wanted was a second opinion from someone who might be able to answer her questions. At this hour, with the weather so appalling, she could surely gain time by asking the doctor to confirm the cause of death. Taking a deep breath, she rapped on the door.

'Hello?' Michael's voice on the other side of the door was alert.

'It's Mallory, the night manager. I'm sorry to disturb you but I have a problem with a guest that I'd like your help with.'

'Hold on.' She listened as Michael made his way across the room and opened the door. He was fully dressed but had changed from his jumper and jeans at dinner into a navy tracksuit. He noticed Mallory taking in his clothes. 'What's the problem?'

'Can I come in?' Mallory looked down the corridor. There were only two ground-floor bedrooms and number six was unoccupied. Nevertheless, she was conscious someone had roamed the corridor that evening leaving a trail of wet footprints. Michael stepped back to let Mallory in, shutting the door behind her.

'There were two guests who ate by themselves this evening. One of them was wearing a short dress with high heels.'

'I remember. She had a bob and was wearing a lot of makeup.'

'That's her. She called reception in distress about fifteen minutes ago. I used my key to get into the room and I found her lying on the floor. I'm afraid she's dead.'

'Dead?' Michael's voice rose a fraction. 'Are you sure?'

'Very sure, but I'd like you to take a look before I call it in.' Mallory hesitated. 'I have to tell you that I'm treating it as a possible crime scene. This isn't a natural death. Can you look at her without disturbing anything?'

'Of course. I'd better come now.' Michael picked up his key, tucked it in the pocket of his trousers, and reached for his cane. In silence, as they walked down the corridor, Mallory was aware that Michael had a reassuring presence that went beyond the fact he was a medic. Here was someone who'd be good in any crisis. They took the lift to the first floor, Mallory wincing at the loud chime as the doors opened. She half-expected a curious guest to see what the comings and goings were but the upper landing remained silent. Inside Grace's room, Michael bent over the girl's body, his hands lifting back Grace's hair as Mallory had done minutes earlier. She saw him wince as he took in the blood and vomit.

'What do you think?' she asked him.

'She appears to have ingested a caustic substance. I wouldn't like to look at the state of the girl's oesophagus or stomach.'

'It's as I thought.' Mallory groaned. 'I think she drank from that glass by the bed.'

Michael bent down.

'Don't touch it,' Mallory said, holding out her finger. Michael grasped her hand and looked at the burn.

'Does it hurt,' he asked.

'It's agony.'

'But you're used to it.' He kept hold of her hand. 'I've seen you limping too.'

She pulled her hand away. 'What do you suggest for the pain?'

'Take one of your strong painkillers and keep the burn wet. Clingfilm is a good idea. What was the girl's name?'

'I can't tell you. I'm sorry but, even in death, she's entitled to privacy.'

'Of course.' He looked around the room, as if committing it to memory.

'I'll call the police from my office,' said Mallory. 'Then Alex, the manager.'

Michael asked the same question as Tom. 'Do you think this is connected to what happened in reception?'

'I don't know. Alys's injuries were nothing like this.'

'That's true. It's an odd coincidence though.'

'The main thing is to protect the scene. There's something going on I can't get my head around.'

They were both silent as they listened to the weather raging outside.

'Help will be a little while coming, I think,' said Michael. He kept his eyes on her. 'You seem to know about procedure. I noticed it earlier with your receptionist.'

'I'm a former detective. Medically retired. I do know about these things.'

Michael nodded. 'Poisonings do happen accidentally, you know. Stray bottles put where they shouldn't be. I've seen it occasionally. Bleach, drain cleaner, detergents even. It's not necessarily a crime scene.'

'What I'm struggling to understand is how a caustic substance ended up in the glass. She was perfectly fine when Tom knocked on everyone's doors around midnight. Does bleach do this to you?' She showed him her fingertip.

He made a face. 'Not bleach then. Could be an industrial cleaning product though.'

'I know it's late but would you wait a moment while I look through the guest's personal belongings? I just want to satisfy myself I'm not missing anything.'

Using a tissue so her fingerprints wouldn't contaminate evidence, Mallory opened Grace's handbag. It contained a purse, mobile phone and an asthma inhaler. Mallory puffed the Ventolin into the room and wrinkled her nose at the familiar chemical smell. The purse had a few pounds in it and the usual credit and loyalty cards. It also had, folded into quarters, a postcard which contained details of the prize she'd won for her stay at the Cloister. Mallory took a photograph of the card with her mobile phone camera and put everything back as she'd found it. They both jumped at the crash of a wave against the rocks underneath them.

'Thank you for looking.' Mallory thought Michael looked shattered and wondered how much sleep he managed to get every night. 'I'll have to mention your name to the police. Is that OK?'

'Fine by me. Do you need me for anything else? I could talk to the police if that would help.'

Mallory shook her head. 'I'll be fine. Can I ask for your discretion until the boats are up and running? I don't think your fellow guests will appreciate the fact that they're sharing the hotel with a dead body.'

'Of course, I won't say a thing.'

'I appreciate that. Just so you know, neither the staff nor guests are aware of the first death either.' Mallory crossed to the far side of the room, turned down the radiator to zero and opened the window a crack so a sheet of cold air blasted onto the sill.

'I thought as much. I've not mentioned it to anyone either.'

'Thank you.'

It was a moment for asking questions she might otherwise have held back. Death, she'd found, did that. Stripped away the niceties and rules of behaviour.

'Can I ask why you chose to come to the Cloister?'

Michael froze and the mask came down again. 'Am I a suspect?'

'Of course not. I'd hardly have asked you to look at the body if I thought you responsible for the death. But I am interested in why you came here.'

Michael shrugged. 'I'm busy at the GP practice. When I go away, I like to unwind. I'm here for a week of relaxation, that's all.'

'It's just—'

'That I should be in a wheelchair?'

'No.' Mallory blanched. 'I never thought that.'

'You wouldn't be the first to think it. I get by fine and I go on my holidays wherever I fancy. When I booked this place in July, Eldey was what appealed.'

Mallory had had enough. 'Look, I feel I'm constantly offending you. If you're so bloody paranoid about your injuries, don't take it out on me.'

'That's rich coming from you. Has a doctor signed you as fit to work? I'd bet whatever is making you limp is still agonising. You should be on a period of extended rest.'

Mallory stepped forward. 'Let's forget it, shall we? I appreciate your help confirming the death. I'll ask for your discretion again.'

'Fine.' Michael opened the door and she heard him walking away from the room. She wondered what possessed her to get into an argument with a guest, especially given the circumstances. She forced herself to focus on Grace and the glass lying beside her. The police would be able to unpick the timeline of Grace's movements far better than she once they got here. She simply needed to hold the fort until help arrived. The mystery of why Grace had acted so oddly at dinner would be theirs to solve.

23

Mallory dialled 999, not because she thought there was an urgent need for the police to hear the news but because it was a death and an unnatural one. Grace Pagonakis deserved an emergency call. The conversation was brief. The emergency police handler said a member of the team would call back and a craft would be launched as soon as the weather calmed. There was no chance of a helicopter in this weather; it was too windy to launch and, in any case, it was needed to deal with helping residents escape flooding in the town. The lifeboat was on standby but wouldn't assist a land-based incident especially if it wasn't an emergency.

The second call was to Alex who, as she'd predicted, panicked.

'For fuck's sake, Mallory. What happened?'

'I don't know...' Mallory's finger was as agonising as her leg. Not sure how else to relieve the pain, she stuck it in a glass of water.

'Can't you guess? You were in the police.'

'It'll be up to a pathologist to work out the cause of death. I got Doctor Hutton in room five to take a look. He's the same guest who tried to help Alys. He thinks, like me, she drank milk which contained a caustic substance. He told me of cases where these types of accidents occur. I only hope he's right.'

'It was in a glass of milk? Then it must have come from the kitchen.'

'I'll ask Elsa, of course, but Tom knew nothing of it.'

'Poisoned? Do you think it's the same stuff that killed Alys?'

Mallory put her hand over her aching head. 'No, I don't. Did the paramedics say anything at all about possible cause of death?'

'Not much. It'll be in the hands of the pathologist but we're looking for urgent answers. It's a public health issue as I run a hotel. I just hope it's still a viable going concern by the time I get back. One death could put me out of business, let alone two.'

'Don't make any assumptions until I know more. I'm sure Grace Pagonakis didn't die from the same poison as Alys. She drank something corrosive.'

'Christ. All the cleaning stuff is kept locked up. Elsa has a key. Get her to show you the cupboard. I don't like the idea a bottle might be where it shouldn't.'

'I'll do that straight away.'

'Oh God,' said Alex. Mallory could imagine him brushing back his hair with his hands which he usually did when he was stressed. 'I don't know what I'd do if you weren't there. Do you think you can keep Elsa calm?'

'I'll try. What *is* the issue with Elsa?'

'An overactive imagination. She keeps talking about her Auntie Joanne and some poisoned nun. I'm afraid I've been humouring her over that but, given the circumstances, do not let her anywhere near the guests.'

'She'll need to give their rooms a clean. There's nowhere for them to go while she does it unless they assemble in the lounge. I'm not sure I'll be able to help much today.' Mallory removed her finger from the glass and inspected the burn. She'd try ointment and a plaster next.

'Get them to do that then. Tell them over breakfast that they're to vacate their rooms while housekeeping takes place. They'll probably be grateful for the change of scenery. What's the weather doing over there?'

'Listen.' Mallory put her phone to the window. 'Can you hear?'

'Oh God.' Alex sighed down the line. 'Just do your best, would you?'

Mallory put the phone down and checked the time. It was quarter to six in the morning and the hotel would be beginning to wake up. There were always early risers and, judging by the smell wafting into her office, Tom had already started cooking breakfast. Mallory needed to move. Her body was beginning to slow down as if desperate to catch up on the interrupted sleep.

Mallory turned on her computer and brought up Grace Pagonakis's details. She was thirty-three years old with a Hastings address that tallied with her story. Her room had been prepaid, as Grace had said, by a company called Gum Candy. A quick internet search confirmed it was a beauty box subscription organisation where, for a fee, you got a package of products every month. Mallory was itching to give them a call but that was police work and she might jeopardise any prosecution if she meddled in any way. There was no information about next of kin. Again, this would have to be left to the police.

Mallory rubbed her aching head. Everything tallied. Grace's details appeared to confirm she was who she'd claimed to be. A teacher who'd struck lucky by winning a competition to a place that would otherwise have been out of her price range. Yet Mallory was sure that the girl had recognised someone the previous evening. A guest whose birthday she thought it was. Mallory typed Grace's name into a search engine. She had an unusual surname, probably Greek in origin. To her surprise, Grace's name revealed over four thousand hits. Mallory opened the top result and stared at the screen.

24

Extract from *LARA* e-magazine article:
Children Who Kill. Why do they do it?

…Some killings, however, defy even the most rational of explanations. The murders that took place in the summer of 1996 have left psychologists, lawyers and police professionals scratching their heads over the killer's motive. The details have, of course, become legendary. In a Wilmslow suburb, a group of schoolgirls were having high tea to celebrate Bryony Clive's eleventh birthday. Even the very act of having a tea party was unusual in a decade of celebratory cinema trips and pottery painting. Bryony, however, was a precocious child who loved reading detective novels and studying the flowers in the family's well-stocked garden. When she grew up, she wanted to be a botanist, she told her doting mother.

It was Florence Bowden's faint that first alerted the other children that something was wrong. She slid down the chair, her legs flailing against the stripped pine table decorated with home-made bunting. She began convulsing on the floor and was dead within seconds. Ruth Watson died soon after because she'd eaten a second helping of pavlova, encouraged by Bryony who gave her a glassful of elderflower cordial to help down the slightly dry meringue. The cordial was poisoned too.

Olivia Clarke was taken to the local hospital with hopes that she'd survive. A life of dialysis before a kidney transplant was her likely fate, doctors informed her parents, but the havoc wreaked by plant-based toxins is difficult to predict. She died later that evening despite everyone's best efforts.

Only Grace Pagonakis made a full recovery, mainly because she didn't like elderflower cordial and had instead opted for a glass of lemonade. She'd only ingested a spoonful of pavlova when Florence passed out and required just a brief stay in hospital.

Bryony Clive, the perpetrator of the crime, survived. Her claim to also have symptoms of poisoning meant the much-needed antidote of atropine wasn't administered to the surviving girls. Her actions came to light in hospital when a nurse became suspicious of Bryony's manner. Under questioning, the pre-teen admitted to having deliberately added the crushed leaves of two foxglove plants she knew to have poisonous properties to the jug of cordial and to the pavlova cream after distracting her mother in the kitchen. When asked for her reasons for killing her school friends, she said that she was entitled to as 'it was her birthday'. It is this comment that shocked the public and has added to Bryony's infamy. It also gave her the nickname by which she has become known throughout the world – The Birthday Girl.

After a short trial, Bryony was found guilty of the murder of her three friends and of the attempted killing of Grace Pagonakis. She was jailed for a minimum of seventeen years, the sentence more lenient than you might expect on account of her being a minor, although still above the age of criminal responsibility. Although her anonymity was ensured during the court proceedings, the judge agreed that it was in the public interest for her name to be published following the guilty verdict, although strict reporting conditions meant that no photographs have ever been released. Bryony's current location is unknown, and she will also have been given a new name on release. There have been many attempts in the popular press to discover her new identity and in 2018, in response to a particularly aggressive media campaign, a new whole life order was made protecting her anonymity and that of her family.

The whereabouts of Bryony Clive, The Birthday Girl, can never be revealed.

25

Mallory sat back in her chair, her mind racing. Surely it was impossible that another girl with the name Grace Pagonakis had survived a poisoning twenty-five years earlier while a different Grace was lying dead upstairs killed by a toxic substance. Mallory forced her mind to quieten and considered what assumptions she'd have made as a detective. The first thing would be to confirm for certain that the Grace of the Wilmslow poisonings was the same Grace lying dead in her room. Mallory went into the image search and, although she found nothing of Grace as a child, eight years ago, there had been a 'Where are they now' feature in a weekly celebrity magazine on victims of crime. In the article, Grace sat in a high-backed armchair in a small apartment overlooking the sea, her gaze pensive. Mallory scanned the accompanying article, feeling sorry for the girl. She was working as a teacher but still unable to shake off the reputation she'd gained as a survivor of a tragedy that had killed so many.

In the article, despite clearly being the victim of a terrible tragedy, she came across as whiny and insecure. Mallory wondered if it was biased reporting or an accurate reflection of Grace's personality. The papers hadn't liked Bryony Clive so there should have been some sympathy towards Grace given she was clearly a victim. The main thrust of the article was that it was her life that had been ruined by the poisonings, not Bryony's. The family had been forced to move away from Cheshire and begin a new life in the south. She'd also not been given the same anonymity as Bryony. Journalists had made periodic attempts to track Grace down, something they were not allowed to do with a killer who had an anonymity order. Mallory felt a flash of sympathy for the girl. It wasn't the first time a criminal had been afforded more privacy than their victim.

Grace stated she was giving this, her only interview, to draw a line under her past. Her justification for the media piece sounded off to Mallory. Plenty of victims of crime never gave an interview to the media. More likely Grace needed the money these magazines paid. It couldn't be easy surviving on a teacher's salary. Mallory amended her search term to include the girl's name and 'interview'. Although there were no more media articles connected to Bryony, towards the bottom of the screen, Mallory spotted a link to *Primary* magazine. It was a chatty, light-hearted publication aimed at teachers. In the spring edition of the previous year, Grace was featured in the 'about you' feature. A list of dull questions had been answered briefly but it was the final two that made Mallory frown.

Q: Favourite treat?

A: My monthly Gum Candy Beauty Box.

Q: How do you relax in the evenings?

A: Watching Netflix with a glass of milk before bed.

Mallory put her head in her hands, thinking. Coincidence was becoming an increasingly desperate explanation for what had happened last night. Here, on the internet, Grace had given away two clues to her life that had resulted in her coming to Eldey and ultimately dying. She had also mentioned a birthday. As Mallory was considering whether to call the police again and demand a lifeboat bring some detectives over, a knock on the door startled her.

'Come in,' she shouted, shutting down the page and looking at her watch. In the doorway stood Beth.

'Is everything all right?'

'I wondered if I could have a glass of milk for Edith. I know breakfast isn't for an hour, but I don't think she can wait that long.'

Mallory swallowed. 'Milk?'

Beth looked embarrassed. 'Is that OK? It needs to be whole milk for the baby not skimmed.'

Mallory shook herself. 'Of course. I'll fetch some for you. Do you want to wait in the lobby?'

Tom was pale and regarding two half-full plastic bottles he'd placed to one side – one blue topped, the other red – plus cartons of almond, oat, and soya milk. 'I'm sorry, Mallory, but I had to check. I unscrewed the caps with my gloves on in case they're tested for fingerprints and tried a bit from each bottle.'

'Are you mad? Did you see what it did to Grace?'

'I only touched the contents with my fingers first. If it was the same substance, it would have burnt the skin the same as yours. They're both fine, Mallory. None of the bottles have been tampered with.'

Mallory sighed. 'That's something at least but we assume the milk came from here until we know otherwise. Put those opened bottles on a shelf somewhere for when the police get here. Not back in the fridge.'

'I've plenty of fresh milk with the seals intact. There was a delivery Friday. We'll be fine for breakfast.'

'Mrs Gregory wants some milk for her daughter. It'll need to be full cream. Can you open a bottle and test it in front of me?'

Tom pulled out a fresh blue-topped bottle of milk from the fridge. She watched as he checked for leaks and then examined the plastic seal. When he was satisfied, he poured a glass and handed it to Mallory. He also poured a glass for himself and, after checking it with his finger, took a sip, then a healthy swig. Despite his pallor, he managed a wink to Mallory.

'From a local farm. Tastes delicious.'

'Thanks. Use that one for guests who want whole milk. I'll take this glass to Beth.'

In reception Beth was staring, as she'd done the previous evening, at the wind through the huge window. When Mallory approached, she pointed at the gate to the winding path down to the harbour.

'How will we be rescued with the trees over the path?'

'They're easily moved once help gets here. I'm just not risking it until the storm dies down. There's too much debris flying around. Try not to worry.'

'What about the building next to where the ferry berths? It looks like a boathouse.'

Mallory frowned. 'There's no boat on the island as far as I'm aware and even if there were, it's far too dangerous to risk it. It's only lifeboats that can deal with this sea.'

'Won't they come to rescue us?'

Mallory shook her head. 'They're an emergency service. Unless we were in trouble on or near the sea, there's no reason for them to get involved.'

Back in her office, taking advantage of precious minutes before the guests came down, Mallory forced herself to concentrate. Grace, over twenty years earlier, had been a victim of Bryony Clive who was no run-of-the-mill poisoner. The name of her attacker was instantly recognisable. Bryony Clive had achieved infamy of sorts; it was impressive, given that no photograph of the girl had ever been released. It was one of the few nods given to Bryony's age given that, in the 1990s, they were still treating children accused of crimes as adults.

The age of criminal responsibility was ten years of age and Bryony had been tried in an adult criminal court. Some of the more socially aware commentators had written about the unfairness of this and that no lessons had been learnt since the trial of the killers of Jamie Bulger three years earlier. That a girl who was evidently still a child sitting on a bench dwarfed by her legal team and social worker should be treated as an adult was nonsensical. However, for every concerned writer, there was one ready to heap contempt on Bryony. How the girl was intrinsically evil and that she was bad rather than mad. Mallory was pretty sure a former colleague of hers had got in on the act, writing a memoir about her days as a detective investigating the famous poisonings.

Mallory massaged her temples. Was this who Grace had recognised when she'd stood on the threshold of the dining room? She'd made that cryptic comment about a birthday and now she was dead by poison. Typing the name Bryony Clive into Google, she realised the extent to which Bryony's anonymity order stretched. There not only wasn't a photo of the girl, but no description whatsoever. She could have had blonde hair and blue eyes, be a red head, have olive skin. There was no clue to the girl's identity. All Mallory had was an age. Bryony would be in her early thirties now.

Mallory pulled her guest list out of her pocket and examined it. Beth Gregory could be Bryony. Jesus, she hadn't considered that when she'd given her the milk. What the hell had she been thinking? She should have looked closer at the woman's reactions. In her early-thirties, she was the right age. She had dyed dirty-blonde hair and pale blue eyes. It was worth making a note of these characteristics in case she could get some inform-ation from police or a rogue newspaper article about what Bryony might have looked like. However, she didn't really think Beth was a contender. The Bryony in the article shouted arrogance and intelligence. She couldn't comment on Beth's intellect, but the woman was far from egotistical.

Charlotte Vass was about the same age too. She had mid-brown hair with dark blue eyes. Could an awkward Bryony morph into cool Charlotte? Mallory didn't think so. Charlotte had an accent that shouted privilege, which would surely have been blurred by years of incarceration. Noah, with his arrogance and assurance of his place in society, would not have married a Bryony Clive unless anonymity orders gave Bryony the right not to tell her partners of the crimes she'd committed. Mallory took two paracetamols from a blister pack and looked at the list. The third possibility was Mona Rubin, which was also hard to believe. Her flame-coloured hair was striking. Was it dyed though? Mallory was no expert but she suspected it had come from a bottle. Mona was sensitive, creative, with a warm aura. She didn't sound like Bryony either.

Mallory drummed her pencil on the desk and considered the other women on the island. Stella Atkinson was far too old to be Bryony and Elsa too young. So, if Bryony was on the island, there were only three possibilities: Beth, Charlotte or Mona. The odd thing was that all three women were physically, if not similar in looks, of a similar body type; above average in height and of very slim build.

She picked up the phone and called her former colleague Shan. She could see him in his white shirt, a little too tight for him, his tattooed triceps bulging under the short sleeves.

'Mallory? This is an early call.' He was surprised to hear from her. She could hear him munching on his breakfast. Probably one of the almond croissants he loved. 'What you up to?'

'I have a new job. A night manager at a hotel.'

'OK. You enjoying it?'

'Great if you like being in gale force conditions.'

'Bad?'

'Bad as in we're cut off with a dead body and my boss is stuck in the nearby town.'

Shan whistled. 'You're not calling me for reinforcements, are you? Not much I can do from here.'

'Look, we've a guest who died in the night called Grace Pagonakis. The thing is she was a victim of a poisoning in the nineties. Remember Bryony Clive?'

'The Birthday Girl.'

'Right. I've called in the death to the local force, and they'll get here as soon as the weather clears. But I've just discovered the background to Grace and, given how oddly she was acting the other evening, I need to try to find out the identity of Bryony when she was released. I need to ensure the safety of the other guests.'

'You think she might be there.'

'I think it's a possibility, but I really hope I'm wrong on this one.'

'Bryony Clive was just a kid, wasn't she? She'll be subject to a whole life order.'

'She is.'

'Then there's no chance of getting any information. It'll be restricted. Is the death suspicious?'

'Definitely, although part of me is hoping it's a horrible accident. She died by swallowing poison.'

'Not suicide?' asked Shan.

'I don't think so but it's not my call. The thing is, we lost our receptionist yesterday from food poisoning.'

'Lost, as in died?'

'I'm afraid so.'

'Bloody hell. Then just wait for the local CID to get there. Come on, you know the drill.'

'Shan, I'm stuck here with a body. The guests will be asking where she is at some point and she made a reference to a birthday when I last saw her at dinner. There's no one whose date of birth tallies with that comment but I have found a connection with Bryony Clive who poisoned her friends on her birthday. So, what I'd really like to know is if Bryony is part of the party.'

Shan, always one for a warped sense of humour, sniggered. 'Stay away from anything that smells of bitter almonds.'

'Very funny. I'll strike the Bakewell pudding from tonight's dessert.'

'Look, why don't you try Anna Kirby? She was one of the DSs who worked on the case.'

'Why her in particular?'

'She retired a couple of years ago and wrote a book about her experiences interviewing Bryony. It was a bit of a pot boiler, but a good story. I read it on the plane one holiday. It caused quite a stir, I remember. The force isn't that hot on ex-coppers writing about their cases, especially when there are whole life orders involved. She won't be able to give you Bryony's new name, of course, but she'll be able to describe what she looked like, any character traits. She must look a little like she did as a child if your victim recognised her. Anna might be able to give you some inside gossip too. Which county she'd been relocated to, for example. You might be able to match something with the details guests have provided on their booking information.'

'What's this DS's contact details?'

'Haven't a clue.'

'Shan!'

'Find it on the internet. It's what I'd have to do given she's retired. You're the former detective, remember. Do some detection.'

It took Mallory five minutes to find an email for Anna Kirby online. The author had a basic website, which hadn't been updated since 2015. The only reference was to her book, *The Birthday Girl*, published in 2004. Anna hadn't embraced a career in writing but had wanted to set down her story in relation to the Bryony Clive trial. That was fair enough, she supposed. Mallory hammered out a message and went to find Elsa.

26

'It's like the dead nun. Mam said this was a terrible place.' Elsa, trying to control her fright, was close to tears. As she watched Elsa panic, Mallory realised how young she was, not much older than Toby. Mallory put an arm round her thin shoulders as Elsa's chest rose and fell in shallow gasps.

'It's nothing like the nun, I promise you.'

'But you say she was poisoned.'

'She's ingested a liquid that has ruined her oesophagus and most of her insides. It's not berries I'm looking for. It's a substance much more corrosive. Can you show me the cleaning cupboard? We need to get to the bottom of this.'

They passed the hum of the dining room where a few of the early guests were helping themselves to a buffet breakfast laid on by Tom. Mallory spotted Mona at her usual corner table and Noah breakfasting without his wife. Mallory hurried Elsa on. She'd have to leave the food to Tom this morning as Elsa couldn't be trusted to keep it together in front of the guests. At the back of the building, near to the spa suite, a small room housed the fresh towels and bed sheets brought over from Tenby each day. From a set clipped onto her waist, Elsa found the key and slipped it into the lock. To one side, the linen was stacked high while through another door was a dedicated cleaning space with electric floor cleaner, industrial vacuum and an array of dusters and cloths. On the back wall was a metal, ceiling-height cupboard warning of hazardous contents. Elsa used another key to open that lock. Bottles of bleach and disinfectant were lined up on the shelves along with weedkiller sprays, wasp repellent and Jeyes Fluid.

'Lost your keys recently?' asked Mallory.

'Oh no.'

'Who else has a key?'

'Alys, the two other room attendants, and Alex.'

'Anyone mention losing their key?'

'Not to me. We have to report every missing key to Alex.'

'Does it look like anything has been disturbed?'

'I don't think so.'

No, Mallory didn't think so either. Alex had made every effort to keep the caustic products safe and any would-be poisoner would find it easier to bring their own bottle of drain cleaner, if that's what it was, readily available from any shop, rather than break into this cupboard. Mallory looked down at the clearly frightened girl.

'And you definitely didn't take a cup of milk up to Grace's bedroom.'

'Of course not. I've never had a guest ask me for a glass of milk late at night.'

Elsa was right. A glass of milk would have been an unusual request, but Grace's interview had made it clear it was her late-night drink of choice.

'Would you like a cup of tea in my office before you start cleaning the rooms? There's no need to go back to the breakfast room.'

'I'm drinking no tea.'

Mallory grimaced at Elsa's logic, but she was, of course, right. Until they found how the substance had got into

Grace's glass, everyone would need to be careful. But Elsa, she suspected, was more resilient than she looked and Mallory needed any help available. 'Elsa. Would you help me?'

Elsa looked up at her. 'How?'

'When you're cleaning the rooms, I want you to look for something out of the ordinary. I don't know what, so just look for anything you wouldn't expect to see in a hotel room or something different from when you cleaned the rooms yesterday.'

'You want me to look for a murderer?'

'Of course not.' She saw she'd failed to reassure the girl. 'Listen, I won't go back to the lodge tonight. I'll stay in your room – it has twin beds, hasn't it? We can keep each other company. If it's your safety you're worried about, I'll make sure you're not on your own.'

Elsa's lip began to tremble. 'Is that OK?'

'Of course. If there's a problem and I'm not around, speak to Tom. You can also trust Doctor Hutton, I think. He's the only guest who knows about Grace's death. If he asks you her name, though, please don't tell him. I need to keep things quiet until the police get here.'

'OK.' Elsa swallowed, looking unhappy.

Mallory looked at her watch. 'When everyone's had breakfast, I'll come to find you and give you a hand. Alex is sending an e-mail asking guests to vacate their rooms while you're tidying them. If anyone hasn't seen it, just ask them politely to go to one of the public rooms downstairs. Any problem, come and find me.'

'All right.'

'And Elsa, please, don't call anyone. Especially not your mum. This has to remain private until help gets here.'

Elsa bit her lip and nodded.

27

MONA

The weather meant that Mona would have to change her plans.

After the productivity of the previous day, Mona felt sluggish. That was the problem with bursts of creativity – you couldn't keep up the momentum. Today, she realised, would be back to the grindstone trying to give the wonderful story she was working on some decent illustrations. She allowed herself half a croissant and a cup of black coffee and left the breakfast room. If truth be told, she didn't feel comfortable with the other dining guest. She'd seen him throw the glass of red wine over his wife the previous evening and that was enough for her. It was a shame as she'd have liked to gauge the mood of the other residents. If the weather forecasts were right, she had the pleasure of another twenty-four hours in their company. Enforced isolation affected people in different ways and it would be an interesting study to watch peoples' reactions. However, she wouldn't get her chance that morning and she didn't blame her fellow guests for having a lie in. The day would be long enough as it was.

Mona saw Mallory pass with the chambermaid. They had an air of co-conspirators about them. Mona yawned. She wondered how Alex was doing on the shore. Mallory looked like she could cope with anything so none of the guests particularly felt his absence. In fact, Mona thought she was probably the only one missing him at the moment. For all his insecurities, he made for interesting company. He also had a business brain. She'd negotiated a decent weekly rate for her stay here and he'd known immediately that it would keep him in profit.

Mona wondered if she should go upstairs and open her paints. Another picture wouldn't get done unless she applied herself. First, though, she needed to clear her mind with a swim in the long pool. She left the dining room, feeling the man's eyes on her backside. In her room, she changed into her swimming costume and put on the hotel's dressing gown and slippers. She tucked her key into the pocket of the robe and left everything else in her room. As she walked along the corridor, a door opened, and Stella poked her head out.

'Off to the sauna?' she asked.

'Having a swim.'

'Mind if I join you?'

Mona frowned. She did mind. The plan was to get into the zone for her next task and she was hardly likely to do that with Stella chatting next to her. However, caught on the hop, she couldn't think how to say no politely. 'I'll meet you down there. Perhaps we can have a chat in the sauna once I've had my swim.'

Alex had been very clever in designing the spa suite. It would have been so easy to have done it wrong but he'd installed a long thin pool down the side of the building. Most architects would have put it outside the building encasing it in glass but the windows would have been a nightmare to clean and it would have made for uncomfortable swimming when the weather was terrible.

Instead, it ran along the interior of the building, giving swimmers complete privacy. To one side there was the exterior stone wall with no windows for prying eyes. On the other, behind smoked glass, the three exercise machines were deliberately placed so they didn't face the pool.

It suited Mona well. Sick of being ogled in the local gym, she'd given up swimming but here, as she went into the water, she felt her body relax as her limbs stretched out. She was on her fifth lap when she heard a door bang. Stella must have decided to have a swim first. She moved to one side of the pool to make space for whoever was going to join her. The narrow space was only suitable for two swimmers doing lengths at a time. As she swam towards the end nearest the entrance, she saw no other guest. Perhaps Stella had decided to go to the sauna instead. Ploughing on, Mona became aware she was being watched. Damn the person who was doing this to her. She sped up, refusing to be intimidated but her peace had been disturbed.

At the end of her twentieth lap, she gave up and reached for a towel. As she wiped her face and her eyes cleared, she saw a thin shape the other side of the darkened glass. Someone was watching her. She pulled on her dressing gown and marched to the door, wrenching it open. The wellness room was quiet. A massage bed in one corner was draped ready for a customer. Mona crossed to the sauna and pulled open the door, giving Stella a start. 'Bloody hell. You made me jump. Is everything all right?'

'I thought I saw someone watching me in the pool.'

'Are you sure?' Stella fanned herself in the heat. 'I didn't see anyone when I came down.'

'It was just now. Did you hear a door bang?'

'In here?' Stella gestured around. 'Can't hear a thing.'

'Oh, don't worry. No mystery, I suppose. I just don't like being stared at.'

Stella snorted. 'It's a long time since it happened to me. Enjoy it while you can.'

'Not bloody likely,' said Mona, laying a towel on the slats.

28

Mallory, in fact, didn't believe in coincidences at all. Her job had taught her that if it was a toss-up between chance encounters and criminal intent, it was usually the latter. Take the coffee issue. Alys had admitted to drinking coffee like it was going out of fashion. Perhaps it wasn't the hummus that had made Alys ill, but the coffee. Shit. She, Stella, Grace, and Alys had all drunk coffee and fallen ill to some degree. Alys, who drank the stuff by the bucketful, had died. Of course, Mallory couldn't be a hundred per cent sure that poison had deliberately been put in the coffee on reception, but Tom's hygiene standards were high. It was a big coincidence Alys's death had come the evening before Grace's death by ingested poison. Here, she was on surer ground as Grace's likely cause of death had been confirmed by Michael Hutton, a trained doctor. Unless she was so distracted she'd poured something poisonous into her milk then her killing was deliberate too.

Mallory would use criminal intent as her working hypothesis – she simply couldn't see how an accident could have taken place. The problem was how different the types of poisonings were. Alys had died but not through the ruining of her throat like Grace. Meanwhile, she and the guests had merely struggled with a headache. This suggested someone either didn't know what they were doing or they had simply intended to make the coffee drinkers ill, nothing more. Perhaps Alys did have an underlying condition. Mallory was certain of one thing: Grace had been meant to die, there was no doubt about that given the corrosive nature of the substance.

Then there was the issue of Bryony, which Mallory needed to think through properly. It would help if she had a clearer head, not the dull achy one which pounded every time she moved and which her medication was not touching. Mallory massaged her temples, trying to conjure a scenario where Bryony might be on the island. Beneath the salacious tone of the news reports, it had been clear that Bryony had an obsession with poisons, which had appalled those following the case. Mallory doubted addictions ever faded. An alcoholic would be forever drawn to drink while a former anorexic would likely have a complex relationship with food. Whatever support Bryony had received in the secure unit she'd been sent to post-conviction, Mallory guessed would only dull the girl's obsession, not overcome it.

And now, on an island known for a nun who'd eaten poisonous berries, was a dead girl who'd once been the victim of Bryony Clive. Mallory was happy to risk the scorn of the investigative team when they got here by assuming that Bryony was also here. She would call the police again, this time asking for CID. If they needed a court order to reveal the identity of Bryony Clive, then now was the time to start the process. First, however, she was conscious she'd left the guests to fend for themselves this morning. She'd check on the breakfasters.

In the dining room was Charlotte Vass, eating alone. The insouciance of the previous evening had gone, replaced by a mannered boredom. She picked at her bowl of fruit and yoghurt while her eyes strayed to the window overlooking the lawned front although there was precious little to see through the rain-smeared glass. It was impossible to ignore the crack of the waves and intensity of the wind that was rattling at the windows. Scott and Edith Gregory sat at a corner table, both waking up. Edith was licking the butter off a piece of toast in between yawns. Beth had either decided to skip breakfast or have a lie in. On one of the tables next to the window sat Michael. He met Mallory's gaze for a moment before returning to his food. She wondered if it was bravery or foolhardiness that led him to sit next to the glass. Either way, the other guests were giving the window tables a wide berth.

Mallory crossed to Charlotte Vass.

'Is everything all right? Anything I can get you?'

Charlotte leant back in her chair and Mallory was once again struck by the woman's coolness. She gave the impression little would faze her.

'Everything's fine. I'm enjoying my breakfast, which won't be the case when my stepdaughter arrives.'

'I saw your husband in here earlier.'

'Noah likes to get up early. He doesn't know what to do with himself now he's had his breakfast. I've told him to go and have a swim. It might take the edge off his temper.'

'Will you be all right?'

'I'm used to it.'

Mallory despaired. She wondered about the dynamics of long-term marriages where people stayed with partners who clearly despised them. The decision to leave Joe, once taken, had lifted a weight from her shoulders. The years of affairs had eroded away at her confidence but one day, after the final dalliance where she'd caught him with his latest fling, she'd left with a small suitcase and her dented pride. She wondered if one day, maybe, Toby might respect her for this act of defiance. She felt she had to at least try to convey some of her concerns to Charlotte.

'You know, however comfortable your life, there is help for you. Counselling, for example, might help you see how dysfunctional your situation is.'

Charlotte folded her arms. 'I owe a lot to Noah, not that it's any of your business.'

Mallory frowned, wondering what Noah had done to bind Charlotte to him. The relationship sounded dysfunctional with the balance of power in Noah's favour. 'I just wanted to let you know. I hope the wind didn't keep you up at night.' She would keep a close eye on both Charlotte and Julia in the coming hours. How would a man like Noah act in a confined setting?

'It did a bit,' admitted Charlotte. 'I heard a bit of a commotion in the early hours. Is everything all right?'

Mallory tensed and saw, out of the corner of her eye, Michael glance across to them. Mallory considered. She and Tom had crept around Grace's room making sure not to wake any of the other guests. It had been the same when she'd brought Michael to the room, with only the ting of the lift bell to disturb the silence. 'What do you mean, commotion?'

'I heard muffled sounds outside our room. I thought someone was walking about the hotel.'

Mallory met the woman's eyes. They were sea blue in colour with an intensity she hadn't noticed before.

'I'm sorry you were disturbed. It was a rough night and tonight will probably be the same. The only consolation is that by the early hours, the storm will have dropped.'

Charlotte grunted. 'Makes no difference to me. We won't be leaving until Noah's got his money's worth. He doesn't like to be short-changed.'

Mallory frowned. It was an odd choice of phrase and out of keeping with the rest of Charlotte's demeanour. Mallory wondered if she'd just seen someone's mask slip a little. It was possible. Charlotte had class – from the way she dressed to her confidence in the world despite her shaky marriage – but she'd hinted that just a small part of what she showed to the world was an act.

'I'll let you finish your breakfast,' said Mallory, forcing a smile.

In the kitchen, she found Tom busy but grim-faced. 'I've been thinking. Caustic substances don't just end up in a glass. How the hell did that happen? I've been worrying about it all morning.'

Mallory wanted to collapse into a chair to relieve her pounding head and leg but contented herself with perching against the counter. 'Look, help is coming soon. In the meantime, we just need to ensure the safety of the remaining guests and try to limit the damage to the hotel's reputation. We owe Alex that much.'

'You think it's a tragic accident?'

'Um…' Mallory did some quick thinking. Tom was an ally and she needed as many of those as she could to get her through the next twenty-four hours. 'The previous evening before I went to bed, I saw wet footprints coming into the kitchen. I'm thinking of a scenario where milk was taken from the fridge, a substance mixed in with it during the day yesterday, it was stored somewhere cool and then transferred to Grace's bedroom.'

'Jesus.'

'It's only a possibility, but I have to consider it. I'm also worried about the coffee too. If that's been tampered with then there's the possibility that other food isn't safe. What can you a hundred per cent be sure hasn't been disturbed?' she asked him.

'Anything in the walk-in freezer will be fine. There's a lock on it and only Alex and I know the combination. I open it when I need to get joints of meat or whatever. There's also frozen milk, cream, cheese and so on in case of a storm. I haven't given the combination to anyone else.'

'Frozen is good. I don't know much about poisons but my guess is freezing won't help toxicity and, in addition, any cooking might destroy its potency.'

'Using that logic, the fruit and vegetables should be fine.'

'Check everything and wash it before use. No salad, no raw fruit. Cook everything. What about the rest of the contents of the fridge?'

Tom shrugged. 'There's no lock.'

'Shit. Get a black bag and let's see what we must get rid of. Don't put it in the rubbish. Everything will need to be tested.'

Together they threw out butter, opened tubs of yoghurt and cream. Vacuum-packed cold meats and cheeses were put on the counter while Mallory inspected them to see if the plastic had been broken. When she was happy there was no tampering, she replaced them in the fridge. 'These are reserves. If we can get away with not using them, I'd be happier. Use the frozen meat and fish, overcook the vegetables – I can cope with complaints for one night.' Mallory's eyes caught sight of a Z-bed in the corner. 'What's that.'

'I'm one step ahead of you. I'm sleeping in the kitchen tonight. No one will get past me.'

–

In the office, Mallory took a call from DI Harri Evans. He sounded tired and distracted.

'It's been one of those nights. For some, the storm's an opportunity. There's been some looting in town and I'm expecting more. Now this. I'm going to see if there's any chance of getting a boat out to you. It's not fair you having to deal with this alone.'

'I'd appreciate that. I need you to talk to my boss, Alex, as soon as you can. Our receptionist, Alys Thomas, died yesterday with a doctor in attendance. We thought at the time we were dealing with a severe reaction to food poisoning.'

'I've the file in front of me.'

So, Harri with an 'i' was nobody's fool. 'Do you have a cause of death?'

'Give us a chance. She only died yesterday and the pathologist doesn't usually work Saturdays. You're not in Scotland Yard now.'

'Fair enough.'

She heard him sigh down the line. 'As it is, I've called the duty pathologist and she's scheduled the autopsy for this morning. I'm going to attend myself.'

'Will you call me with the results?'

A pause. 'Sure.'

'It's important. I'm pretty sure someone deliberately killed Grace. I can't make an accident scenario work.'

'And you think this Bryony Clive is responsible. Jesus, this is a minefield. Murder is rare enough round here but a mass killer? You sure Bryony Clive's been released from prison?'

'According to the news reports I've read. How do we go about finding out her real identity?'

'She's a section 45 case. I think it might need the Home Secretary's permission to reveal her new identity to us. I'll have to speak to my boss about this. I doubt she'll know so she'll escalate it up too. It'll probably take days, not hours. You say all the other guests are OK? What about the ones with headaches?'

'I think they're fine. I can't be sure about my coffee theory. It doesn't fit with the violence of Grace's death.'

'So all is calm amongst the guests.'

'They don't know anything about this, with the exception of the doctor, Michael Hutton.'

'And the killer, if you think it deliberate.'

'And the killer,' agreed Mallory. 'I've made steps to check that any food given to the guests is checked. I'm doing it quietly but if Bryony is amongst the guests, she may well spot something is up.'

'Christ, I don't envy your job. You're retired, you say?'

'Medically, but I'll be fine.'

'Keep your mobile handy and I'll call you back as soon as I have more news.' Harri hesitated. 'Don't try any heroics. The storm is abating about five a.m. tomorrow. You just need to get through today and tonight. Even if you suspect who Bryony is, don't approach her.'

29

CHARLOTTE

The weather meant that Charlotte would have to change her plans.

Alert, she watched Mallory leave the room, the night manager's gaze dropping to the man with the cane who was bent over his book. Mallory had done a pretty good job of pretending nothing had happened in the night. She'd got the impression Mallory had been trying to work something out about her, which suggested the woman was sharp. Charlotte was also conscious that she had been under scrutiny, which meant that she was in danger. She would have to be more careful during the time she remained on Eldey.

Charlotte was aware of the air of privilege she gave off. Oddly, it had not taken her that long to acquire it and she wrapped her acquired gentility around her like a precious mink coat. The intensity of Mallory's gaze suggested she'd spotted a flaw and that worried Charlotte. She wondered what she'd done to give herself away. She shook her head. It probably didn't matter anyway. Mallory would have enough on her plate over the coming hours. She shouldn't go looking for problems rooted in her own imagination.

The funny thing was she'd once worked at Mallory's job. In her early twenties, she'd got herself a job as a night receptionist at a local hotel. She wasn't officially a night manager but given she was the only member of staff on duty, she'd been in charge during the long evenings. In the centre of a town, she'd had to deal with drunken guests and those absconding from paying their bills. In fact, it couldn't have been more removed from the understated luxury of the Cloister. But she remembered the effort it had taken to ensure that any mishaps went unnoticed by guests.

Charlotte sighed and caught the eye of Michael, who was looking more relaxed now Mallory had left the room. She noticed he had his arm across the cover of the book he'd been engrossed in and she wondered what was making him so defensive. In looks, he was the opposite of Noah. Dark clipped hair starting to go grey at his temples and lean in build. He also had none of Noah's animal magnetism. But there was still something about him. Perhaps it was his scars, which would have been disastrous on a woman but gave him a piratical look. Sexist bullshit was what Julia would have told her if she'd shared the observation, which was probably true. But as a woman, she wouldn't have liked to carry the scar that he wore well.

He interpreted her gaze as the desire to chat. 'It's going to be a long day,' he said, tucking his book into his jacket pocket.

'I know. What are your plans?'

'A bit of reading, maybe. I don't get much chance to watch TV so maybe now's the time to catch up on some programmes.'

'Don't try streaming them. Julia, my stepdaughter, has done nothing but complain about the wi-fi connection since we got here. I complained to the owner but he said that was one of the attractions for guests. Slow living, he called it. He's even thinking of installing buttons where you can turn off the router for your room.'

'Most people choose Eldey to get away from it all, I suppose. I'll stick with the Blu-rays then.'

Charlotte paused, stirring her coffee. 'You lead a busy life?'

'I'm a GP. So, yes, the practice takes up most of my time.'

'A doctor? At least we have someone on hand if anyone gets sick.'

Was it her imagination or did his smile slip? She wasn't sure. 'I'm certainly here,' he agreed. 'I think I'll have a leisurely breakfast. No point rushing things. Would you like some more coffee?'

'Not for me.'

They both stood at the same time and Charlotte averted her eyes as he reached for his cane.

'Why's that man got a stick?'

The little girl was staring at Michael with the unashamed curiosity only children can get away with. Michael turned and waved it at her. 'I can fight off any monsters I meet.' Charlotte noticed he was adept at using the cane to steady himself as he poured himself some coffee from the jug.

The girl giggled and buried her head in her father's arm.

'What's her name?' asked Charlotte.

'Edith.' The man smiled. 'I'm Scott.'

He was nondescript and geeky, the type who'd bore you for hours, which was the last thing she wanted when she was stuck with nowhere to go.

'Big storm,' Edith told her. 'I'm going to find Mummy.'

'She is in the room at the end.' Scott was back looking at his phone as Edith sped away.

Charlotte smiled. Never much interested in children, she was always at a loss what to say to them. She crossed to the window and looked out at the trees. Whoever had planted the garden had been prepared for storms and high winds. The trees were supple, their trunks bending in the wind without snapping. There would be damage to the branches, of course, but at least the trunks held firm. Charlotte, however, was less interested in the garden than the building that couldn't be seen from this window. She'd spotted the place on arrival but had deliberately kept away from it until today. Now, with Storm Ettie at its worst, the hotel's three staff, and yes she had counted them, would be busy feeding guests and ensuring the hotel maintained its immaculate appearance. It would give her a chance. The weather, which had seemed like a disaster, now opened new opportunities. Charlotte reached into the bottom of the bag and made sure the key was still there. She felt the touch of metal against her fingertips and looked around. Scott was contemplating the drawing Edith had been crayoning at breakfast and the rest of the dining room was empty.

Now was the time.

30

At nine o'clock, Mallory called Toby. She felt more relaxed contacting him at the weekend as these were the days in the legal agreement when Toby should be staying with her. As she waited for him to answer, she briefly considered a parallel life where she was still in London doing a mundane job and wondering whether Toby would agree to stay with her that weekend. Shan had been right and not for the first time. What the both of them had needed was a break from each other.

Toby answered as she was about to cut the call. 'Mum. I'll be late. I'm going skateboarding this morning.'

'Skateboarding? Is this a new thing? You're not hanging around on the streets, are you?'

He sighed down the line. 'Just some friends I've made in school. We go to a proper park so you don't need to worry.'

He'd made some friends. Thank God for that. 'I'm not worried. I just wanted to check you were OK.'

Mallory heard a muffled voice and Joe came on the phone. 'Why the hell are you ringing him this early in the morning? We have an agreement—'

'That I'm allowed to be with Toby at the weekend. Surely now I'm not seeing him, I can ring on the days he'd normally stay with me. You know I'm currently doing night shifts. This is a reasonable hour for both Toby and me and nothing to do with you.'

'Listen,' hissed Joe. 'Every time he speaks to you it takes an hour or two for him to settle. He's got these new friends who seem to be doing the world of good. Can't you try later?'

'I've an emergency situation here. We're trapped in Storm Ettie. I don't know when I'll be able to speak next.'

'Hard luck.' Joe was a cop too and had decided early on that the Roads Policing Unit gave him the testosterone-fuelled environment he craved. His brushes with dismembered limbs on motorways, however, had left him with a callousness she suspected had always been part of his personality.

'Dad!' Mallory heard a muffled sound and Toby came back on the line. 'Are you OK, Mum?'

For a moment Mallory nearly broke down. Not just with the weight of responsibility of looking after all the guests with Grace's body upstairs, but from being on this island in the first place, away from her son who'd called her Mum for the first time in God knows how long.

'I'm fine, Toby. Just missing you.' Her voice cracked and she winced, knowing how embarrassed he'd be if he realised she'd been close to crying.

'Are you OK, Mum? What's that sound?'

'I'm in a really bad storm, that's all. The island is cut off until tomorrow.'

'Cut off? Will you be OK?'

'Of course I will. Don't worry about me.' Mallory used a sleeve to wipe away a tear that was sliding down her cheek.

'I miss you too, Mum. Can we speak later?'

'I'd like that very much.'

Mallory felt both invigorated and exhausted after the conversation. The weather was making her jumpy. The storm had gathered a head of steam and outside was a maelstrom of flying branches and eddies of rain. As she crossed the lobby, she saw Julia Vass lounging on the sofa flicking through a magazine. Elsa must be cleaning her room. Mallory studied her for a moment and remembered what Charlotte had told her at dinner. She climbed the stairs to room ten and knocked before going in.

'Elsa, it's me.' She looked around. Teenagers have a reputation for messy spaces and Julia was no exception. Toiletries spilled from the bedside table to the floor and a novel was lying on the bed, its spine split and covered in what looked like red wine. Mallory looked under the bed and rifled through the drawers.

Elsa came out of the bathroom. 'Is anything wrong? I thought I was going to be looking through the rooms.'

'I'm trying to find where Julia keeps her alcohol.'

'In the wardrobe behind the spare blanket.' Elsa smirked at her.

'Great.' Mallory put her hand to the back of the shelf and retrieved three mini bottles of red wine. She opened each one and poured the contents down the sink. 'Put the bottles in the recycling. She'll have fun looking for them when she comes back in.'

'You think…' Elsa chewed her lip.

'Nothing to worry about. I just want to make sure the vulnerable guests, in this instance the under eighteens, are kept as safe as possible. Where next? I'll give you a hand.'

'Room eight.'

Mona's room overlooked the front of the hotel giving a view, Mallory saw, of her cabin tucked in the corner of the plot. It was this vista that probably accounted for Alex sprucing up the exterior of the cabin while neglecting the interior. Mona's desk had been pulled in front of the window, although Mallory wondered how much of a distraction the view would be while she was trying to paint.

'How are you getting on?' Mallory asked Elsa.

'Everything seems to be going fine. I've done a quick tidy of the other occupied rooms. Most just needed clean towels and beds making. I've also wiped over the bathrooms and given the carpets a vacuum.'

'Any complaints?'

Elsa shrugged and gave Mallory a look which suggested no more than usual.

'Anything you need to tell me about then?'

'I don't think so. Just the usual lot, aren't they?'

Are they though? Mallory had been inclined to dismiss Alys's comments, but she'd been right in noticing they were a disparate group. Not the hotel's usual demographic of wealthy professionals. Only Noah Vass and his family and, possibly, Michael Hutton fitted that description. Mallory decided not to share her views with Elsa who had relaxed now Mallory was taking charge of their situation. Mallory's eyes dropped onto a roll of canvasses peeping through the top of a cardboard tube next to the desk. She resisted the urge to pull out the roll of paintings and see what was in Mona's imagination. It seemed Mona had decided to make herself scarce while her room was cleaned.

'I think we're going to need to change this,' said Elsa nodded her head at the rumpled sheets, not meeting Mallory's eyes.

'I'll do it.' Mallory began to strip the bed amused at the girl's prudishness. Mallory was intrigued by the state of the bedclothes – there were plenty of day visitors to the island every day and perhaps Mona had a boyfriend over. It was really none of their business. She threw the soiled bedding into a pile in the corner of the room and pulled a fresh sheet over the mattress. Elsa had the heavier cleaning but went about the task with gusto, her body shaking as she cleaned the claw-footed bath.

'I did say a light clean, Elsa.'

'Might as well get it done properly.'

'I don't want to tire you out.'

'I'll be fine.'

Oh, to be a teenager again, thought Mallory. 'Did you come over here to visit your Aunt Joanne when she was resident?'

'Of course.' The top half of Elsa remained hidden in the bathtub, her muffled voice answering Mallory's questions. 'We never stayed the night though. Auntie Joanne was in the cabin you're using. There's not much space for guests, is there?'

'I suppose not.' Mallory rubbed her head. The aspirin she'd taken earlier had begun to wear off but the thudding in her head remained. She'd try another painkiller when she finished this room.

'Tell me about the poisoned nun,' she called to Elsa, laying the duvet on the bed and resisting the urge to climb between the sheets.

Elsa's head popped up from the bath. 'Really? I thought you weren't interested. Mam says I talk too much about it.'

'I've changed my mind. What was her name?'

'Bridget Marsh. I told you yesterday afternoon. She came from a well-to-do family and wanted to join the order of the Companions of the Good Shepherd from when she was fourteen. It was founded in 1924 by Margaret Taylor, the daughter of a rich family who built this house for her. She started the order with three of her friends and when women they knew came to visit, they liked it and stayed. They were all drawn from the upper classes.'

'Very select.'

Elsa didn't react to Mallory's sarcasm. 'After the First World War, there were lots of single women, not all who wanted to remain in the family home as spinsters. It was a chance of a bit of freedom.'

'How many were here, then?'

'Twelve according to Auntie Joanne. She said it was like in the Bible, you know.'

The reference was lost on Mallory. 'And this Bridget Marsh wanted to come here?'

'She was the last of the Companions to arrive. It was the early 1930s. Her family were sure her wanting to become a nun was just a fad. She'd been launched into society. Auntie Joanne showed me a photo of Bridget she found in a magazine. Bridget was wearing this silk dress with long gloves and looked ever so stylish. She was thinner than me, thinner than you even.'

'Thanks very much,' said Mallory, conscious she hadn't put on much weight despite Tom's cooking. 'Did she come to Eldey and fall in love with the place like the others?'

'She already knew about the community from a cousin who had come here on a retreat so she paid the convent a visit and was hooked.'

'But the family disapproved?'

'Yes, and as she was under twenty-one, they went to court.' Elsa came into the bedroom rubbing her forehead.

'So, Bridget ate poisoned berries.'

'Exactly.'

'Perhaps it was a mistake.'

'You can't mistake berries from the cherry laurel bush. They don't look like fruit or anything. They're jet black for a start.'

Mallory froze, clenching the duster in her hand. 'Laurel?'

'Of course. You know the big bush that shields the garden from the westerly window. It's called a cherry laurel.'

'I know it. She ate berries from there?'

'Go and take a look at it. The berries are there now it's autumn.'

Mallory was thinking furiously, wondering if the lack of sleep was getting to her. She saw the figure near the hedge *after* Alys had died. Her imagination was running riot after a night of disturbed sleep.

Elsa hadn't returned to her cleaning but was catching her breath after the exertion. 'Do you want to know about why people think Bridget was murdered?'

Mallory sighed. 'You can tell me in the next room.'

Out in the corridor, Beth Gregory was scrolling on her phone. 'Is everything OK?' asked Mallory.

Beth jumped and put her phone in her pocket. 'Just getting a bit of peace.' From behind the door they could hear the muffled drone of Edith's sobs.

'It does get better,' said Mallory.

'Does it?' Beth's eyes swept over the dishevelled pair. 'When?'

'Um.' Mallory stopped. 'When they go to school.'

That, at least, got a laugh out of Beth who knocked on her room to be readmitted.

They went down in the lift, Elsa wheeling her trolley while Mallory slung the heavy laundry bag over her shoulder.

'Where next?' asked Mallory.

'We can finish with the rooms of the guests who left yesterday. I left them to last. It's not as if we're going to be checking anyone in.'

As Elsa opened room six, Mallory casually turned to look into the room opposite, occupied by Michael Hutton. He was sitting in an armchair with his door ajar, engrossed in the book he was reading.

'I'll be with you in a second,' Mallory told Elsa as she tapped on Michael's door. She saw him close the book, turning it over so she couldn't read the title.

'I'm just checking everything is all right. Believe me, I'm asking all the guests the same thing, so please don't take offence.'

He rose immediately, making Mallory feel guilty.

'You don't need to stand. Please, I just wanted to see if you needed anything.'

He came towards her anyway, brushing his hand through his cropped hair. 'I'm fine. I'm feeling a little closed in with the weather so I decided to do a bit of reading with the door open onto the corridor. It makes things feel less claustrophobic.'

'You're not disturbing anyone. We just need to give the room opposite a clean. I also wanted to check you're OK.'

She saw she'd offended him again. 'Because I've mobility issues?'

'As I said, I'm checking on everyone, including staff.'

He turned his face away, unconvinced. 'I'm fine.'

Rather than watch his progress back to his armchair, Mallory followed Elsa into the spare bedchamber and shut the door behind her.

'I keep offending the guest in room five. Don't you think having mobility problems makes you a little more vulnerable in difficult situations?'

'Vulnerable to what?' asked Elsa.

'Well, fire for example.'

'The hotel's not on fire,' said Elsa.

Fair point, thought Mallory, noticing the girl was desperate to finish her story of Bridget Marsh. 'Go on. Tell me about Bridget's supposed murder.'

Elsa began stripping the bed. 'By the 1980s, the community was down to five. After Bridget's death and the publicity surrounding it, they closed the community to new recruits. So, basically, the order was only ever one generation of women. They all got old together. Margaret Taylor, the original founder, was a tyrant and bossed the other sisters around. My Auntie Joanne thinks she was showing signs of dementia and, in the end, because she refused to leave the island along with one other surviving sister, they had to pay for a nurse to live in the convent. They couldn't expect people to be coming and going to the island on a regular basis.'

'Was it around the time your aunt was staying here?'

Elsa's voice lowered to a whisper. 'Exactly. Auntie was only here about ten months, the island didn't really suit her, but the nurse used to give her all the gossip. Margaret was babbling on about the fact that she'd encouraged Bridget to eat the poisoned berries. There would still be twelve on the island, you see. Margaret didn't care if her companions were alive or dead. They just needed to be here. But it didn't work out.'

'Bridget's family took the body away.'

Elsa paused. 'You do know the story then.'

'Of course not, but the family were never going to allow the burial of Bridget here. I'm not sure this tale of murder makes any sense.' Looking at Elsa's crestfallen face, Mallory relented. 'It's a great story, though. I'm wondering how well known the story is. I mean, I've never heard of it before but would it be possible that a guest has read about it somewhere?'

'It mentions poisoning on the website and in the history of the Cloister that we leave in each room.'

'I know the one. Julia Vass, the teenage girl you were telling the story to, brought the pamphlet down to dinner. You've definitely piqued her interest.'

'I didn't need to. She knew all about the nuns already. Shame there wasn't actually the tour she was expecting. She's as obsessed as I am.'

'Somehow I doubt that very much.'

Elsa pouted. 'All right. Nearly as obsessed as me. As I told you, the story's there for everyone to see. I don't understand why Alys was so upset.'

In the gloom, Mallory peered out of the window of the downstairs room, trying to catch a glimpse of the mausoleum on the other side of the island. She'd taken a trip over the previous week, but there was little to see. A small stone building with pillars either side of a long narrow door. It wouldn't have looked out of place in a Hammer film but, once you'd taken in its general creepiness, you were keen to get away.

'So how many coffins are in the mausoleum.'

'Eleven,' Elsa whispered.

'The door is covered with an ornate gate like the one at the bottom of the hill. I can understand they wanted to keep people out of the mausoleum but why at the bottom of the hill?'

Elsa shrugged. 'People have always been trying to land on the island. It was to keep unwanted visitors out.'

When they'd finished preparing the room, Mallory sent Elsa to have a shower and rest before lunch. Back in her office, Mallory opened the hotel's website and there, as Elsa had stated, was the story of the nun. It even mentioned the cherry laurel. I hope to God it's just a weird coincidence, thought Mallory and shut down the computer.

31

BETH

The weather meant that Beth would have to change her plans.

She'd spent a sleepless night with the wind and rain battering their windows and had sent Scott and Edith down to breakfast without her. She'd hoped a long bath might restore her balance but, instead, her mind played over and over what had happened the previous evening. She'd felt the strain of her fellow guests and it had made her jittery. Beth had spent the rest of the evening in a high state of tension, but the meal had progressed like those of previous nights. Scott had attempted to engage her in the latest chapter he'd written, which sounded as dull as the previous one. Edith had started off well but had grown bored and begun to play up. She'd been the one who wanted to take her to the room, but Scott had insisted and she'd not wanted to draw more attention to herself by making a scene.

Of course, it was too late. What had happened, had happened. It made no difference. Except Beth suspected there were more surprises to come, which meant she had to change her plans.

In the bathroom, she took a long shower instead of the bath, hoping it would wake her up. Afterwards, she wiped the steam from the mirror with a towel and stared at her indistinctive features in the glass. Scott always said that he'd fallen for her neck, which was supposed to be a compliment but suggested her face wasn't much to look at. Edith had inherited her looks, which was a shame. Beth sighed. It was too late to do anything now and she must carry on as if everything were normal.

Going downstairs, she avoided the other breakfasters although Scott spotted her and gave her a chilly smile. She ignored his martyred expression and went to the sitting room. On one wall was the group of nuns, their expressions serious. On the other side of the window, the storm rallied, shaking the glass. Through the murk she saw a figure battling their way through the trees. What a fool, thought Beth. No torch or high-vis vest. If they had an accident, they'd perish before anyone realised. She leant forward and tried to identify who it was. A woman she decided. Definitely a woman.

'Mummy.' Edith ran to her and hugged her legs. She tensed. Edith had gone through a biting stage a year earlier and had nipped her thigh. Today she contented himself with holding on tight.

'Where's Daddy?'

'Talking to the man with the stick.'

'Did you tell Daddy you were coming to see me.'

'Of course.'

Beth wasn't so sure this was the case, but decided to let it go.

'Mum? Why is that lady crying?'

Beth froze. 'What do you mean?'

'I heard a woman crying.'

'Show me.'

She allowed Edith to lead her by the hand, out of the room into the passageway. 'I can't hear anything.'

'There was,' Edith's voice rose. 'I heard a lady crying.'

Absentmindedly, Beth patted her daughter on the head, straining to hear anything above the howl of the storm.

32

In her office, Mallory found the number for Gum Candy and called the customer service helpline. She'd promised herself she wouldn't interfere with a police investigation but her chat with Elsa had raised the possibility that the island had been chosen because of the story of the nuns. The tea party had been an act of theatre. A group of school friends on a summer's day having a birthday tea. It suggested setting was incredibly important to this poisoner. And if Bryony liked theatre, didn't plays usually have three acts?

'We don't give information out about our subscribers.' The woman's voice was cool.

'I just want to speak to someone about your competition prizes. One of the guests staying at our hotel who won one of your competitions has died tragically.'

'Oh.' The woman was nonplussed. 'It's Saturday. I'm not going to be able to contact anyone until tomorrow.'

'It's an emergency. Can you try?'

Mallory was put on hold and tinny music tinkled down her ear. She lifted her leg and rested it on another chair, the pain marginally easing off.

'Can I help you?' A more helpful voice came onto the line.

Mallory sat up and repeated her request.

'We only give away hotel stays as prizes at Christmas and for our summer promotions.'

'Perhaps Grace won it during the summer.'

'I don't think so. The hotel was in Scotland. What was the name of your hotel again?'

'The Cloister on Eldey island. It's off the Pembrokeshire coast.'

There was a short silence. 'We've not used your hotel for any prizes. I'm sorry.'

'Hold on,' said Mallory as the woman was about to ring off. 'I've an account that pre-paid the hotel. Gum Candy UK.'

'That's not right. All our finances go through our parent company, AltaX. Your guest died, you say?'

'It doesn't matter.' Mallory cut the call and looked at the photograph she'd taken of the postcard in Grace's room.

'Very clever,' she whispered, aware of the opponent she was facing.

Mallory snapped on a pair of latex gloves left on reception for the COVID-wary guests and went up the stairs. There was little of the bustle she was used to. Most of the Cloister's occupants were staying in their rooms, although she passed Mona sitting in reception, flicking through a magazine. Julia was playing music, the tinny sound seeping out from under the door. In other circumstances, she might have asked the girl to turn it down, but Mallory needed every guest comfortable while she worked out what the hell was going on.

It took all her confidence to open the door to Grace's room and step inside the frosted space. Grace was lying where they'd left her. Of course she was. Get a grip, Mallory told herself. She went over to the girl's handbag and retrieved the card. The postmark was illegible. Neither the posting location or date could be deciphered. She then began a thorough search of the room now she was alone. She began with the bathroom, checking each item in Grace's bulging makeup and washbags.

What was nagging at her was Grace's reaction to spotting Bryony. She hadn't been frightened. OK, she hadn't wanted to sit with her fellow guests but neither had she retreated to her room. She might have been poisoned by her schoolfriend twenty-five years earlier but she wasn't frightened of her. So Grace hadn't thought she was going to be a victim and had assumed her meeting Bryony on the island was nothing more than chance. If she'd had any inkling Bryony had been responsible for her trip here, she'd have been on high alert. The question was what had Grace thought about in the couple of hours between recognising Bryony and drinking the milk. Tom had been under the impression that Grace had looked over his shoulder when he had undertaken the guest count at Mallory's request. Perhaps she had hoped Bryony was going to pay her a visit to discuss that fateful day in 1996. Mallory would never know, but Grace would not have drunk the milk if she had any sense that she was in danger. Perhaps she'd been tired and her defences down, or the coffee she'd drunk in reception, if it had been tampered with, had dulled her wits.

Mallory crossed to the table which ran alongside the wall opposite the bed. There was an empty saucer to one side, the same design used for the dinner service. Underneath the table was another bin she hadn't spotted earlier. It was empty except for a card lying face up.

With compliments.

Mallory didn't recognise the handwriting. It fitted the scenario she'd constructed in her head. Grace had been killed after Mallory had seen the footprints into the kitchen after Friday dinner. This was after the coffee had been tampered with so the killer was likely to have been seeking out the milk. It was easy enough to leave a glass of milk on a tray outside the door, give a slight knock to alert the occupant and hurry away. Perhaps Grace had assumed the hotel was gifting all the guests a hot drink because of the weather. It was clear Grace hadn't instigated the murder by recognising her old friend. The card from Gum Candy and the milk suggested the killing had been planned all along. Mallory replaced the card where she'd found it.

Her phone buzzed in her pocket and she fumbled for it, hoping it was Toby calling her back now he was away from his father. But it was DI Harri whose voice she heard. She sneaked a look at her watch.

'How's it going?' he asked.

'I don't know.' She told him about the card and her conversation with Gum Candy. She waited for the explosion. Her old boss would have been furious with her interference but Harri was cut from different cloth.

'I'd have done the same as you in your shoes. We'll follow it up here.'

'You don't have a name for me?'

'No, I don't, and my boss is doing everything by the book. You should have seen the look on her face when I told her Bryony Clive might be on Eldey. She's going for the chief super exams next month. The last thing she needs is mention of The Birthday Girl on her record.'

'I just need a name, Harri.'

'And that's going to take time. I'm sorry. I'd ring the bloody Home Secretary myself if it'd help. Anyway, look, that's not why I called. The pathologist has done the autopsy and Alys had chronic lung disease. Its official name is bronchopulmonary dysplasia and he's convinced that played a factor in Alys's death. However, the official result of the PM is "inconclusive" pending other tests.'

'You mean she wasn't poisoned.'

'I'm not saying that. The blood work is going to take twenty-four, even with me asking for it to be rushed. But unless Bryony, or whatever name she goes by now, knew about Alys's condition, she couldn't have assumed the poisoning would be fatal.'

'That's not making me feel any better.'

'It isn't?'

'No, because it means that Bryony's playing around with drugs, which means any of us could be her next victim.'

'Then you just be bloody careful what you eat and drink over the next few hours. A fine reputation the Cloister has but I'd prefer you ate beans on toast until the storm clears.'

33

You can't do everything by yourself. Mallory had known this from her very first day in the Met. Your colleagues aren't your friends. They're your lifeline. Here on Eldey, she'd never felt more dislocated from the outside world, not even when she was in hospital. At least then Toby had paid her reluctant visits, sitting in the uncomfortable armchair beside her bed and playing with his phone. Assessing her options, she recalled a piece of advice issued on the first day of a new posting by her new boss. Choose your allies carefully. Not everyone is on your side.

So, who were her allies at the Cloister? Tom, certainly. You couldn't fake a reaction to the discovery of Grace's body. He might possibly be connected in some way to Bryony Clive but she doubted it. He had a Somerset accent, a world away from the wealthy Cheshire town where Bryony had lived. She was also prepared to put Elsa in the ally camp. The girl was fanciful and jittery but surely not a killer. Both she and Tom, for example, could have knocked on Grace's door with a complimentary glass of milk and Mallory would have been none the wiser. The fact that the killer had gone to the effort of preparing a signed card suggested it was a guest not a member of staff behind the plan.

So, Tom and Elsa were safe, but she needed someone else to talk through her suspicions with. A person with more knowledge of human nature and that, she thought, was Michael Hutton. He was a doctor and death, however shocking, was surely not a huge trauma for him. The problem was that they'd parted on bad terms, which meant Mallory would need to apologise to get him on her side. For a moment, she felt sorry for him, an unusual emotion for her. He'd had to look at Grace's ruined face and was now sitting with his fellow guests banned from mentioning the dead girl. With a sigh, she went to find him.

Scott was finishing his breakfast alone although Mallory could hear Edith's squeals coming from the sitting room. The little girl was finally waking and had upped her noise level. Mallory wasn't sure how that would go down with other guests. Many people, she'd realised, came to the Cloister to escape children and their presence was an added worry during crises like this. When this was all over, she'd talk to Alex about the possibility of making the hotel adults only. Children would still be able to travel over by boat for the day and there were plenty of quayside family hotels in Tenby to accommodate them.

Mallory guessed Michael had a restless nature like her own and she was unsurprised to find her knock unanswered. She found him in the small bar area, which Alys had insisted on referring to as the parlour. While from the front-facing rooms you could get glimpses of the sea, the bar faced the back of the hotel and a bank of conifer trees planted as wind breakers. The room had been designed for intimate evenings, the furnishings a cocoon of dark wood and teal blue to match the colour of sea roaring in the distance.

Michael was with Stella – they'd helped themselves to glasses of Orangina from the bar and had been there a while judging by the empty cans on the table. Michael glanced up at her, his gaze hard to read.

'We've left an IOU on the counter. You can charge it to my room.'

'That's fine,' said Mallory. 'How are you, Stella?'

'I'm well, thank you.'

'No aftereffects from the coffee at least.' Michael's words held a double meaning and they gazed at each other over Stella's head.

'That's great to know. As long as you're feeling OK.'

Stella kept her back to Mallory. 'I'm fine. I'd better get going.' Stella picked up her drink and left the room.

'I don't know what I've done to offend her.'

Mallory pulled across a chair and sat down, taking the weight off her leg. Michael, she thought, looked well despite his broken night. He clearly got on well with Stella and their conversation had brought colour to his face. He looked animated as he gestured to a chair. Mallory was embarrassed to be sitting so close to him. A quick look in one of the mirrors had confirmed her fears that she had the appearance of someone dragged through a hedge.

'I wouldn't worry about it. How are you feeling?' he asked.

'Not brilliant,' said Mallory. 'Look, I seem to keep offending you whenever I see you and I'm sorry.'

He looked down at the table, fiddling with the can in his hands. 'I think we were both under a lot of stress given the circumstances. I haven't been able to get the image of her out of my head. It's a terrible way to die.'

'Look, I need to talk to you about something. I've just been back to the room to check on things. I don't know who else to trust and I'd like to run a theory past you to convince myself I'm not going mad.'

'OK.'

He wasn't as surprised as Mallory had expected. This wasn't good. She was on the verge of sharing the possibility they might be trapped with a killer and his composure was unsettling her.

'I need to ask you first where you got your scars from. I'm not being nosy. It's relevant to the death of the guest.'

She thought he was going to refuse to answer. He turned his face, keeping his eyes on the weather outside.

'All right. In 1999, I was a student at Bristol University. I was at a party one evening and a fire broke out. One of the candles set alight a pair of curtains on the ground floor. I was upstairs and became trapped along with all the others who were in the same room as me.'

Mallory looked at him. 'You jumped?'

'Exactly. I later learnt it was the worst thing I could have done. What you should do is stay in the room and wait for help to arrive.'

'I'm afraid Grenfell told us that isn't always the best advice.' An image flashed at Mallory. She'd been on duty the night of the fire in the tower block and had gone down to the scene to see if she could help at all. So many lives lost because people had followed the advice. Stay where you are and await rescue.

'But it's your choices that haunt you, isn't it? Two of my friends in that room died from smoke inhalation but I was at the window. I might have been all right if I'd waited for the fire engine. Anyway, I jumped, which badly broke my leg, and I glanced off a railing, which gave me the piratical scar on my face. I've had numerous operations on my injuries and this is now as good as it gets for both my face and my leg.'

'And the scars on your neck?'

Michael put his fingertips to the burnt flesh underneath his jawline. 'I was alight when I jumped.'

'Why do you beat yourself up about it?' Mallory couldn't keep the harshness from her voice. 'Part of your body had caught fire and your friends were dying around you. Anyone would have jumped.'

'Thank you, Mallory. While we're at it, would you like to tell me about your injuries that you're doing your best to hide?'

Mallory laid a hand over her agonising leg, thinking. She was trying to put that fateful day, when her career and future fell apart, behind her. He'd been honest enough with her but she suspected he'd told the story over and over again. It was different for her. Eldey was her first job since leaving the hospital and she hadn't yet perfected the narrative to explain her situation and injuries.

'I was attacked by a paedophile, nicknamed Icebox Pete, we'd been sent to recall to prison. He'd been approaching young girls in the street, which obviously breached his parole conditions. He had absolutely no remorse nor intention of reforming. However, he didn't want to go back to prison, so he got out his Bowie knife.'

Michael winced. 'I'm sorry to hear that. I remember dealing with knife injuries during my stint in A and E when I was training and they could be horrific. He stabbed you in the leg?'

'And in the lung. That was the injury they thought might kill me. I lay on a London pavement while my partner, Shan, spoke to me while trying to staunch the blood seeping out of me. It's funny but it's something I've been trained to do, you know, keep the patient talking while waiting for paramedics. I never expected to be that victim.'

'But policing, especially in the capital, is dangerous, isn't it?'

'Of course, but, I dunno, I hadn't envisaged a life where I'd be injured so badly, I couldn't be a cop anymore.'

'Didn't they offer you a desk job?'

Mallory looked towards the window, which rattled violently as a gust slammed against the frame. 'Of course, but it wasn't for me. I got divorced just before the incident and it was time for a change anyhow. The trouble is, I'm just marking time until I know what to do next. I don't feel I can move on until my leg heals properly.' It was the most honest she'd been about her injury. She'd played it cool when Alex had asked about her injuries in the interview but Michael's quiet questioning opened up the reality of her situation.

Now they were talking about her medical conditions, Michael was more confident. 'Healing can be a long process.'

'Didn't your injuries stop you from becoming a doctor?'

'Not really. I had to take two years out from my Biosciences degree but once I'd graduated, I went on to medical school. They knew of my disabilities from the start. It closed some doors to me in the medical profession but not as many as you might think.'

'A GP? So you don't know anything about poisons.'

'I did five years at medical school. I know a little about them but I'm certainly no expert. I've told you as much as I know about the guest's death. She ingested something caustic and it will have caused catastrophic damage to every surface it touched. Lips, mouth, throat, stomach.'

'What do you actually die of when that happens?'

'I don't know, but perforation of the oesophagus for example would kill you. It'll have been an agonising death.'

Mallory considered her options. She suspected her few sips of that bloody coffee had affected her judgement but she had to assume Michael wasn't a killer. If she'd made a mistake, she was too exhausted to care.

'Does the name Bryony Clive mean anything to you?'

'Yes, she killed her schoolfriends with a poison tea party on her birthday.' Was it her imagination or was a flush spreading under his skin? Mallory looked hard at Michael who returned her gaze with clear eyes. 'Don't look so surprised. She is famous, you know,' he said.

'You told me you were in Bristol in 1999. Where were you three years earlier?'

'I went to the university in the autumn of 1997. Before that I was living with my parents in Cumbria.'

'Which is nowhere near Wilmslow.'

'Nowhere near,' he agreed. 'Why are you mentioning Bryony Clive?'

'One of Bryony's friends survived. Her name was Grace Pagonakis, which matches the name of the girl in the room. I've seen a photo on the internet of Bryony's surviving victim. It's definitely her.'

'And Bryony is no longer in prison.' There it was again, an odd note in Michael's voice. Mallory wondered if she'd made a fatal mistake in confiding in him. It was too late now to backtrack.

'She was released in 2013.'

'And you think there's a possibility she might be on the island?'

'Grace won the room in a competition, which the company say they know nothing about. I've a horrible feeling it's Bryony's hand behind the invitation, which means Grace was deliberately brought here to be killed. At this stage of the investigation, I'd be looking at motive. Why bring Grace here to Eldey? If Bryony wanted to settle old scores, she could have travelled to Hastings where Grace lived and killed her there. In the context of Alys's death the night before, I now need to consider protecting everyone else here.'

'You mean the food.'

'Tom is sorting that out. I trust him and, if I have to taste everything before it goes out, then I will. We need to eat until help arrives.'

'But, do you think there's a possibility that Bryony is here on the island and there's a grand plan behind this?'

Mallory rubbed her face to clear the fog creeping through her brain. 'I think there's a strong possibility.'

His voice was preternaturally calm. 'Surely, though, when the storm came in, Bryony must have considered changing her plans. It's one thing to poison your enemies and return to your home and hope you've got away with it, another to be stuck in a hotel without any means to escape.'

'She never would have got away with it, would she, though? As soon as the detectives ran the names of the guests through the computer, it would have flagged her. I don't know exactly how the system works but, at some point, the investigating team would have realised the girl known as Bryony Clive was a guest. This is about revenge, not trying to get away with murder. People's personalities don't change. When Bryony was caught after the tea party, she made no attempt to deny her involvement.'

'So we wait it out until the police arrive and Bryony's identity is revealed.'

'I thought that would be the best plan but now I'm not so sure. Stella drank the coffee too. She said it was off and I had a few sips of it to check it was all OK. I've felt terrible ever since.'

'Stella mentioned a headache.'

'I need to talk to her to see if she has a connection to Bryony or whether it's a random event.'

'I wouldn't do that.'

Mallory frowned. 'Why not?'

'Stella's a little prickly. I think I should speak to her first. She'll open up to me.'

Mallory folded her arms. 'No.'

'She really won't speak to you, Mallory. Let me talk to her first.'

'What have I done—?' Mallory stopped at the sound of shattering glass.

'I think a window has broken.' Michael reached for his cane.

Mallory was on her feet. 'I'll go. Take your time.'

She reached the lobby at the same time as Mona Rubin came hurtling down the stairs. 'Oh my God,' she said, lifting her arm to her face.

The wind howled through the lobby, its maelstrom causing chairs to tip over and magazines to fly above their heads. In the middle of the chaos, white with shock, stood Beth Gregory covered in evil-looking slivers of glass which glinted under the light. Mallory moved closer, holding the shaking woman's arm.

'Stay still. You're covered in glass but not many have punctured your skin. We'll need to pick off each shard one by one.' Mallory turned to see Michael appear behind her. 'Is that the best idea?'

'Agreed.'

'Beth! What the—'

Scott appeared at the bottom of the stairs holding a sobbing Edith in his arms.

'Don't let her see me like this,' shouted Beth. 'Take her back to the room.'

It was Mona who went first to comfort the trembling woman. She picked a sliver of glass from Beth's cheek.

'Your face is fine,' she murmured.

Mallory marvelled at Mona's insight. Of course, the first part of the body a person would worry about, once they realised they weren't seriously injured, would be the damage to the face. Mallory crossed to the other side of Beth and together the two women began to remove each shard, Mona murmuring comforting words. Up close, Mallory thought Beth looked younger than the date of birth on her record. She certainly had none of the malevolence the newspaper reports gave to Bryony. She was nondescript, surely not an attribute of the infamous poisoner. While she was close to the two women, Mallory also cast a glance at Mona whose face was covered by a smattering of freckles. Again, it gave her a younger look than the intimidating appearance she presented to the world. There was something slightly aloof about Mona that dissipated when you got closer to her.

A huddle of guests had gathered at the bottom of the stairs, joined by Tom and Elsa, who was stuffing a book into the front pocket of her apron.

'Could I ask everyone to return to their rooms or go to one of the other rooms? Please stay away from the windows. Michael, I'd like you to check over Mrs Gregory.'

'Where's the first aid kit?'

The wind continued to howl around the lobby. Mallory needed to move Beth away from the splintered glass but the woman was rooted to the spot.

'It's in the office. Elsa will show you.' Mallory turned her attention back to Beth. 'Can you come further into the lobby? Tom, do we have anything we can use to secure the window?'

'There are boards in one of the outbuildings. Alex thought something like this might happen. I'll go out now.'

'Be careful outside.'

When Mallory and Mona had finished, they stepped back for Michael to examine Beth. By some miracle, only four shards had punctured her skin including one on her face. Michael dabbed antiseptic ointment into each of the wounds and covered them with a plaster.

'I'm fine.' Some of Beth's shock had abated and she'd begun to shiver. 'I just need to lie down.'

'I'd rather you had some hot, sweet tea first.' Michael stepped back. 'You've had a shock.'

'How about I make some,' Mallory said. 'Mona, could you take Mrs Gregory up to her room.'

In the kitchen, Mallory opened a fresh packet of tea, checking for any signs of tampering. She'd take the pot straight to the guest to ensure there was no meddling. As she was pouring in the hot water, Tom came staggering in.

'Problem,' he announced.

'What now?' asked Mallory.

'You'd better come and look at this.'

'I don't want this tea left unattended.'

'You don't need to leave the kitchen. Take a look out of the window.'

Mallory crossed to the back door and stared, straining to make sense of the destruction visible through the glass.

'It's the telephone pole. It's come down. It was one of the cables that smashed into the window causing it to shatter. A bit like whiplash.'

Mallory groaned. 'So we have no phone line or internet.'

Tom rubbed his forehead. 'That's about the size of it. Until the storm dies down we're cut off from the outside world.'

Well, that's just bloody brilliant, thought Mallory. 'Right, Tom. I need everyone in the sitting room. Start knocking on the doors and I'll get Elsa to do the same. We all congregate in half an hour.'

34

Mallory's first thought was that with the telephone lines down, she wouldn't be able to take Toby's call later. He'd promised to call her back and this tiny movement towards her had given her hope that their relationship might be salvaged. But, without the internet, the call to her mobile would not connect. She hoped Joe had enough decency to show him the weather reports. Scott, the guest in room one, had said he'd been following the storm on national news. It wouldn't take Alex long to realise he couldn't get in contact with the hotel either. She was now wholly responsible for the safety of the guests without any contact with the mainland. DI Harri Evans, she saw, had been a comfort. A supportive professional. She would have to trust he was getting on with things while she held the fort here.

Mallory went to the sitting room and began to pull the heavy chairs together so she could address the guests. She'd have to make an excuse for Grace's absence but her focus would be on putting the lid on any potential panic. She could hear Tom hammering the panel to cover the window. She was relieved it was the cable from the tele-graph pole that had smashed the glass, which suggested an extraordinary one-off event. The other windows would presumably hold in the storm, but she'd still need to tell the guests to stay away from the glass. She couldn't take a chance on more serious injuries.

Footsteps along the corridor alerted her to someone approaching. She turned and saw Elsa in the doorway, her face flushed with excitement.

'Are you all right?'

Elsa came into the room, shutting the door behind her. 'You told me to look for something out of the ordinary, remember, I couldn't immediately see it. So I decided to look for the ordinary if you see what I mean.'

Mallory smiled. She'd have made a good investigator. 'Go on.'

'Well, I looked to see what was in people's wardrobes, on their bedside cabinets. I thought I might find an object hidden in plain sight.'

'And did you?'

'I found this.' With a flourish, Elsa produced a paperback book and handed it to Mallory.

'What—?' Mallory stopped when she saw the title. *The Birthday Girl: A Portrait of a Murderer.* 'Jesus. Don't tell me you know about Bryony Clive?'

Elsa blanched at Mallory's tone. 'I've heard of her. What's the matter?'

Mallory took a deep breath. Elsa might be eighteen but she was still young enough to be vulnerable. 'I'm just surprised to see the book, that's all. Where did you find it?'

'That's the thing. I found it in Doctor Hutton's room while I was hoovering. He put it in his bedside drawer, but made such a song and dance about it, I had a look to see what it was. It's not the sort of thing you'd expect a doctor to read, is it?'

181

No, it bloody well isn't, Mallory thought. No wonder he'd been blushing when she'd mentioned Bryony Clive to him. He'd been reading a book about her, which he'd covered up the previous evening when she'd spoken to him outside his room. Mallory turned the book over in her hands. Bloody hell. Not only was it a book about Bryony Clive but it was written by Anna Kirby, the ex-detective she'd emailed that morning. Well, that line of inquiry was a waste of time. Whether Anna called or emailed her a reply, there was no way she'd receive it.

'The Birthday Girl. She's famous, isn't she?'

'Yes, she is. I guess it was all before you were born though.' Mallory flicked through the pages. When she looked up, she saw Elsa was holding out her hand. 'What do you want?'

'I'm going to have to put it back, aren't I? We can't be taking things from guests' rooms.'

'I'll give it back to Doctor Hutton. There are some things I want to ask him.'

'You won't drop me in it, will you?'

Mallory glanced at the girl's pale face. 'Of course not. I'll say I was conducting a search myself. I'll keep you out of it.'

'*Diolch*.' Elsa clutched Mallory's hands. 'Is she here?'

Mallory didn't bother to plead ignorance. There was something about Elsa that demanded an honest response. 'I think so.'

'So do I,' whispered Elsa.

'I'll keep us safe, I promise,' said Mallory. She pulled the girl closer. 'I promise. Did you find anything else?'

'Not really. I'll go to help Tom in the kitchen. You don't want us at the meeting, do you?'

'No need.' Mallory looked at her watch. 'I've fifteen minutes. I just want to have a quick look at the book.'

'OK.' Elsa made to leave, before turning and coming up close to Mallory. 'She's here, because of Bridget Marsh, isn't she?'

Mallory, engrossed in the book, heard the click of the door as Elsa left the room. Mallory skipped the intro, flicking through the pages while she looked for the detective's description of Bryony. Finally, in chapter four, she found it. Under the eye of the Companions of the Good Shepherd, she began to read.

35

THE BIRTHDAY GIRL BY ANNA KIRBY

Bryony Clive is sitting in the custody suite, her thin legs pressed together and her arms crossed. She's an unprepossessing child, although we're not supposed to make value judgements about a suspect's appearance. Many a good looker has turned out to have a heart of coal and vice versa. But we're only human and I don't have any experience of interviewing a child accused of murdering her friends so I'm going to rely on every iota of experience I have. And that includes what the suspect looks like.

Bryony's eyes are an attractive blue, which she's clearly proud of as she keeps taking off the spectacles we know she's been prescribed for her myopia. She's a mixture of smug and arrogant which, of course, sets my teeth on edge because there's nothing I hate more than a conceited killer. I shouldn't be surprised. Not really. Except for the morons I meet, and there are plenty of those in my job, any villain with a speck of intelligence thinks they're superior to us coppers.

DC Ellis is struggling with the case, I can see. Between interviewing Bryony Clive and Grace Pagonakis, she's gone to the toilets to have a cry. I don't have a problem with this. Crying is as natural as sleeping and eating. The problem is when you allow your emotions to cloud your judgement but fortunately Janice isn't showing any signs of that.

We've gone to interview Bryony after Grace's statement. Grace is an ordinary child with dark brown hair and a shy smile. In the way children do, she both likes and despises her friend Bryony. I can remember a similar child in my own class at school. A girl brighter than everyone, a little boastful and not suffering fools gladly. That girl was an outsider too but that's where the comparisons with Bryony Clive finish. Bryony is a watchful, assessing child with an air of smug satisfaction.

'Can I just run over a few things again, Bryony?'

'Of course,' says the girl rolling her eyes. The duty solicitor is sitting with her, a prematurely balding man in his late twenties. He has a nervous cough, which he's trying hard to hide. In the corner, rather than Bryony's mother, there's an appropriate adult. My DI has insisted we follow all formalities to the letter when interviewing Bryony. We're operating under intense media scrutiny and everything is to be done by the book. The appropriate adult represents a set of independent eyes to safeguard the rights of this child.

Which is what I need to remember. Bryony, despite her crimes, is a child and I need to balance that with the fact she's also above the age of criminal responsibility. Just.

'So, Bryony. You put the crushed leaves of the foxglove plant—'

'Digitalis,' interrupts Bryony.

'Digitalis, of course.' I frown, temporarily losing my train of thought. 'But commonly known as foxglove and often found in gardens like your own. And what gave you the idea to use it?'

'It's the poison in a crime novel I just read.'

'But that's a work of fiction, isn't it, Bryony?' asks Janice. 'You do know what we mean by fiction, don't you?'

The girl's look is one of pure contempt. 'Of course I do. I wanted to see how well the writer had researched the novel. Digitalis usually only causes minor discomfort in small doses.'

'How do you know that, Bryony?' I ask.

Bryony sighs, irritated by my question. 'I read about it. I just wanted to see how it worked in practice.'

'And by seeing how it works, did you for a moment think that it might kill your school friends?' I lean forward to make my point.

'That's the thing with poisons, isn't it?' says Bryony. 'Anything can happen.'

'But you did realise that you might end up killing your school friends.' I need to get Bryony to reaffirm that she knew the likely outcome of her actions.

'Oh, yes.' The girl has adopted a nonchalant tone but, for a brief moment, I'm sure I've seen the mask drop and an expression of uncertainty appear.

'And you definitely didn't tell any of your school friends what you intended to do.'

'Of course not.' Bryony's voice drips with scorn. 'None of my friends would be willing to deliberately take poison.'

'So why do you think Grace survived?'

Bryony shrugged. 'She wouldn't drink the cordial. She insisted on a glass of lemonade so it was just the pavlova she ate. She took ages to start eating it as she'd had too many sandwiches. I thought for a moment she wouldn't take anything at all.'

'And did you push her to eat it?'

'I just waited. I didn't want to bring attention to myself. Eventually Grace took a spoonful but Florence had already started to be sick by then.'

I sit back in her chair, frustrated. Janice's eyes are on me. She hadn't wanted to reinterview Bryony again this evening but had pushed for us to have a good night's sleep, or as near to it as possible, and try again in the morning. I'd agreed it was a good idea so why had I pushed for this second interview? Bryony has confessed. The killings were pre-meditated and meticulously planned. The girl shows little remorse and her lawyer will have a hard time, even at eleven, showing that she wasn't aware of the consequences of her actions.

With a nod to my colleague, I get up. We need to get the CPS on board, but Bryony will be charged in the morning.

36

Mallory stared at the group of faces feeling a little like Poirot at the finale of one of the Agatha Christie novels she often read in bed. She'd had just enough time to put Anna Kirby's book in her office before coming back to the room to address the guests. Shan had been wrong when he'd called it a pot boiler. It was much better than that and she'd desperately wanted to read more. She'd made a tactical error talking to Michael when he was clearly a man with his own secrets. It couldn't be coincidence that he had a book in his possession relating to Bryony. He was somehow connected to this bewildering set-up and she needed to work out how much danger he posed. He was sitting in the far corner of the room, his face partially in shadow. Next to him was Stella, her expression tense, and Mallory again felt her intense scrutiny.

She studied the rest of the guests. Beth, drowsy with the codeine administered by Michael, had stayed in her bedroom with Edith. Scott had perched himself on the seat nearest the door, ready to bolt if he heard either his wife or child cry out for him. A medium-sized man, with long, thin limbs, he was folded into the chair like a bat. His face showed signs of strain and he'd temporarily lost his boyish appearance. Next to him, on the small sofa, sat Noah and Charlotte Vass. Noah's huge leg was jigging up and down, a sure sign of repressed energy, but Charlotte was once again unusually calm. Mallory, trying not to stare, looked again at the features of Charlotte but all she could see was the slightly aristocratic coolness of a woman who knew her place in the world. Julia, she'd been told, was in her room fuming over the lack of internet.

Mona Rubin was sitting on the other side of Stella. She'd changed since helping Mallory in the lobby, possibly worried about shards of glass sticking to her clothes. She wasn't wearing one of her long dresses but had put on trousers in a thick weave. Mallory had been impressed by how Mona had tended to Beth. Now she was murmuring something to Stella although Mallory could see it was having little effect on the woman's mood.

'Where's the other guest?' asked Charlotte. 'The girl with the bob. She was at dinner last night. I haven't seen her today.'

Mallory closely watched the group. 'Grace is staying in her room for the moment. This meeting is purely voluntary.'

If the killer was present, they'd know the statement was a fudge. Grace was certainly in her room, so Mallory was hardly lying. However, none of the guests paid much attention to the news, waiting instead for Mallory to issue her reassurances.

Mallory took a breath. 'As you all know by now, the phone line has gone down. It's not a fault either Tom or I can repair. The pole is damaged and the cable has snapped. We're therefore not able to contact anyone on the mainland or to put calls through to each other's rooms or to reception. I do, however, have a walkie talkie. I'll carry one handset around with me, the other I'll leave on reception. If there are any problems, come and use the handset to get in touch with me. I won't be far.'

'Problems like what?' asked Scott.

'Anything at all. I've called this meeting to reassure you that everything is in hand. The storm is expected to last until the early hours of tomorrow morning, after which weather conditions should improve enough to send over a boat. Given my conversations with Alex, the owner, I'm expecting it at first light.'

'Will they know we're incommunicado?' asked Stella.

'Of course. Alex will know immediately that a line has gone down. He's been calling the hotel regularly.'

'There's no mobile signal on the island at all?' asked Michael.

'None whatsoever.' Mallory wasn't so sure about this. On her first day on the island, she'd overheard a guest tell her child that they'd go to the cove just beyond the jetty where a faint signal could be picked up. Mallory had never tested it, preferring to rely on the hotel's wi-fi. She had no intention of telling anyone that a signal might be possible. It would be lethal to even attempt the walk in this weather. 'I understand it's frustrating and upsetting but I want you to hold on to the fact that this time tomorrow, you'll be back on the mainland.'

'What if we want to remain on Eldey?' asked Mona. Mallory saw that the hems of her trousers were wet. It was perfectly possible she'd gone outside. Mona had a mind of her own and was unlikely to listen to instructions. She might also know about the signal hotspot.

'I doubt you'll be allowed to because the fallen telephone pole is a hazard.' The police would also want the hotel to themselves. It wasn't like in classic detective novels where everyone would be kept in situ and interviewed. Witness statements would take time and the safety of the residents would be paramount. Guests were likely to be ferried to the local police station to be interviewed away from Eldey.

Mona shrugged. 'I've paid for a month's stay.'

'You can discuss a refund with Alex. I'm sure he'll be in touch with all of you. What I'd like to do is put together a schedule of who leaves first. The boat holds up to six passengers. I suggest that Scott, Beth, and Edith Gregory go on the first trip. Would the Vass family like to join them?'

Noah nodded at Michael. 'We're all fine. Perhaps those less able should go in our place.'

Michael flushed. 'I'm happy to wait.' He looked directly at Mallory. 'I'll wait.'

'Suit yourself,' shrugged Noah. 'The three of us will go on the first trip too.'

'Excellent. The rest of you can go on the second boat – Mona, Stella, Grace, Michael and I think Elsa, our staff member who's eighteen, will want to go with you.'

'And you,' said Noah.

'As well as being the night manager here, I'm also responsible for security. I'll be staying on with Alex when he arrives. Tom also lives here and might want to remain. Are we all happy with the plan?'

Mona shrugged, clearly reluctant to leave the island.

Scott, who Mallory had pegged as the quiet type, had obviously been building up his annoyance. 'It's outrageous we're stuck here. Suppose Edith falls ill? There's absolutely no way to get help. How can you run a business like this?'

Mallory opened her mouth to reply but was beaten to it by Mona. 'The website makes it perfectly clear that the Cloister is on an island.'

'And it's a fucking stupid place to bring a child,' said Noah, turning to address Scott. 'If you're looking for someone to blame, maybe find a mirror.'

Scott stood. 'I've heard enough. I'll go back to my family.'

A room of curious eyes watched him leave the room. He had a faintly ridiculous air but Mallory would still have to check on his well-being after the meeting.

'Does anyone else have any questions?' asked Mallory.

'How are we doing for provisions? I'm a little worried about the food.' The question came from Stella, the second time she'd asked the question.

Mallory paused. 'We have plenty of food, but we'll be altering the menu to take account of missing ingredients. We're incredibly lucky that we have our usual chef so you won't notice a drop in quality.'

'Plenty of alcohol, at any rate,' said Noah.

'There *is* plenty of drink, but please be careful. If there's an accident, I can't get help until tomorrow morning. Any other questions?'

The room was silent.

'Can I now ask you to go back to your rooms?' said Mallory. 'Lunch will be at one p.m. and it'll be a slightly restricted menu to ensure we concentrate on feeding you a substantial dinner, which will be at the same time as yesterday.'

From outside, overlaying the roar of the wind, Mallory could hear a thump-thump down the stairs. She wondered if Elsa was clomping around but the sound had an air of panic, feet tripping over each other as they stumbled down the stairs. Mallory immediately thought of the Gregory family, but it was Julia Vass who stood on the threshold of the room, her face puce.

'The girl in the room next door to me is dead. The girl with the red lipstick at dinner last night. She's dead.'

37

The group clamoured towards Julia. Charlotte was quickest on her feet, putting her arm around her step-daughter who, for once, made no move to shake her off. Noah headed towards the door, closely followed by Stella and Mona. Mallory had to move fast. For a split second, she wondered whether to play along, pretend that she was as shocked as they were at the announcement. What made her mind up wasn't that she'd be unable to maintain the charade but that they'd all be questioned about the essential accuracy of their accounts when the police arrived. Even she would be asked to provide a statement in order to be eliminated from the inquiry. The closer she kept to the truth, the easier it would be for the investigation.

'Stop.'

The note of authority in her voice brought everyone to a standstill.

'I don't want anyone going upstairs. Julia, you need to tell me how you got into the guest's room.'

'Aren't you going to go up and check on the girl?' asked Mona.

'I'll certainly be going to the room,' said Mallory, 'but, first, I need to know how Julia found the body.'

'The door was open,' said Julia, her face blotchy from crying.

'Open? What do you mean? Slightly ajar or wide open?' Mallory looked across at Michael who shook his head slightly.

'Hold on.' Julia's father had finally found his voice. 'What the hell's going on here? You're telling me you *knew* about this?'

Mallory flushed. 'I want you all to stay here. Julia take me to the room and show me how you found the door. One of your parents can come with you.'

Julia glanced at her father and nodded. Charlotte looked put out but, after a glance at her husband, reclaimed her seat on the sofa. Mallory looked over at Michael. 'Perhaps you can come too.'

They made a subdued group as they made their way to the room. Tom had come into the lobby at the commotion, but Mallory just inclined her head back towards the kitchen. She didn't want the kitchen left unattended. If Bryony was on the island, and Mallory was pretty sure she was, then her modus operandi was poison delivered through food. Better she deal with irate guests than dead ones. She hurried up the stairs with Noah and Julia while Michael took the lift. From behind, Mallory heard another tread on the stairs. She turned to see Stella on the bottom stop.

'I'd like to come too.'

'And I'm telling you, you can't. Please wait in the sitting room. This has nothing to do with you.'

'Fine.' It clearly wasn't, but Stella, for the moment, would have to wait. As they reached the entrance to Grace's room, Mallory took in the door flung open, the tips of the dead girl's fingers just visible.

'You don't need to go in, Julia. I know it's a distressing sight. Tell me, was the door like this when you saw it open?'

'Um.' Julia bit her lip. 'I'm not sure. I walked past and saw the door slightly open, which I thought was a bit strange. I thought she'd forgotten to close it or something, so I knocked.'

'The door was only partly ajar?' asked Mallory. 'Like this?' Mallory pulled the door towards her.

'I guess so.'

'That's OK. So you rapped on the door and when you didn't get an answer, what did you do?'

'Knocking on the door pushed it open a bit, I think. I just went in. I thought she might be sick or something. I hadn't seen her since dinner yesterday. As I got further into the room, I saw her lying there.'

'And did you touch anything?'

Julia hesitated.

'It's really important, Julia. Did you touch anything?'

'I knelt down next to her and felt her hand.'

'It's all right, sweetie,' said Noah. 'You can count on me to sort this out.'

Mallory sighed. Another set of fingerprints. She'd underestimated the killer, probably not for the first time. Her working assumption had been that Grace was lured to Eldey so Bryony could get her revenge. That had, to some extent, reassured Mallory that she'd be able to keep the death quiet. It would be in both the hotel's and Bryony's interest. Why sow chaos when all you want to do is exact your own terrible justice?

'Will you wait here? I just want to check the room.'

'I'm coming with you. I want to see what my daughter saw,' said Noah.

'Fine,' said Mallory, sighing. More contamination. 'You might as well come in too Michael. You'll be able to see if anything's been disturbed.'

Grace was lying where they'd left her, the window was still ajar letting in an icy cold draught of air.

Mallory stopped by the bathroom. 'I'd rather you didn't go any further into the room. I'm sorry that Julia had to see this. As you can see, it's not pleasant.'

'Which arm did you touch?' Noah called to his daughter.

'The one reaching towards the door,' Julia said, her face turned away from them.

Mallory frowned. Noah was no longer the buffoon she'd seen in the dining room but trying to take charge of the situation.

'Why is it important to you which arm Julia touched?' asked Mallory.

Noah ignored the question, his eyes on Grace. 'The funny thing is that she's vaguely familiar.'

'She was in the dining room yesterday evening.'

'I didn't notice her then.'

Mallory wasn't surprised. Noah had been seated with his back to Grace and she'd been at pains to keep away from other guests.

'Familiar in what way?' Mallory pressed.

'I'm not sure. Maybe I've seen her in the papers.'

That might account for it. Although there were no photos of Bryony she could access, the adult Grace had been tracked and pestered by various publications since the birthday tea. Mallory decided to keep her name secret for the moment. She had told it to Michael and now bitterly regretted it. The fewer people who knew the better.

'I'd like to shut up the room again. Michael was with me when I locked it last time but perhaps you could both watch me secure the door again.'

They both looked on as Mallory closed the door and tried the handle to make sure it stayed firm. It was pointless worrying about fingerprints given the number of times she'd touched the handle.

'I think you should go back to your room, Julia,' said Mallory when she was happy the door was secure. 'I want to speak to your father. Shall I get your mother to come and join you?'

'Stepmother.' The girl's tone was flat. 'I don't want to see her.'

'How about I get your father to put his head around your door once I've spoken to him.'

Julia nodded and opened the door at the end of the corridor. She was subdued but not terrified. She must surely be able to work out the reason Mallory had left the room intact. So, it seemed, did her father.

'It's a crime scene,' Noah asked her once his daughter was out of earshot. He didn't even bother to phrase it as a question.

'It's what I believe. I'm a former detective and that's what my instincts are telling me.'

'I see. And at what point were you going to tell us that we were sharing the hotel with a corpse?'

'I wasn't. The safety of the guests is paramount. I need to make sure no one panics while we're stranded here.'

He swung his eyes down to her. 'You told him.' He pointed at Michael. 'Is he an ex-cop too?'

'I'm a doctor.' Michael, she saw, was unafraid of this giant of a man. 'I was able to confirm death. We left the scene as we found it and locked the door after us.'

'Then who opened it?' asked Noah.

'We don't know.' Mallory, jittery, tried the door handle again just to make sure she wasn't going mad. The door held.

'Well, it's perfectly obvious that someone has a key. If you'd installed an electronic system, it'd be easy to see who had come and gone. As it is, you've got old-fashioned brass keys like something out of the 1950s.'

'That was the owner's decision. In a remote place, perhaps an electronic system isn't ideal. We have to deal with what we've got.'

'Well, as I said, someone's got a spare key, haven't they?' Noah folded his arms. 'Who has access to this room?'

'I have a master key,' said Mallory, 'and I can assure you it's not me. Elsa, the room attendant, has one too. I'll talk to her now but she's aware of the body and has been told not to open the room. I don't for a minute think it's her.'

'If someone has a spare master key, then they can get into any of our rooms. We shall also be taking steps to protect ourselves.'

'Please don't do anything rash. All the bedroom doors have bolts which can be used from the inside. The master key is only useful to access rooms if they're empty.'

'Or have a dead body in them.' Noah's humour wouldn't have been out of place in the Met police. 'How did your guest die?'

'I don't know,' lied Mallory.

Noah turned his attention to Michael. 'You're the doctor. What do you think? There's vomit and blood everywhere. Is it something she ate?'

'It's possible but I've seen accidents happen. Until we know for sure, Mallory is right to treat it as a crime scene.'

'Well,' said Noah. 'This weekend break is turning out to be more of an adventure than I'd anticipated. I shall certainly be claiming compensation when I'm back home.'

'Of course.'

He swung around. 'And you're sure you can't tell me the guest's name?'

Mallory tried a smile. 'Even the dead are entitled to their privacy.'

38

'We need to talk,' said Mallory to Michael.

Noah had left to speak to Julia in her room. Judging by the hushed words coming through the door, Julia had calmed down. Noah's reaction had been a surprise. He'd have been perfectly entitled to call Mallory out on the fact she'd left a dead body in the room next to his daughter's. Noah's questions, however, had been measured and shrewd. It suggested a more complex personality than she'd originally credited him with. She wondered why he had told Julia that he would sort it out. The arrogance of the rich, probably, who thought throwing money at any problem solved most things.

Before she tried to unpick who might have a spare master key, she needed to confront Michael about the book in his room. She suspected she was in the middle of an intricately plotted scheme and her problem was that she hadn't even worked out who the players were yet. Michael, however, had other plans.

'I'll speak to you later. There's some things I need to do first.' He headed towards the top of the stairs not even giving her a backwards glance.

'This is important,' she shouted after him, but he stepped inside the lift without looking back at her.

Mallory sighed. The issue of how someone had entered Grace's room was important but, she suspected, insolvable.

Bryony must have gotten hold of the key sometime this morning. Mallory had seen the wet footprints into the kitchen after everyone had retired for the night. For Grace to drink the poisoned milk, it would have to have been left outside her room. She wouldn't have taken a glass of milk from her infamous childhood friend. The hotel was short staffed and there were a number of master keys although she couldn't now contact Alex to ask him the exact number. The open door was no accident. What Mallory couldn't fathom was why a killer would want to sow disquiet amongst the guests. If Bryony was the killer, she'd presumably achieved her aim with Grace's death, so why announce it to everyone? Mallory stood for a moment thinking, tapping a pen between her teeth. Bryony had been a show-off, that's what Mallory had taken away from the article she'd read. On that fateful day in Wilmslow, she'd chosen an event to gain maximum impact. The girls had been killed in front of their parents during a birthday party and Bryony had become, from that moment, The Birthday Girl. Perhaps that explained why she'd opened the door. It was an action that shouted – look, see what I've done. Mallory had a horrible thought that she'd played into Bryony's hands by not announcing the death of a guest. The silence and hastily rearranged plans must have been eating away at the girl. Mallory was sure, more than ever, that Bryony was on the island.

She would confront Michael once she had reassured each guest that everything was in hand. As she entered the dining room, however, she saw that the little group had dispersed. This again was unusual. People were usually agog over unnatural deaths waiting for any news that might be drip-fed to them. Only Mona Rubin remained in her chair, her hands clasped around her knees. She looked up at Mallory as she entered.

'What's happened?'

'There's been a death in the hotel. One of the guests who was with you at dinner last night died in the night.'

'The girl dining by herself?'

'Yes, exactly.'

'Died? How?' Mona smoothed her trousers then froze as if she'd realised she was drawing attention to her clothing.

'I'm afraid I can't tell you that. It's a sudden death so it'll be investigated as such.'

'But the girl, Julia, found the body.'

'She says the door was open, which is a mystery as I certainly shut it this morning.'

Mona hesitated. 'You don't think—'

'What?'

'That there's something odd about the death, do you?'

'It's a sudden death of a young woman so of course it's odd. Why do you ask?'

'It's just I thought I saw someone watching me this morning when I was in the pool. It was only a moment. Perhaps just fancy, but it left me uneasy.'

'Someone was watching you. Did you see who?'

'I'm afraid not. When I left the pool, the person had gone.'

'Man or woman?'

'I'm afraid I can't even tell you that.'

Mona didn't appear particularly perturbed. 'It's probably nothing but I think it's wise to keep vigilant,' said Mallory.

'Of course.' Mona stood, trying her hair back into a bun.

'Can I ask what made you choose the Cloister?'

Mona frowned. 'I told you, I needed a month to myself to work on my art.'

'But why here specifically? It's not a run-of-the-mill place. Something must have brought you here.'

'I had a bit of money left to me by an aunt and I'd seen the website somewhere. It seemed a wonderfully creative place. The old nunnery, the mausoleum, the little coves. The discounted prices in the autumn helped too.'

Someone's certainly being creative, thought Mallory grimly. 'It was a random choice, then. You weren't specifically invited here.'

Mona frowned. 'Invited? I certainly wasn't invited. I might have received a promotional email. My inbox gets clogged up with them, but occasionally there appears one advertising just what I'm looking for.'

Mallory considered Mona. She could be a killer or a potential victim. Mallory didn't like the news that she'd chosen the Cloister after receiving an email. Her next question was conflicted by the need to protect what she knew about Grace while taking advantage of Mona's willingness to talk. 'I saw you speaking to Stella when we were all assembled in the room. Is she OK? I got the impression she was agitated about something.'

Mona wrinkled her nose. 'She seems wary of you. Have you done anything to upset her?'

Mona's answer was hardly a surprise. 'What did she say, exactly?'

'She whispered that she didn't trust you.'

That's great, thought Mallory. I suspect everyone and Stella's got her suspicions about me. Time for a chat. 'I'll talk to her. In fact I need to speak to everyone. I'm surprised the group disappeared given the news.'

'Julia's mother went back to her room. I think she was a bit miffed she wasn't allowed to accompany her daughter upstairs. Stella couldn't wait to get away. Scott obviously wanted to check on his wife and child, which is perfectly understandable after the accident earlier. I thought she was unnaturally calm afterwards, didn't you?'

'Shock,' said Mallory, suddenly distracted. 'That's odd, Edith's not crying. She must be still dozing with her mother.'

'Makes a change,' said Mona with a wink. Mallory remembered how much she liked Mona's wry humour.

'I'll check on them in any case. I'm going to do a quick knock on everyone's door.'

As she passed room three, she could hear Noah and Charlotte bickering but their words were muffled. She knocked on Stella's door but was met only with silence.

'Stella, are you there? It's Mallory.' Mallory was convinced the guest was listening but the door remained shut. Mallory was clearly pariah of the moment as Julia refused to open the door to her either.

'Go away,' she shouted and Mallory could hardly blame her. She couldn't remember her own first sight of a dead body. For reasons only a shrink would be able to unpick, the memory of her first professional death had been subsumed by other more violent fatalities. But she knew about shock and how some recollections were impossible to erase.

'Please, Julia, I just want to see if you're OK. I'll use my master key if necessary.'

In response, Mallory heard the door latch being secured. She sighed. 'OK, but I'm here if you need me.'

Third time lucky, thought Mallory as she waited outside the Gregory family room but again was met by silence. Unlike with Stella, the lack of noise felt ominous. A complete absence of sound. After banging on the door for a second time, she used her key to open the room and looked at the scene of devastation. The bed covers were strewn across the floor and shoes, toys and heaps of dirty washing were piled around the room. Elsa had said she'd cleaned every room so the wreckage must have happened in the last hour. Mallory crossed to the wardrobe and saw that there'd been an attempt to pack various items. There were no sign of coats, scarves or hats and very few of Edith's clothes were to be found. Mallory pulled at bedside drawers but couldn't find any wallets or personal papers. The devastation in the room masked the fact that the Gregory family had left the place, taking their essentials with them.

Mallory tried to imagine where they might have gone. Outside, Storm Ettie was doing its worst – they'd be lucky to get a few feet away from the building. Mallory went downstairs and looked in the sitting and dining room. Charlotte had stopped bickering with Noah and was helping herself from the coffee pot. She jumped at Mallory's appearance.

'I was just—'

'Have you seen the Gregory family? The couple with a young child?'

'I saw them pass with their coats on. I told them they shouldn't be going out in this weather and the husband told me to fuck off.'

'They went out the front?'

'No, towards the spa suite out the back door.'

Mallory followed the corridor around to the left and saw the door leading to the back garden ajar. Shit. She hurried back towards the kitchen. Tom was making a soup from cans of lentils piled on the counter.

'Trouble?' he asked.

'I think the Gregorys have gone outside.'

'Idiots. Do you want me to look?'

'I'd better do it. I don't for a minute think they've gone for a walk.'

'Where else is there for them to go?' asked Tom.

'They were asking earlier about the boathouse at the bottom of the jetty,' said Elsa. 'They wouldn't leave the room while I cleaned it. A right mess it was too. No wonder they've been feeling cooped up.'

'They asked me something similar earlier. Don't tell me there's a boat there.'

'Of course not,' said Tom.

'There is, you know.' Elsa jumped down from the counter. 'Alex bought it when he arrived. He wanted to use it to row around the island but the first time he tried it, he got caught in the rip tide by the cove. It frightened the life out of him, so he's not used it since.'

'But how would the Gregory family know that?'

Elsa bit her lip. 'I mentioned the boat to the family because they were asking. I didn't actually think they'd try to use it.'

'They're not going to try to row a boat in this weather. That's a death wish,' said Tom. 'Let me go and find them.'

'Neither parent struck me as having a death wish. Oh God.' Mallory remembered telling Beth the lifeboat would only be launched if someone was in trouble at sea. 'I think they're hoping to be rescued by the lifeboat. There'll be flares on board, I'm sure. I'm going to have to go down there.'

'Let me go.' Tom grabbed his jacket.

'I'm security, I do it.'

'You look terrible, Mallory.'

'I'm going,' she said. 'If anything happens to me, you're going to have to be the one who looks after things. Can you do that? Keep the kitchen secure and reassure any anxious guests. I'll be as quick as I can.'

39

Elsa came running to her as Mallory shrugged on her waterproofs. 'The Gregorys are making their way down the slope. I could see them from the dining room. I tried to run after them but I saw—'

'Saw what?' asked Mallory.

'I saw the nun,' shouted Elsa. 'Don't laugh. I saw her dressed in her long habit. It was Bridget Marsh.'

For crying out loud, thought Mallory. 'The nuns didn't have long habits,' she said as she pulled a woollen hat over her head. 'I don't have time for this now, Elsa. They were an Anglican community. You told me that yourself. Look at the picture hanging on the wall. Bridget Marsh is wearing a knee-length skirt and short head covering.'

Elsa stared at her open-mouthed. 'You're wrong. I know what I saw.'

'Take a look at the photo again,' said Mallory, exasperated. 'Please, Elsa. Take a look at what Bridget Marsh's ghost should look like before you start describing her.'

The exchange had given her a headache and as soon as a gust of wind battered into her, Mallory found her temper darkening. She set off down the hill, keeping clear of the trees bending in the wind. She looked around for the telephone wire – it could do some serious damage if it hit her – but she saw Tom had secured it to one of the remaining poles. She was nearly blown off her feet twice before she reached the garden's edge. When her foot hit the path, the slick cobbles sent her flying, winding her as she landed on her back. As she struggled to her feet, her eyes caught a figure looking out of the window. It could only be Noah Vass, his huge bulk filling the window frame.

Mallory put her head down and powered forward. When she got to the top of the slope, she saw the danger of trying to make her way down even in her walking boots. The path was strewn with debris and the salt water and rain was gushing down the cobbled stones. Only the thought of Edith out in this weather made her plough onwards. She used one side of the cliff to brace herself, clinging on to jutting rocks and ivy spilling from above. The sea roared beneath her as her legs slipped and skidded. At each corner, she expected to see the Gregory family also struggling, but they were more sure-footed than her.

She slid down the final part of the slope on her knees coming to a halt outside the open metal gates. Underneath the steps where guests queued to wait for Owen's boat was a building with high wooden doors. Already ajar, Mallory wrenched them open further and clung onto the handles. In front of a sturdy inflatable raft with an engine at the back, three forlorn figures huddled. Edith, unsurprisingly, was screaming her head off.

'What the hell do you think you're doing?'

Scott kept his eyes on the boat. 'I thought it was a rowing boat. We were going to put it afloat just by the jetty and set off flares so we could be rescued.'

'And whose brilliant idea was this?'

Mallory saw him give his wife a side glance. Beth's face was worse than when she'd last seen her after the accident. Puffed up, as if she'd been crying, the single sliver of glass which had punctured her cheek looked as if it might leave a scar. She should get Michael to take another look. Michael. Mallory grimaced. She had to speak to Michael.

'It's my fault,' said Beth, her voice a strange monotone. 'I'm worried about Edith. I just wanted to get away from here.'

'What's wrong with her?' Some of Mallory's anger dissipated. She went to the girl screaming in her father's arms and put her hands on her forehead. 'Her temperature feels OK.'

'It is fine but she was very dopey this morning.'

Oh God, not Edith, thought Mallory. 'What's she eaten today?' she asked.

'Just breakfast with me. Some toast and the glass of milk earlier.'

The bread would have been from the freezer so should have been OK and she'd supervised the opening of the milk herself. A crash outside brought her to her senses. 'Edith's best in bed. She might have a mild infection. We have some tins of baby food in the kitchen. Perhaps if you try to tempt her with that later, she'll feel more like eating. I can get Michael to look at her in the meantime.'

Beth kept her eyes on her little girl. Mallory could see the scar beginning to weep, blood mingling with water. 'I'm a terrible mother. The window breaking shook my nerves and then Scott told me about the body, I just flipped.'

But she didn't sound like a woman who was at the edge of her sanity. If anything, she sounded deadly calm. 'This situation is making fools out of us all. I'm worried about you too, Beth. Let's get back to the hotel.'

She reached out to touch the woman's arm but Beth shrugged off her touch. 'We'll go back. It was a stupid idea in the first place.'

Mallory watched the couple as they began to battle the winds back to the hotel. Mallory hunted around the boathouse and found an empty container. It was easy enough to find the fuel tank and, using a piece of rubber hose, she syphoned off the petrol left in the boat and stored the can behind a rock. If anyone else had the bright idea of taking the boat, they'd find their plans thwarted.

Mallory went to follow the Gregorys back up the path, staying behind them to make sure they all made it up safely. Her phone began to beep over and over as a stream of text and voicemail messages found the weak signal connection with the mast over on the mainland. Mallory hesitated. She'd called in Grace's death. There was nothing more to tell the police, either they'd taken her concerns about Bryony being on the island or they hadn't. She saw message after message from Alex and those could wait too. There was precious little she could say to reassure him.

Her heart leapt when she saw she'd missed two calls from Toby. He hadn't forgotten. She tried accessing her voicemail, but the signal was too weak. Finally, she picked up her first message. It was from Joe.

'Mallory, what the fuck did you say to Toby this morning? I've had a message that he's on his way to see you. You'd better have a fucking good excuse ready.'

Mallory stared at her phone, feeling sick. She'd no idea why Toby had decided to pay her a visit. She'd almost broken down on the phone to him but that hardly accounted for him making his way to the island. He'd be unlikely to even get to the town in this weather. She tried to call Toby's mobile but the signal was dancing around in the wind. Only on the final try, did she get through to him.

'Where are you?'

'Reading.' She could hear a station announcer in the background.

Mallory swore. 'Will you do me a favour and turn around. Listen to the weather around me. You'll be safer in London.'

'I want to talk to you Mum. About everything that happened.'

Oh, God. Not now, she thought.

'OK. I promise, as soon as I can get off this island, I'll come and see you in London?'

'I want to talk to you now.'

'But I'm stuck here. Listen—' The phone went dead as rain battered down on the handset. At this rate, she'd have no working mobile. Mallory pushed open the gate and began the arduous climb back to the hotel, her legs slipping beneath her. She caught up with the Gregorys, Scott grim, Beth expressionless and Edith sobbing.

'You run and get Edith back inside,' she told Scott. 'Go to your room and give her a hot shower. That'll wake her – I'll help Beth.'

Scott sped off without even looking back at his wife. Mallory gripped Beth's arm and half-helping half-dragging her pulled her up the incline.

'I can't stay in a hotel with a dead body.'

'You don't have any other options.'

'Can't you just move it to an outhouse?'

'No, I can't,' said Mallory, pushing on. The rain battered down on their heads and a rumble of thunder could be heard in the background. Beth was shivering despite the thick coat she was wearing. It would have been useless if they'd set out to sea.

As she approached the entrance, through the rain-smeared glass, she could see Michael anxiously staring out of the window as she dragged Beth towards the warmth. When they were finally in the lobby, he moved towards her.

'She's fine,' Mallory said. 'Everyone's just drenched through. I've told them to have hot baths but I'd like you to look at Edith first.'

'Send up a pot of tea and coffee. They need to increase their body temperature. I'll go and organise it.'

'No, I'll do it once I've put Beth in her room. I want to have a talk with you before you look at Edith.' She used the last of her strength to get Beth up the stairs and into the bedroom. Beth wrestled herself free from Mallory's grasp and ran to the bathroom, slamming the door behind her.

'I'll deal with her,' said Scott, refusing to meet Mallory's eye. He continued to clutch his laptop containing his precious manuscript.

'How long have you been married?' Mallory asked, trying to sound casual.

Scott hesitated. 'Just a year. We got married when Edith was two. Why do you ask?'

'I was just wondering. Did you meet your wife through work?'

'Of course not.' Scott's eyes narrowed. 'What's with all these questions?'

Both turned as Beth stood in the doorway watching them. She was getting nowhere with her oblique questioning. Maybe it was time to be bold. Start actively trying to provoke potential suspects into revealing their true selves. 'Are you all right, Bryony?' asked Mallory.

'It's Beth,' said Scott. 'Beth not Bryony.'

'Of course,' said Mallory, still watching Beth whose tear-stained face remained impassive. 'Apologies.'

40

CHARLOTTE

The night manager was sharp and she'd need all her wits about her to get through the next eighteen hours.

When Charlotte realised all communications had gone down, she'd packed a bag containing the items most likely to condemn her. She was torn between fight or flight and, at the moment, flight was winning. She had come to the island full of plans but the weather had intervened. She pushed her overnight bag to the back of the wardrobe before Noah came back into the room. He'd guess the contents and then it'd be game over.

On cue, he came into the room, rubbing his hands. 'Fine day for a walk.'

She couldn't judge his mood. 'What do you mean?' she asked.

'Everyone's outside. The family with the young child. Mallory. And that woman with the long, red hair.'

'Mona. What are they doing out in this weather?'

'No idea. Trying to get away from sharing a space with a dead body, I guess.'

'Grace Pagonakis was the girl's name. Let's at least give her a name other than the "the body". She deserves that at least.' She saw him freeze.

'How do you know that's her name?'

Charlotte stopped. 'I asked the girl who cleans the rooms. She didn't want to tell me but I wheedled it out of her. I promised not to tell anyone she'd given me a name.' She looked at him. 'What's the matter?'

'What do you think is the bloody matter?' But Noah was thinking hard. She could feel his mind ticking over.

'Did you know her?' Even as she asked, she was sure that they hadn't been lovers. The girl simply hadn't been his type. Mona, yes. Even Beth Gregory. But not Grace with her unflattering hairstyle and too tight clothes.

'It's an unusual name.' He said the words slowly.

Charlotte gave up. 'All right. I'm going for a walk. Is Julia OK?'

'Not answering the door.' He looked across at her briefly. 'No point in you trying. She won't let you in.'

Charlotte slid off the bed. 'You know, I think I'm going to knock anyway. She's had a shock and I'm not the monster you think I am.'

'I don't think you're a monster.' He had an odd note in his voice and Charlotte turned but he'd settled himself on the bed. 'I'm here if you need me, you know.'

'Need you?' Charlotte's veins turned to ice.

'You heard what I said. I'm here if you need me.' He looked at her. 'There are a lot of bloody coincidences happening this weekend. Don't think I haven't spotted them.'

Charlotte grabbed her coat and pulled it on. 'I'll check on Julia now.'

'Why are you wearing a coat?'

'Because I can't stop shivering,' she shouted back at him.

Julia opened the door on the second knock, Charlotte's first rap drowned out by the sound of tinny music. Julia appeared flushed and Charlotte could smell brandy on her breath.

'I need the bottle please,' she said, holding out her hands.

Julia, to her credit, didn't bother to deny it. She reached under her bed and pulled out a half litre of ten-year-old Armagnac. The girl had expensive tastes like her father.

'How much have you had?' asked Charlotte, looking at the bottle now only a third full.

'You going to pump my stomach?' jeered Julia.

'I know how to. I just need a funnel and a piece of tubing.' Charlotte let her accent drop for a moment and watched in satisfaction as the girl paled.

'I've had two glasses.'

She'd probably halved the amount but even four glasses wouldn't kill her even though it'd probably give her a sore head in the morning.

'Are you OK? I know finding the body must have been upsetting.'

'Upsetting?' said Julia slamming the door. 'You need to be drunk to put up with all this.'

Charlotte paused for a moment and looked towards the window. No time like the present.

41

Michael was waiting for Mallory in the lobby. For the first time, she was aware of his strength. She'd been guilty of what she most dreaded for herself. People saw your disabilities and they became your defining trait. Michael with the cane. Mallory who walks with a limp. It was Michael, in fact, who they were having to rely on. The only resident currently on Eldey who had medical knowledge. Who knew how to treat the sick. Their eyes met and he smiled, trying to mask his embarrassment.

'I need to talk to you,' he said.

She considered a response, aware of the need to choose her words carefully. He had a thin shell, his touchiness a defence mechanism against the world.

'Fine,' she merely said.

'Perhaps I should check on the Gregory family first,' said Michael.

'Give them half an hour to have showers and then go to see them. I think they're a little ashamed of their attempts to flee.'

'Let's hope no one else tries to copy them.'

Mallory wiped her face with her sleeve. 'I've drained the boat's tank. It won't happen again.'

'We'll talk now then.' He stepped back, anxious to get the conversation over with.

'The bar will give us some privacy. Hold on a moment.'
She hurried into her office and retrieved Anna Kirby's
memoir from her locked drawer. He looked at the book
in her hands.

'Did you take that from my room?'

'I really do hope you have a good explanation for
this,' said Mallory leading the way. When they got to
the small bar, she shut the door and leant against it, her
body in an agony of exhaustion. 'When I spoke to you, I
needed to talk through with you my fears about finding
Grace's body. I mentioned the name Bryony Clive, more
commonly known as The Birthday Girl. You said you
knew her story but not that you're reading a book about
the poisonings.'

Michael kept his eyes on her. 'What exactly are you
accusing me of here?'

'Goddamit.' Mallory walked across to him, gripping a
chair. 'You saw the state of the body. This isn't a question
about your reading choices. I told you I thought Bryony
Clive was on the island and at no point did you tell me
that you were reading a book about her. So, I'm asking
you, why did you come to the island with that book?'

'I didn't.'

'Well, I doubt it was in the sitting room library. It
doesn't look like Alex's choice of reading material. So
where did you get it?'

Michael reddened. 'I don't think I can tell you that.
Someone gave it to me.'

'Who? Who gave it to you?'

He hesitated. 'I feel like I'm betraying confidences.'

'Of a killer?'

'She's not... OK, it was Stella who gave it to me.'

'Stella?' Mallory's head began to thud. 'What's going on? Why would Stella give you the book?'

'Because she wrote it.'

Mallory, for a moment, thought she was going mad. That the rotten coffee had contained some hallucinogenic drug. 'She wrote it? But the author is an ex-detective called Anna Kirby.'

'It's a pseudonym. Her real name is Stella Atkinson.'

'Fuck.' It accounted for Stella's strange behaviour on Eldey although not her animosity towards her. 'And what is she doing on this island?'

'She had an anonymous tip-off that she would find Bryony here this weekend. The book made her a fair bit of money at the time. It certainly helped her police pension. She'd not sold many books recently though so she'd decided to write an updated edition. She'd been trying to track down Bryony's whereabouts but had no luck.'

Mallory thought of Shan's reaction. No one who wanted to keep their job would have been willing to pass on that sort of information even if they'd been able to access it.

'So, who told her Bryony would be here?' she asked.

'She doesn't know – the tip-off was anonymous, as I said. She assumed one of her former colleagues was doing her a favour.'

'Christ. First Grace gets an invite from a beauty company who denies all knowledge of the alleged prize and now I find Stella has been lured here too. What was she hoping to achieve? An interview with Bryony? A girl who's spent much of adolescence incarcerated and has been given the benefit of complete anonymity. Are you telling me Stella really thought Bryony would just say yes to an interview?'

Michael frowned. 'Stella's not stupid. She arrived this week ready just to identify Bryony and think of a way of approaching her. You never know how people are going to react. I've learnt that as a doctor. There was a slim chance Bryony would agree to speak to her.'

'And how did you discover this?'

'Stella and I had an early morning breakfast on Friday. She was on edge but clearly proud of her achievement in writing the book. She told me about the case and leant me a copy of the book.'

'So why the hell didn't you tell me all this when I spoke to you this morning?'

'Because she asked me not to.'

'And you agreed? Come on, Michael, you know the situation we're in. This isn't the time to make rash promises. I need all the information I can get.' She was sick of being lied to and the desperation of their situation was beginning to dawn on her. 'Given the fact we may be sharing an island with a murderer, I'd really appreciate the truth, Michael.'

Michael exhaled. Mallory saw that stress had inflamed his scar and she wanted to reach out and touch it. 'When Stella arrived, she assumed by Friday evening she'd have spotted which guest was Bryony. But there were a number of possible women who might match Bryony's description and she couldn't work out who she needed to approach.'

'She couldn't recognise her at all? Wasn't she one of the investigating officers?'

'Yes, but she only interviewed her once on the day of the killings. After that, it was escalated to a larger team so she never actually got to question Bryony again. That was left to specialist officers.'

'So she couldn't recognise Bryony. Did she even have an inkling who it might be?'

Michael kept his eyes on her. 'She thought it might be you.'

In her exhaustion, Mallory was seized by a desire to laugh. '*I'm* Bryony? Good God.'

'You're about the right age and you have her colouring. Light brown hair and blue eyes.'

'That's it? All of us have blue eyes – me, Mona, Charlotte, Beth. As for hair colour, that's easily changed.'

'I'm just telling you what Stella said.'

'For God's sake, Michael.' The man was infuriating. 'I am not Bryony Clive. I grew up in Guildford not Wilmslow. I couldn't tell the difference between arsenic and baking soda. What I don't understand is why she's been avoiding me? If she thinks I'm Bryony, then she'd want to speak to me, surely.'

'Obviously she came to the island desperate to speak to Bryony but she thinks she was poisoned the other evening when she drank the coffee. It upset her terribly, I found her crying in her room this morning and had to try to calm her down. The little girl who's staying here looked frightened.'

'And fear made her stay away from me?'

'She complained to you about the coffee but she was watching you closely to see how you reacted. I'm not sure you reassured her.'

Mallory rubbed her face, immediately regretting it when a dart of pain shot up her hand from her finger. 'I need to speak to Stella as soon as possible because she might help me identify Bryony from amongst the guests.

You're going to have to come with me. She won't answer the door to me on her own.'

But this time Mallory could tell the silence from behind the door was genuine. Mallory used her key to enter the room. It was neat as a pin in contrast to the chaos left behind by the Gregory family. Elsa had no doubt cleaned the room but the lack of beauty products, books and other bits and pieces suggested Stella lived a contained life.

'She can't have got far,' said Mallory. 'I'll look through the hotel for her. You check on the Gregorys and then come and find me. Is there anything else you're not telling me?'

'No, but you're not one to talk. What is it you're not telling me?'

Mallory stopped. 'I think Bryony is going to kill again and I think Stella is the next target.'

42

MONA

The night manager was sharp and she'd need all her wits about her to get through the next eighteen hours.

The hotel was on the move, she could tell. The stasis of the morning, everyone dull and sluggish after a night's incarceration, had been replaced by a sense of energy and purpose. Mona would harness this energy for what she needed to do next. She wondered why Charlotte was so jumpy and what was with the outdoor coat. She'd tried to speak to the woman, warn her that the weather was lethal, but Charlotte had said she was simply wearing it to keep warm. Mona had let it drop but was positive that Charlotte had her sights set on the outside. She just hoped that whatever the woman was up to, it didn't interfere with her plans.

In her room, Mona took out her paints from her bag and checked the space under the false bottom. It was vitally important mix-ups didn't occur, especially when time was so short. Snapping her case shut, Mona lifted it and picked up a sketch pad she could afford to ruin in the rain. She slipped on her long, tatty mac she'd hesitated about bringing to the island, knowing its artistic scruffiness would be at odds with the carefully cultivated luxury of the hotel. Now she was just grateful that it would keep her warm and disguised.

The corridors were quiet but Mona wasn't fooled. The occupants of the hotel were on high alert, which meant that she'd have to be careful. However, now it had been decided that they'd be leaving by boat as soon as help arrived, she had to make some urgent decisions. As soon as she opened the door, she realised the foolhardiness of her plan. The gusty wind was strong enough to lift her off her feet. Still, she ploughed on, her end goal alive in her mind. This was her only chance.

43

Mallory cursed that she hadn't spent more time talking to Stella. Admittedly, she'd been giving Mallory a wide berth but she had, Mallory remembered, wanted to come to Grace's room when Julia had burst into the sitting room to announce her news. If Mallory had been thinking straight, she would have asked Stella what her interest was in Grace. She clearly hadn't recognised Bryony's childhood victim or she would surely have warned Grace that the two of them on the island must be more than mere coincidence. Now, with Stella missing, Mallory began a hurried search of the hotel beginning with the public rooms. In the sitting room, she found Elsa staring at the photo of the Companions.

'Are you OK?' she asked the girl. 'Can you see why I asked you to look at the photograph? If you saw someone in a long black outfit it's not going to be the ghost of Bridget Marsh. These were modern Anglican nuns. Forget *The Sound of Music*.' The island might be geographically remote but the sisters had brought twenties fashion to the island, including calf-length skirts.

'Yes.' Elsa continued to stare at the picture, her brow furrowed.

'What's the matter?'

'Just something I haven't noticed before.'

'What?'

'This is Bridget Marsh.' Elsa pointed at a sister near the back.

'I'm sorry, I really don't have time for this.'

'Please.'

Mallory leant forward, conscious that time was ticking away and she needed to urgently find Stella. She also was aware that keeping Elsa calm was of utmost importance over the next few hours. Bridget Marsh looked older than Mallory had expected. She had none of the freshness of youth but appeared anxious and closed off. She had her gaze downwards towards the woman sitting in the middle of the nuns, Margaret Taylor.

'Can't you see it?'

'See what, Elsa? Please, I need to look for someone.'

'She looks like Alys. I never saw it before but I haven't looked at the picture properly for a while. I think it's the weather, it heightens your senses.'

'Alys?' Mallory peered at the nun again. In looks there was nothing that reminded her of Alys except, perhaps, the glance she was giving Margaret. 'I'm not sure I can see the resemblance.'

'She definitely looks like Alys,' said Elsa. 'I'd heard some of the family settled in the area afterwards. I'll have to ask her when I see her next. She must have some tales to share too.'

Stories that would never be told. Mallory wondered how Elsa would take the news of Alys's death. Harder, she was sure, than that of Grace who was a stranger to the girl. It was a good spot by Elsa but hardly surprising given the girl's interest in the island. It also solved the mystery of why Alys had taken offence at Elsa's relish as she told the story of the dead nun. Family ties ran deep and Bridget's death would surely be a sore point.

Mallory sighed, darting a glance at Elsa. She was intrigued by her spot of the family resemblance but Mallory wasn't sure that Elsa turning over the story of Bridget would be particularly helpful in the tragedy that was unfolding.

'Look, Elsa. Have you seen Stella Atkinson? The guest in room nine.'

'I saw her this morning when I cleaned her room. She didn't want to go downstairs but I can't clean with a guest present. She left eventually.'

'You haven't seen her since?'

'No. What's the matter?'

Mallory took in Elsa's worried expression. 'I just want to ask her something. It's fairly urgent. I have my radio on me. The other handset is in the office. If you see her, will you call me?'

'Is it about the dead girl?'

'Sort of, but it's nothing to worry about.' Mallory looked at her watch. 'Lunch is in five minutes. You need to get to the dining room soon.'

'Tom has done soup and sandwiches. The soup is Tuscan lentil and it's delicious. Everything he's prepared he's tasted himself.'

Mallory blanched. 'It's not laid out in the room for everyone to help themselves, is it?'

'Of course not. I'll be taking orders and carrying them to the table.'

'Thank God. Please radio me if Stella's there.'

But Mallory was pretty sure Stella wouldn't be at lunch. Now that a guest was dead, her senses must be on high alert. It was urgent Mallory find her before Bryony did. In the lobby, Charlotte Vass was rifling through papers on reception.

'Is there anything I can help you with?'

Charlotte jumped at her voice and pulled her tweed coat tighter. 'Sorry. I was just looking for details of this tour Julia keeps mentioning. With the internet down she can't access the email she received but I wanted to check the details. I appreciate we can't go outside but perhaps an indoor discussion of the story might pass the time.'

'There's no tour. There's been a mistake.' God, she thought, once I've found Stella I have to talk to Julia. She must find out who had emailed her about this mythical tour. Charlotte turned to go, drawing the arms of her sleeves down over her hands.

'Have you seen Stella Atkinson?'

'The older woman? She was in here about half an hour ago,' said Charlotte. 'She seemed a bit agitated. Perhaps the isolation is getting to her. Is there something the matter?'

Mallory gave Charlotte a quick look. The question was asked with a studied casualness. 'Nothing wrong. I'll carry on looking.'

The dining room was empty but through the round windows of the kitchen doors, Mallory could see Tom preparing drinks. Engrossed in his task, he didn't see her watching him but turned to smile at Elsa who was cutting up a loaf of bread into thin slices. Mallory next tried the spa suite although she didn't think Stella, if she was feeling vulnerable, would be using the pool or sauna. Ignoring the sign telling guests not to enter in outdoor shoes, Mallory pushed the door open. The pool was empty but when she opened the door of the sauna, she saw Beth relaxing on a towel.

'I've not seen her since breakfast,' she told Mallory in response to her question.

'No problem.'

'Is anything wrong?' Beth sat up. 'You look worried.'

'It's nothing to concern yourself about. I want to check where everyone is. How are you feeling now?'

Beth shrugged. The scar on her face was still inflamed. 'I need a bit of time by myself. Children are great but they're draining. I think that's why I overreacted. When Scott told me about the dead body, we panicked. I'm really sorry you had to go out in the rain after us.'

'It doesn't matter. As long as you're all right.'

Mallory closed the door behind her and sat next to the woman. She was as thin as Mona and Charlotte but her height, she saw, came from the woman's long body, rather than her legs. 'I found it helped when Toby went to school. I felt I'd got a bit of my personality back. He was a difficult toddler but him starting full-time education meant I was able to return to work. I think I made a decision after that never to completely lose sight of what I wanted in life.'

'You have a child? Where is he now?'

Making his way towards the island, thought Mallory, swallowing her worry. 'With his father in London.'

'You're not together?'

'No.' Mallory stood shaking out her leg. 'But, as I told you the other day, it does get easier. Sort of.'

Beth smiled. 'I shall hold on to that.'

44

BETH

The night manager was sharp and she'd need all her wits about her to get through the next eighteen hours.

It had been good to chat to her. Beth had a small social circle of mothers she'd met through her NCT classes and at nursery, but they all seemed to revel in motherhood. No one found it a challenge as she did. The endless sleepless nights followed by days where it felt like she was wading through treacle. Mallory had been kind but that didn't mean she wasn't very, very dangerous. She'd soon have to get dressed and face the others at lunch. It was a danger point and the best thing for her to do really would be to eat in her room. But, although it was hard to admit it, there was that part of her that thrived on tension.

She would go and dress and come down to lunch as a family. She picked up her towel, rammed her feet into flip flops and opened the sauna door, letting out a blast of lavender into the spa suite. In the pool along the far wall, she saw her husband dunking Edith in and out of the pool as she screamed with delight.

'There's Mummy,' shouted Scott, which put Edith in a frenzy of excitement. Her heart swelled with a love she hadn't known possible all those years before she'd had kids. You loved them and resented them.

'I'll go and get dressed. You carry on.'

Scott's face fell. He'd clearly been hoping she'd take over so that he could go back to the room and write. Nice try. Beth only had a short window between lunch and dinner and she intended to use it to her advantage. In her room, she put on her warmest pair of trousers and added the fisherman's sweater her mother-in-law had knitted the previous winter. To go out through the back door, she'd need to slip past the entrance to the spa suite. It was hard to get out of the building unseen. It wasn't Scott she had to explain herself to, but the flaxen-haired chambermaid come waitress. She was dressed for serving lunch but for some reason was hanging about the spa suite. She looked at Beth in concern as she passed.

'You're not going outside, are you?' asked the girl.

'I just need a bit of fresh air. I'm only going to stand underneath the eaves and let the wind blow me about a bit.'

'Be careful.' Elsa pushed past her, giving her a quizzical look over her shoulder.

45

Mallory pulled on her outdoor coat and changed into her walking boots. She still wasn't dry after her last foray outside. The cuffs on her sleeve and neck collar were giving off the stink of wet wool and her trousers clung to her legs. At some point, she would need to go back to the cabin and put on a fresh change of clothes but a damp jumper and trousers would have to do in the meantime. Stella clearly wasn't in the hotel and Mallory now believed the woman was in danger. She would search the outbuildings first, which also meant a trip down to the boathouse. There, she would try to contact DI Harri Evans and warn him another guest was missing. That should surely add urgency to the rescue mission.

She was desperate for a stiff brandy. She'd maxed out on her meds, which meant no more painkillers. Mixing them with alcohol would be dangerous but she was at the stage where she needed anything to take her mind off her leg. She wanted to rip off her jeans and bathe the wound under tepid water but she didn't even have time for that. She zipped up her jacket and made her way to the lobby where Michael was waiting for her. He looked terrible, his gaunt face badly shaved and eyes rimmed with red.

'I'm still looking for Stella. I now need to try outside.'

'She still thinks you're Bryony. Let me come with you.'

'I can't. It's treacherous out there.'

'And I'd be more of a hindrance than a help.'

Mallory stopped. 'It's not that. I can sense danger. I'd like you on standby here.'

'What do you mean?'

'If Stella's outside then I don't know what shape she's going to be in. It would be a great help if you were ready at the hotel for a possible emergency. I'll go out the front. I need to check my own cabin and some of the outbuildings. Then—' Mallory stopped at the sound of Elsa shouting her name. 'What now?'

They turned to see Elsa in the doorway wearing what Mallory called her dead nun face.

'Mallory. Come and see.' Elsa's cheeks were flushed and her eyes glittered in excitement.

'Wait here,' Mallory told Michael. Swallowing her nausea, she allowed Elsa to lead her away from the lobby, up the stairs and into the corridor.

'What's wrong?' asked Mallory.

Elsa stopped in front of Stella Atkinson's room but didn't open the door. Instead, she pulled back the curtain to one of the passage windows which overlooked the back of the house. 'See,' she said.

Mallory crossed to the window and used the cuff of her sleeve to wipe condensation from the glass. Across the dark of the afternoon, a light burned in the distance.

'Who's out there?'

'Not a person. A thing.'

'For God's sake. I thought we'd had this out about the nuns.'

'I mean a building. It's the mausoleum.'

'There's not going to be a light inside there.'

'It has a lamp hanging about the door. It's always been there. I used to play around the building when I was younger. I thought nothing of it. The lamp was there but you couldn't turn it on from the outside. There was a switch inside.'

'You sure?'

'Yes. Someone's been inside and turned the light on.'

Mallory moved her forehead closer to the glass. The light shimmered in the gusts of wind but the beam was steady. The lamp had been lit and was flashing its beam across the island.

'Which rooms face the back?' she asked Elsa.

'Rooms one and ten, either end of the corridor.'

'Right, do me a favour. We'll draw the curtains in this passageway so guests aren't tempted to look out over the back of the hotel. For the two rooms at the end, could you knock and check on the Gregory family and Julia Vass? Just explain it's a welfare check. While you're in the rooms, draw the curtains. If you're asked, and only if you're asked, tell them it's to protect occupants from the possibility of smashing glass. I don't want anyone looking out there until I've turned off the light.'

'You're not going there?' Elsa's grip on Mallory tightened. 'You can't go out in this.'

'I've been out in it once already and I'm going to go again. I haven't been able to find Stella. If she's there, she might be in trouble.'

'You'll be blown into the sea. You need to use the path and it's not straight across the fields. It goes near the cliffs in places.'

'I'm not going to walk. I'm taking the quad bike from the shed. I'll be able to drive across the fields. The ground will be rocky but hard. I'll switch the lights on and off three times when I get there so you know I've safely arrived.'

She ran down the stairs, almost colliding with Scott and Edith.

'Is everything all right?' The skin beneath Scott's eyes was paper thin, the blue veins standing out.

'Everything's fine.' Mallory went into the back office and put in the password for the key safe. The quad bike key was there, and she grabbed it, slamming the safe shut. 'I'm just going to do some final checks before night falls. Don't worry.'

Satisfied, Scott nodded. 'At least the lights haven't gone out.'

'We have food, heating and light. We've just lost contact with the outside world until the phone line is reconnected. Try not to worry.'

She brushed past the pair and stepped outside, closing her eyes for a moment as she braced against the wind. Mallory's feet sank into the dewy grass as she crossed to the outbuilding where the quad bike was kept. The door was shut fast and she felt her wound crack and seep as she pulled hard. It wouldn't give until she managed, with two hands, to tug on the door.

The room stunk of engine oil. She put on the helmet left on the driver's seat and turned the ignition. The bike started straight away although the engine was cold. This was reassuring at least – there weren't any signs of recent use. She set off, focusing all her energy on keeping a steady speed. If she turned the bike, she'd almost certainly perish. At first, inside the confines of the hotel grounds, her grip held as she steered the bike across the lawn. Once she was past the hateful laurel hedge, however, she faced the full force of the storm blowing across the peninsula, battering the island. The quad bike was top of the range and Alex's high standards might just save her life. Each time a huge gust pushed the bike sideways, it stayed upright, helped by the even ground.

The gloom hadn't completely descended although there was precious little light. Mallory kept her eyes fixed on the light coming from the mausoleum. The orb grew larger as she neared it but there was no sign of anyone else out in the elements. Guessing most of the gusts were coming from the west, Mallory parked the bike next to the east-facing wall and pulled out the keys. She wasn't going to risk anyone taking it while she checked the building.

The door was unlocked and opened onto a room with two neat rows of coffins. Margaret Taylor and her cohort had come here to live together and to die, one by one. Mallory got out her torch and shone it around the room. They were all identical, stripped pine and placed on an iron rack. There was none of the disorder and decay Mallory had feared. Like the rest of the complex, the place had a managed look. Obviously, the nuns had looked after their own while alive but Mallory wondered who had ensured this place remained cared for.

Mallory needed to step inside to check no one was hiding there but her courage was failing her. She could cope well enough with the dangers posed by the living, but this place gave her the creeps. There was an odd, smoky atmosphere to the air, which clogged her lungs. She stood at the entrance peering into the darkness. The overhead light, although strong, didn't shine into the far reaches of the building. She had a fair idea why the light had been left on. Bryony was playing jokes again. A wave of nausea threw her off balance. She should get back to the hotel. It wasn't a night for adventures. As Mallory, facing out onto the wild landscape, put her hand to the light switch to turn off the power to the light at the front, she heard a movement behind her coming from the crypt.

46

Mallory spun round, reaching out for a pillar to steady herself. She sensed danger – the same menace she'd recognised the previous evening crossing to her cabin. What she now expected to see was who The Birthday Girl was. Mona, Charlotte or Beth. As a bubble of hysteria rose in her throat, Mallory clung on to the last of her sanity. The ride across the island should have cleared her head but now the crypt was a carousel of images, the faces of the three women grinning as they spun around her head. Lifting the front of her jumper over her mouth as a makeshift mask, Mallory removed her head torch and shone it around the crypt, the wild beam bouncing off stone and wooden coffins. Another sound echoed around the chamber, this time recognisable as a groan of pain. Mallory ploughed forward, coughing in the pungent air. At first, she thought it was her imagination. A body on one of the spare racks. It took all her courage to go to the figure retching at the foul miasma.

Mallory bent down to look at Stella, careful to keep the strong beam from her torch out of the woman's face. Even in the small act of crouching, it was impossible for her to keep her balance.

'Stella,' she whispered, feeling the woman's pulse, which fluttered against Mallory's fingertips. 'Stella, are you all right?'

'No.' The words came out in a long hiss. 'Don't come near me. Poison. In the air.'

Mallory recoiled. 'Are you sure?'

'Can't you feel it?'

Mallory was assailed by another rush of nausea. 'Yes. Is this what's making me hallucinate?'

'Probably. You need to get out of here.'

'I'll let the night air in.' Mallory stumbled across the room and dragged open the heavy wooden doors, letting in the blowy wind. She could see piles of smoking, evergreen leaves stacked up in the corners of the crypt. Laurel, she was sure. Pulling her jumper further over her nose, she pulled the branches out of the building and chucked them into the night, their sparks dancing in the wind. Remembering her promise to Elsa, she found the light switch, an old-fashioned lever type and clicked it off and on three times.

She vomited onto the grass, immediately feeling better. Inside she could see the foul choking smoke. Stella would die if Mallory didn't get her out of there. She ran back into the crypt almost blind from the singeing smoke.

'Stella, I have to get you on the quad bike.'

'I can't move.' Stella rolled over and retched on the ground beneath her. Her juddering caused a nearby coffin to rock.

'I have to get you out. You need help. Laurel is poisonous, isn't it? It can't just be the berries. The atmosphere in here is foul.'

Stella was stupefied with pain. 'Pull me over to the door.'

Mallory looked around the mausoleum for something to use as a stretcher but apart from the eternally sleeping sisters, the place was just cobwebs and rotting leaves. She had little choice but to drag Stella outside by her arms while the woman's heels scraped along the concrete floor.

She lay Stella flat on the ground, the rain spraying the woman's face. It brought back memories of Mallory's own brush with death nine months earlier. She prayed the sharp air outside would revive Stella enough to transport her back to the hotel.

'Why did you come to the crypt?'

The woman licked her lips, her voice hoarse. 'You know. Bryony. Bryony brought me here.'

'But who is Bryony? Please, Stella, this is important. Michael told me you thought I was Bryony. You don't still think that.'

Stella gave a shake of her head.

'Then who is it? You're the only person here who's met her in real life.'

'I don't know. Bryony had brown hair... a mousy colour, I think.' Stella coughed, a rattling sound as if her lungs were struggling to work. 'Her eyes were blue – it's what I wrote in my book – but I don't actually remember them.'

'You don't recognise her from amongst the guests?'

Stella didn't answer but turned her head away from the beam light. 'I feel terrible.'

Mallory knelt next to the woman. 'I can get you back on the quad bike and give you an emetic at the hotel. That might help. At least let Michael look at you. He might be able to mitigate the effects of whatever laurel leaves do to you.'

'They produce cyanide. Every gardener knows it. I was so careful what I ate but I was struggling with staying indoors. I had a note under my door. Bryony was going to meet me here. She knew I'd come here even in the most terrible of weathers.'

'Was there anyone here?'

'I think so. The light was on but as I stepped into the building I was overcome by a feeling of sickness. Then someone hit me on the head. When I came round, I was on the rack.'

'Let me see.' Stella's cropped hair made it easy to check for injuries and Mallory couldn't see any blood. Internally, she had no idea what damage had been done to the skull. A gust of wind reminded her of their vulnerability. She pulled the radio out of her rucksack. 'Elsa are you there?'

The radio crackled to life. 'Are you OK? I saw the light signal. It's not Bridget Marsh, is it?'

'Don't be ridiculous. I've found Stella and she's feeling a bit under the weather. Can you get me Tom? He won't leave the kitchen so you're going to have to go to him yourself.'

'Wait a minute,' said Elsa and the radio went silent.

Mallory turned her attention back to Stella. 'We'll get you back to the hotel in a jiffy. Michael said you'd been invited to the island.'

Stella made a stab at laughing. 'I fell for an obvious ruse. I received an anonymous message that I'd find Bryony here this weekend. It seemed to be sent from heaven. I'd put some feelers out to see if I could track down Bryony. I'd approached her legal team and put in a request with the Home Office that I'd like to get a message to Bryony. No one replied but when I got the email, I wondered if someone had seen my letter and decided to help me along a bit.'

'A leak or something.'

'Exactly. I made the booking for this weekend but when I got here, I couldn't spot Bryony as an adult. There were women of about Bryony's age but not one of them was recognisable. That's when I thought Bryony might be you.'

'Mallory, are you OK?' Tom's voice came over the radio.

Mallory, her head pounding, updated Tom on what she had found. 'I'm going to bring Stella back to the hotel. Find Michael and take him into the spa suite. I'll bring Stella through the back door.'

'Is she OK?' asked Tom.

'She'll be right as rain.' Mallory met Stella's gaze and the woman shook her head slightly. Mallory bent down to her.

'You're sure you don't think I'm Bryony, do you?'

'I don't know.'

'Listen, I'm Mallory Dawson. I was brought up in Guildford not Wilmslow. My mother lives in Australia. I'm divorced with a child.'

'Bryony had a child.'

'What?'

'Bryony had a child. How old is yours?'

'Nearly sixteen.'

'Then they're too old. You can't be Bryony.'

'Why not?'

'In 2018 when Bryony got lifelong anonymity it was because of the existence of an offspring. The court order covers her child too.'

'You're sure?'

'I've still got contacts in the police. They couldn't tell me much. I knew at least that.'

'You think Beth Gregory is Bryony?'

'I don't know. How long has Charlotte Vass been married? I heard her daughter shout "you're not my mother" this morning. My contact might not have got all the details right. Perhaps it was on her marriage to her husband that the court order came into effect. To protect a stepdaughter.'

'Shit. Then we're no nearer to the culprit. Mona doesn't give the impression of someone with a child in tow.'

'She looks at the child a lot.'

'I'm sorry?'

'Mona looks at the little girl. When she doesn't realise she's being observed, she stares at the girl.'

'Edith Gregory? You think Edith reminds her of another child. Do you think if Bryony had a child, it might have been taken into care?'

'Would you trust The Birthday Girl with a child? Bryony was obsessed with poisons. Anyone close to her would be in danger. Can't you question the women?'

'I have no official role in the killing of Grace. Or your attempted murder.' Mallory paused. 'I have to tell you that we've lost a member of staff. Alys, who was working on reception, died yesterday evening before Grace. You were right, there was something terrible about the coffee.'

'Help me,' Stella tried to sit up. 'I'll be damned if I die it's going to be next to these fucking nuns.'

'That's the spirit. Take my coat.' Mallory shrugged off her puffa jacket and helped Stella into it. 'My guess is that the laurel has only been used for you. I don't think it's what was put in the coffee as the timings don't match – I saw someone out by the laurel tree – and I'm still trying to work out what poison killed Grace.'

'The same poison can be used in different strengths. Have you read my book? Michael told me you'd discovered it in his room.'

'Only an early chapter where you describe meeting Bryony for the first time.'

'Read the beginning of chapter six. You'll see some parallels to what's going on here. Listen,' Stella swallowed and grimaced in pain. 'There's someone else I recognise. A face from the past. They might be able to help. He's connected to Bryony.'

'Who?' asked Mallory. 'Who do you recognise?'

'Noah. I recognise Noah Vass.'

47

Noah – who said he'd recognised Grace. Who'd come to the island because Julia wanted to take a tour no one had heard of. Mallory's stomach turned as she considered the danger Noah now faced. He gave the impression of a man who could look after himself but Bryony had shown she could take even the wary by surprise. She shook Stella slightly to keep her awake.

'Tell me. Tell me how you know Noah Vass?'

But Stella had fainted, now senseless to any of Mallory's questions. Her dead weight made Mallory's task much harder as she could barely put any pressure on her painful leg. It took all her reserves to get Stella onto the front of the bike. The rain had started to flow more steadily again. Clamping her arm around Stella's waist, Mallory mounted the bike and started the engine. She was aware that in the gloom her progress was visible if anyone cared to look out of one of the passageway windows. Elsa drawing the curtains might have brought more attention to the west of the island. Perhaps even now Bryony was watching her return with her quarry.

Beneath the roar of the sea, she felt the thin spirits of the sisters urging her on. The darkness, the fear, the knowledge that something terrible was loose on the island pushed her into the land of the living. She drove on, her eyes on the building in front of her. Stella was limp and

Mallory kept her arm around her body as she drove the bike on with one hand.

The lights of the Cloister shone at her as she pushed forward. In the doorway a huddle awaited her. Elsa had her arms crossed, her face hidden underneath the hood of her coat, while Tom was clutching the walkie talkie. But it was Michael who limped out to meet them, his gaze boring into hers.

'Can we put Stella onto the massage table in the spa suite? I'll be able to get a better look there.'

Mallory felt like weeping. 'I can barely walk.'

Tom came forward out of the shadows. 'I'll carry her.'

Mallory climbed off the bike as Elsa ran to her. 'Can you feel them? Can you feel the sisters around us?'

'I can feel them,' said Mallory unsure if she was just humouring the girl or going over to the dark side. She leant against Elsa – the girl was stronger than she looked – and allowed herself to be led into the clear warmth of the spa suite.

'Get her a blanket,' said Michael over his shoulder. 'She needs to warm up quickly.'

Elsa hesitated, biting her lip. 'Do you mean Mallory or the guest?'

'Mallory. Go quickly.'

Elsa left the room, banging the door behind her. Mallory looked across at Michael. 'Thank you. She's gone, hasn't she?'

Michael looked down at the body of Stella Atkinson. 'I'm afraid so. She probably died on the trip back over here.'

'Dead?' Tom was aghast. 'From something she ate?'

'This isn't anything to do with food, Tom,' said Mallory. 'Stella has been poisoned by burning laurel leaves

248

in the mausoleum. Will you please get back to the kitchen and just stay there. We need to decide on a plan of action for dinner tonight and what to tell the remaining guests. Did you lock the doors to the kitchen?'

Tom held up a key.

'Then please get back there and devise a menu using only tinned food. Absolutely nothing else. Not even from the freezer. I'm sorry about this.'

As Tom opened the door to the suite, she could hear Edith bawling, which was what she felt like doing herself. Michael, she saw, was calm. 'Are you any nearer finding out who Bryony is?' he asked.

Mallory told him that Bryony now had a child but she still couldn't be sure which of the women it was.

'I don't think it matters. Whoever is Bryony, it's too late. People are dead, and trying to identify the killer is an impossible task for a single person. The whole point of poison as a method of killing is that the guilty can be far removed from the victim. From what I read of the book, Bryony is an obsessive and very good at hiding it. What's the matter?'

'Stella told me she recognised Noah Vass before she died. I need to speak to him urgently.'

They stopped speaking as Elsa came into the room. Mallory took the blanket from the girl and wrapped it round herself. 'Thanks, Elsa. Why don't you join Tom in the kitchen? He'll need all the help he can get devising a menu from tins.'

'OK.' Elsa cast a glance at Stella but left without asking any questions.

'Shall we leave Stella here?' asked Michael.

'I don't like that idea. Remember Grace's door was left wide open. I wouldn't put it past Bryony to pull the same stunt again.'

'What do you want to do?'

'I think she'd be best in the spare room opposite yours. We can lift the table. Shall I call Tom?'

'We could try ourselves?'

She saw it cost him his pride to offer. The very least she could do was to match his courage. Making sure the passageway was clear, they lifted Stella along the corridor. It was just as well the room was near. She didn't think her leg would take any more weight on it.

'We'll leave Stella on the table. I'll put a blanket from the bed over her.'

'I think we should finish this conversation in my room,' said Michael.

Mallory nodded and pulled the door shut. In Michael's room, she sank on the bed, not caring what he thought of her.

'Before she died, Stella said I should look at chapter six in the book. She said it gave an insight into Bryony's state of mind. Can I look at it now?'

'Of course.' He gave her the book, open at the sixth chapter.

CHAPTER 6

One of the oddest things about this case is the fact that Mrs Clive is frightened of her daughter. I've always assumed that children who commit crimes come from dysfunctional backgrounds but, unless there's something I'm not picking up, the Clives appear to be an ordinary suburban family. Benjamin Clive is a manager at the local Toyota car dealership and his wife, Rachel, owns a clothes shop. Apart from Bryony, they have another child, Adam, two years younger than his sister. DC Ellis interviewed the father at his workplace. He confessed he was keeping away from the house as he has an image of the girls imprinted on his eyelids, which strikes me as odd as he never saw the scene of death. But I do know what he means, and Benjamin Clive comes across as Mr Average.

His wife, Rachel Clive, doesn't want to be anywhere near Bryony. Of course, she's trying to hide it. Her parenting is going to be under scrutiny over the next months and not just by us. The press is having a field day and everyone wants to focus on the mother. How can you bring up a child who is a murderer? So, the natural thing to do would be to stick by your child, say that you love them despite everything. Which, to be fair, is what Rachel is doing. But it sounds forced. At least she's let me interview her at home in the little sitting room at the back of the house which overlooks the garden.

'I'd take you to the living room but I've kept Adam off school and he's watching TV there.'

'How's he coping?'

'Hard to say. I don't think he really understands what's happening. He's only nine. You don't really understand the concept of death then, do you?'

The implication is that Bryony, at eleven, did.

'I'd still like to speak to him.' I sit down on the too-squishy sofa, my fat backside sinking into its depths. 'I appreciate he wasn't present at the party but he may have seen some of Bryony's preparations.'

'That's fine. I'll sit in, if you don't mind.'

There's a silence and I'm sure she's reminded of the fact that neither parent was present during Bryony's inter-views. I ask the question that's been nagging since I was first called to the house.

'Why do you think she did it, Mrs Clive?'

The question makes the woman slump. 'Bryony's always been obsessed by poisons since we bought her a chemistry set for Christmas one year. She began by following the instructions in the pack and when she'd exhausted those experiments, she started using stuff from the garden. I though it harmless enough. I remembered mixing rose petals with water when I was a child. I thought it was just like that.'

'I guess there's a big difference between making a concoction of flowers and deliberately selecting a plant you know to be poisonous.' I see Rachel hesitate and I pounce. 'Had she used poisons before?'

The woman focuses on the swirls in the expensive-looking rug.

'Mrs Clive?'

Rachel looks at me, her face pale.

'Nothing I can prove.'

'But…'

'But I think she's been poisoning all of us for months.'

49

Mallory looked up from the page. 'I don't know why she directed me towards this.'

'It means that Bryony is happy to poison everyone,' said Michael. 'Nothing is a coincidence. Your headache, you've been poisoned. Ditto Edith's drowsiness. There's both a grand plan and a willingness to improvise. That's Bryony's hallmark. These last few hours will be the deadliest. Bryony is happy to target anyone.'

She stood, her body weary from fear and lack of sleep. 'It's simply confirmation of what we already knew. None of us are safe – and that includes you, Michael.'

He said nothing to her for a moment. She took in his waxy skin, but Michael, although attractive with his sculpted features, never looked well. 'I'm all right. Look, this is what's bothering me. You have three suspects for Bryony: Mona, Charlotte and Beth. They don't all look alike, even though they're a similar build. We think Grace recognised Bryony straight away, so why couldn't Stella identify her?'

'She says she didn't see enough of Bryony to get a permanent impression of her. Perhaps it would be more useful to ask how Grace recognised her.'

'We're not going to find that out though, are we? It could be the way she walked, laughed even. The adults, Stella and Noah, wouldn't have known this. Grace would.'

Michael shifted in his chair. 'OK. Let's take their appearances. Mona has bright red hair. Do you think it's dyed?'

'Undoubtedly.'

'What else distinguishes her?'

Mallory considered. 'She's very thin. Far thinner than the others, although a similar build. Stella also thought she takes an unnatural interest in Edith Gregory.'

'Ensuring the safety of the child needs to be our main priority. OK, Charlotte.'

'Mid-brown hair, blue eyes. She has Bryony's colouring but I think her appearance comes from hours at the makeup mirror. She gives the impression of spending a lot of attention on her looks.'

'That's more interesting, but if you wanted to alter your appearance, surely you'd make more of an effort.'

'But that's my point. She does make an effort.' Mallory remembered the powder and ointments at Charlotte's table.

'OK. And Beth.'

'With Beth I struggle to get past the exhausted-mother look. Her fair hair is dyed but the brown roots are clearly visible, suggesting she doesn't have the time to make much effort with her appearance. No makeup, as far as I can see. If she's Bryony, she'd be the easiest to recognise.' Mallory sighed. 'I just feel we go round and round in circles.'

'If we agree Alys was the first poisoning, can we rule anyone out? She was sick about five-ish as she was coming off shift. All three suspects were here.'

'Mona was, I'm sure. She must have been as she wasn't on the last boat coming over. Charlotte and Noah had checked in the day before.'

'That would be quick work on Charlotte's part to go to the kitchens and poison the food.'

'I have a horrible feeling that wouldn't stop Bryony,' said Mallory.

'And Beth?'

'She was out on the mainland. I saw them return but I've no idea how long they'd been there.'

'That's the whole point of poison though, isn't it? The killer doesn't need to be nearby. It removes killer from victim.'

'I don't think that's much of a priority for Bryony, but you're right, it still could be Beth. What gets me is, from what I know about Bryony, she was proud of the publicity she received. That was the dominant part of her personality, the thing that made the press turn against her. I don't see it in any of our three women.'

'Which means she's hidden it,' said Michael. 'Which makes her especially dangerous.'

–

Charlotte was alone in her room. The bed linen was rumpled on the side of the bed Mallory had seen Noah lounging on the first evening of their stay. Mallory could sense his absence. The bathroom door was ajar and hanging from it was a green waxed jacket, the rain falling in rivulets from it and forming a pool at the base.

'Has Noah been out?' Mallory picked up the jacket, which was too large to belong to Charlotte. Yet it was the woman who blushed.

'It was me, I'm afraid. I was feeling cooped up so I stood briefly under the canopy at the front of the hotel. I used Noah's jacket as it's the most waterproof but I got that wet just standing still.'

Mallory looked closely at the woman. It was an unnecessarily long explanation, which put her senses on high alert. She put the heavy jacket back on the door. 'It's your husband I wanted to see. Is he around?'

'He's gone for a wander around the hotel. He seems agitated about something.' She smiled. 'Even more agitated than usual, I mean. He's been like a cat on hot bricks all afternoon so I told him, well as much as you can tell a man like Noah, that he needed to expend some energy.'

Again, that long stream of information. Mallory shifted her opinion of Charlotte again. Perhaps she was just a woman who needed to explain her position in life.

'I'll go and find him.' Mallory hesitated. Here was a chance to find out about Noah if he didn't want to talk to her himself.

'What does Noah do?'

'Noah? He's a criminal barrister. He and his brothers all went into the law. James Vass didn't pay a fortune in school fees for them to lounge about.'

Which explained the ease with which he took charge of his daughter after she found Grace's body. Mallory was aware of being wrongfooted again. She'd pegged Noah down as an arrogant oaf, she was right about the arrogance but, as a barrister, he had as much insight into the criminal mind as she did. He was also a potential victim of Bryony – and Mallory had his wife on her list of suspects. Mallory groaned. She should surely rule Charlotte out. Noah would know if he'd married a killer. And yet, Mallory knew of prison authors who married convicts they'd met in prison, guards who had relationships with their wards. It was possible, just possible, that Noah knew who Charlotte was and had married her anyway. No wonder he had been so insistent when asking questions about Grace's cause of death. Stella's revelation about Bryony and a child could be in relation to Charlotte's marriage to Noah. Even the acquisition of a stepdaughter would trigger interest from authorities.

'I'll go down and talk to him.'

She found Noah in the library. For a man with restless energy, he was oddly still. He was sitting at one of the tables, his elbow resting on the table. He started slightly when she appeared.

'Can I talk to you?'

His eyes narrowed. 'What has Julia been up to now?'

'It's not about Julia. It's about Bryony Clive.'

'Bryony.' He let out a sigh. 'Yes, I thought, at some point I'd need to have a conversation about Bryony. As soon as I heard the name Grace Pagonakis, I had a horrible feeling the past was coming back to haunt me.'

'Who told you Grace's name?'

'My wife wheedled it out of your waitress.'

'You do know Bryony's here? That's my assumption.'

'Is she? I rather hoped we'd be dealing with a pale imitation. She became infamous enough, didn't she? I think there might even have been some copycat poisonings around the world.'

Mallory's heart sank. 'So you haven't recognised her amongst the guests?'

He shook his head, but kept his eyes on the table.

'Noah, it's important. Are you absolutely sure you haven't seen Bryony here?'

'No.' He held her gaze, his amber-flecked eyes reminding her of a lion's.

Mallory sat opposite him. 'Tell me about her. Anything you remember. Anything that will help.'

He put his hands in the air, a gesture of defeat. 'It was one of my first murder trials and, of course, the most famous. I was the junior defence barrister so it was an exciting case to be part of but we never really expected her to get off. The idea of diminished responsibility was hard to argue when confronted with Bryony, who was highly intelligent and perfectly aware of what she'd done.'

'How did she look?'

'Pretty insignificant. She wore glasses, which were pretty, a sort of turquoise blue, but it meant that the rest of her face was hidden. You sort of focused on the glasses, if that makes sense. Brown hair that she wore in a ponytail. At first, I felt sorry for her. She was tiny in a courtroom of adults. She sat at the bench with a social worker next to her. For support, but the social worker was more upset at the evidence in the trial than she was.'

'The newspaper reports emphasised her lack of emotion.'

'Exactly. We tried to argue a diminished responsibility plea but the judge wasn't having any of it.'

'And she was found guilty.'

'Exactly. Except…'

'What?'

'Well firstly she was irrationally angry about the testimony of her friend, Grace Pagonakis. If anyone's got reason to be angry, it would be Grace. She sees her schoolfriends poisoned and then is nearly killed herself. I'd be pretty upset. But Grace was a lugubrious child. A sort of plodder who gave her evidence in this adenoidal voice. I remember the only time I saw Bryony angry was after she'd given her testimony in court.'

'What was it in particular that upset her?'

'I think it was the fact Grace was giving evidence for the prosecution. I think she'd not expected any survivors and Grace laid the afternoon events out in their appalling glory.'

'If she's on the island, it's a pretty good motive for Grace's death. Why was no photo of Bryony produced? We have them for other child killers.'

'That's the problem. A few of them have been identified as an adult. If you have a photo, you have an image to compare it with. There are experts in ageing children's faces. After the guilty verdict, the stringent reporting requirements weren't lifted.' Noah drummed his fingers on the table. 'So, I'm afraid you've only got my memory to go on.'

'And Stella's.' Mallory decided, for the moment not to inform him of the woman's death.

'Stella?'

'The guest with the orange glasses. She was a DS on the case. She wrote a book about her experiences under the name of Anna Kirby. It was called *The Birthday Girl*.'

'Never heard of it. And she's here?' His face darkened. 'Then she needs to be bloody careful. Do you know why we're here? Someone sent an email to Julia saying a great aunt of her mother's was a nun on this island and was involved in a poisoning. There was a tour being organised – a one-off – and it was to come this weekend or forever miss the opportunity.'

'Bridget Marsh.'

'That's not her name.'

'I mean Bridget Marsh was the girl who was poisoned. Julia was sent an email?'

'Exactly. And Julia, of course, loved the story. She's had a rough time at school. She was in a fair bit of trouble last year and, after a lot of therapy, we think she's on the straight and narrow. But of course, that makes her a loser in her friends' eyes. She asked me to book a weekend here.'

'When did she ask?'

'A few weeks ago. Now I'm wondering if I've been played.'

'Noah. You have got to be very, very careful. Stella Atkinson is dead.'

'What?' He stared at her. At last she'd shocked him.

'I found her dead. I can't tell you the whole story now but believe me you have to protect yourself.'

'And my family.' He stood but Mallory saw his hands were shaking.

'Noah. I need you to confirm this one more time. You absolutely don't recognise Bryony now? There are some female guests here about the right age for Bryony. Beth Gregory, for example, the woman with the young child. Or Mona with the red hair. Stella even thought it was me.'

He looked up, startled. 'You?'

'It's not me, I promise.'

He shook his head.

'I know this is going to sound strange, but you're absolutely sure that Charlotte isn't Bryony, aren't you?'

He looked back at her, his eyes shrouded. 'Give me some credit for knowing my own wife.'

50

Mallory pushed the doors open to the kitchen. The conversation with Noah had left her concerned about his attitude towards Bryony. Like Stella and Grace before him, he wasn't fearful of the former child poisoner, more angry about her subterfuge. Did this mean, despite his protestations, that his wife was in fact Bryony? The girl was emerging to Mallory as a chameleon, capable of changing her visage at will.

'How are you getting on?' she asked Tom.

'I was on a submarine for a bit. This type of cooking reminds me of those times. Food from a tin.'

'What are you making?' Mallory felt the deep weariness of the sleep deprived and very sick. Her wound, now pulsating with an infection despite her careful ministrations, plus the legacy of the coffee and burning laurel meant all she wanted to do was curl up under her bedclothes, preferably in her cabin.

'Tomato and chickpea curry, tinned-crab fishcakes, butterbean cassoulet.'

'I'm impressed.'

Tom hesitated. 'I don't want you to think I'm telling you how to do your job but don't you think people should be eating in their rooms? It'd be safer.'

'I promise you it wouldn't. Even if I declare a complete lockdown so no one can leave their rooms, it's harder to check on everyone behind closed doors. It's poison we're dealing with. The person doesn't need to be in the room, which means the damage could have already been done. Putting everyone together means I can keep an eye on the guests. It's the only way.'

'You're not telling the others about Stella?'

'Noah Vass knows, but I doubt he'll be speaking to anyone else about it. We'll make the same plans as we did when Grace died. If anyone asks, we say she's in her room.'

'That went well last time.'

'Listen, Tom. It's six o'clock now. It's less than twelve hours until help. We just need to keep calm.'

'What about Elsa?'

'She doesn't need to know about Stella. Her body is in room six on the ground floor. It's not where she died but there's nothing we can do about that for the police investigation.'

'How do you think this is all going to pan out, Mallory? The hotel will never survive.'

Mallory thought of the ghoulish tourists taking photos of themselves in front of the crypt.

'I wouldn't be sure about that.'

–

The Gregory family were the first down to dinner. Beth had rallied and made an effort with her dress and makeup. It seemed a strange thing to do in the circumstances but if Beth wasn't Bryony, she wouldn't know another death had occurred. It might be a way of keeping up her spirits. Mallory couldn't remember seeing makeup in Beth's room, but a cosmetics bag would have been hard to spot amongst all the mess. Scott, carrying Edith in his arms, was sullen, still smarting from Mallory's rebuke in the boathouse, she suspected. He kept his eyes on his wife, his concern evident. Edith was snoozing in her father's arms. There was a small sofa in the far corner, little bigger than a tub chair.

'Why don't you let Edith sleep on the cushions? She looks exhausted.'

Scott looked at his wife, who nodded. Mallory wondered if she'd got the dynamic wrong between them. Beth had claimed responsibility for their trip to the boat-house and Scott had been willing to let responsibility lie with his wife. Here, he'd also deferred to her. Mallory watched as he placed Edith on the sofa.

Noah came in with Julia and took one of the tables with just two chairs.

'Charlotte won't be coming down this evening. She has a headache.'

'Is she OK?' asked Mallory.

Julia raised her eyes to the ceiling. 'Nerves.'

'How are you feeling?' Mallory asked the girl.

'All right considering I found a dead body.'

Mallory made a stab at humour. 'Something to dine out on when you get back to school.'

'Thanks a lot. My friends think I'm a freak as it is. I still haven't found what I came for, either.'

'What's that?' asked Mallory, keeping her eyes on Noah.

'We, believe it or not, had a relative who was part of the order of nuns. But I've not even had a chance to discover any more about her.'

'I see. I don't think anyone's written a history of the place. There's just the sheet in the hotel brochure. Have you found your relative in the photo?' asked Mallory.

'What photo?'

'I'll get Elsa to show you after dinner. There's a large image in the sitting room. She can finish telling you the story of the sisters.'

Julia, suspicious to the last, smiled grudgingly. 'OK.'

Mona and Michael came into the room together, Mona laughing at something he'd said. Mallory was shocked by the spurt of jealousy she experienced at the sight of the pair together.

'Would you like to sit at the same table?' she asked.

'Perhaps we should save a space for Stella too,' said Mona. 'I'm sure she'd want company.'

Mallory didn't look at Michael but concentrated on Mona whose pale, lightly freckled face gleamed in the discreet lighting.

'Stella is in her room tonight,' she told the woman who was moving away, her eyes on Edith.

Mallory took the order for drinks. Noah wanted a bottle of red, requested with a wink at Julia who would clearly be getting a glass or two too. Mona and Michael were sharing a bottle of white. Scott wanted a beer and Beth a lemonade. With everyone served their alcohol, Mallory placed unopened bottles of fizzy and sparkling water, all with their seals intact, on the tables.

Elsa was hard at work in the kitchen. 'I want us to work in relay,' Mallory told her. 'If you're in the dining room, I can be here. And vice versa. I don't want the dining room left without either of us being there.'

'You don't think there'll be more trouble?'

'I'm not sure, Elsa.' Mallory had decided to tell Elsa about Stella as soon as dinner was over. The girl was bright, if naive, and she could easily stumble over the body in room six. She thought Noah most likely to be in danger despite his assurances he could look after himself. They would also need to work out sleeping arrangements to get themselves through to the morning. As with dinner, Mallory favoured some kind of shift pattern where one member of staff was always awake. Mallory hoped the weather forecast hadn't changed in the meantime. She was holding on to the fact that help would come with the morning light.

Tom had excelled himself in his dishes. 'You should write a cookbook,' Mallory told him as she surveyed the array of pots.

'It was harder without spices. Luckily, I had a new plastic bottle of salt in the shed otherwise they'd have been eating bland food.'

'You definitely checked it?'

'I promise I did. I've also tried each dish in the saucepan. You keep the plate in your hand as I dish up and take it straight to the guest.'

'Thank you.'

Mallory and Elsa were absorbed for the next hour and a half, serving dishes and refilling glasses. The guests were subdued but relaxed and all had clearly decided to ignore the wind, which was having its last hurrah outside. The clouds in the pinkish night sky were blowing out into the sea. The sting in the storm's tail. Mallory could feel the calm coming.

51

After dinner, the guests dispersed slowly, unwilling to return to their rooms, which must surely feel like a prison now. Noah was hugging his bottle of red wine next to his bored daughter. Eventually, Julia left her father brooding as he doodled on a notepad. Stella's absence went unremarked – the guests had turned inward as they awaited rescue. Mona and Michael left the dining room together, but Michael dawdled, looking like he wanted to speak to Mallory. Mona clearly wanted to stay and join in the conversation but, after receiving no encouragement from Michael, made her way up the stairs.

'What's the matter?' asked Mallory.

'What do you think is the matter? I was just checking you were OK. Did you speak to Noah?'

Mallory looked around and grimaced. She pulled Michael into her office and shut the door. 'He was one of the defence barristers at Bryony's trial. So he's in danger but insistent that he can look after himself.'

'That's ridiculous. I can't speak for Grace, but Stella was no fool. She still died.'

'He's a grown man. I've told him that Stella's been killed and made sure that tonight's food was safe. I'd bet my life on it.' She saw Michael's face. 'Sorry, wrong expression I guess.'

'I think you should confine everyone to their rooms.'

Mallory sighed. First Tom and now Michael were advising this. Given that dinner was over, it wasn't a bad idea. It was dark outside and the storm still blustery.

'OK. Let me start by helping shut down the kitchen and the downstairs rooms. Then I'll visit each room individually.'

Tom and Elsa sprang apart when Mallory entered the kitchen, Elsa's face flushed.

'How long will it take you to clean up here?' asked Mallory, taking in their guilty expressions. Tom looked away, refusing to meet her eyes.

'I've been doing it as I went along,' he said. 'Probably another hour or so. I need to run the dishwasher a few times and swab everything down.'

'Fine. Can you do that by yourself? I want Elsa to help me with something.'

'Of course.'

Elsa gave Tom a backwards glance but came willingly towards Mallory. 'What is it?'

'Once you've cleared the dining room, go and knock on Julia Vass's door and tell her the story of the Companions. Take her to see the photo too. Afterwards, I want to make sure everyone is in their rooms and I think the only way to do that with Julia is to satisfy her curiosity. It's the reason she asked Noah to bring her here. A distant relation came here, apparently.'

'What was her name?'

'I've no idea. Sorry. You can ask her that, can't you?'

'OK.' Elsa unpinned her apron. 'I've cleared away most of the tables. It's just that big man with the blond hair left. Julia's father.'

'I'll go and move him along. We've enough to do besides sitting and waiting for him.'

But when they entered the dining room, Noah had left, taking his wine bottle with him. 'Just give the table a wipe. I'll be back in five minutes to lock up.'

Mallory was shutting up the drinks room when she heard a sound behind her. She turned, her senses on high alert, but Mona stood in the corridor. She'd slung a cardigan over the long woollen dress she'd worn at dinner.

'Is everything all right?' asked Mallory, testing the handle to ensure the door was shut.

'I wondered if you had any news when help might arrive.'

Mallory moved on to the dining room. Elsa had left and the tables were cleaned but left unlaid for breakfast. Too much was at risk to leave unattended cutlery on the table. Mallory pulled the door and locked it. She'd still be able to access the kitchen from the door at the end. For now, though, this room was out of bounds. She also wanted to show Mona that every room was being locked.

'Help will be here at first light, I think. The storm's dying down, I'm sure of it.'

Mallory wondered if she was giving Mona the timescale in which her retribution would come, but was too tired to care. Charlotte, Mona or Beth, it would all be revealed soon. 'Are you all right, you look a bit feverish.' Mona lifted an arm to touch Mallory's forehead.

Mallory pulled back. 'I'm fine. It'd be great if you spent the evening in your room. I'm keen that everyone is kept safe before help arrives.'

'Of course.' Mallory followed Mona down the corridor. At the lobby they parted ways, Mallory went into her office while she heard Mona's tread on the stairs. Mallory searched through her drawers for painkillers and saw she'd used most of her stash in the hotel. If she wanted more of the strong stuff she needed to get back to her cabin. After swallowing two dihydrocodeine Mallory tried to stand but her leg buckled underneath her. She didn't dare take off her trousers in case she did more damage to the wound. Once the hotel was shut up, she'd risk a trip to the cabin to sort herself out.

She needed to shut off the living room but Elsa was hopefully taking Julia to see the photo. Instead, she went to the spa suite to close it for the night. None of the guests had shown any indication that they'd be going to the pool so now was the time to shut everything. As she approached the doors, with her radio in hand, she noticed a set of footprints, like the ones she'd seen on Friday evening. This time they were leading into the room. Pushing open the doors, she checked and locked the treatment room where they'd first put Stella. The empty space where the massage table once stood was an unwelcome reminder of Stella lying a few doors down. She made to lock the sauna when her eye was caught by a shape in the hot tub by the far end of the pool. Alex hadn't skimped with the design. Although he didn't welcome parties, the tub was big enough to accommodate a man of Noah's size. He was face down, a grotesque starfish in the turquoise water. Next to it was the bottle of red wine he'd been drinking and an empty glass.

Mallory stopped, spinning around to check she was alone. 'Tom,' she spoke into her radio. 'Are you there?'

'Is everything all right?'

'Can you come to the spa suite? Don't make a song and dance about it.'

As she waited, Mallory entered the water and grabbed hold of Noah to turn him over. The chemicals scorched her leg wound as she ineffectually tugged at Noah's shoulders to try to dislodge him.

'Jesus.' Tom leant over the tub.

'Pull him out, for God's sake,' she said. 'I'll try resus on him.'

Noah was too large for Tom to pull the dead weight of his body from the water. Mallory pushed the man, grasping Noah's knees as Tom heaved him out. Mallory wondered how much damage she was doing to herself in the pool. She now saw poison everywhere, its insidious tentacles extending into every fabric of the building.

'I'll do the resuscitation,' she said, heaving herself out of the water. 'I need to check there isn't still poison around his mouth.' Looking at his throat and tongue, she couldn't see anything suspicious and she began to pump his chest. 'Get the defib from the office. It's worth a try.'

Tom disappeared, leaving her to continue the resus, the spa suite eerily quiet. When water began to spurt out of his mouth, she had a moment of hope, but his heart refused to come to life. She was pretty sure it was useless. Noah had died from his heart or lungs giving way, not from drowning.

Tom returned with the machine. 'I saw Charlotte at the top of the stairs. She seemed to be looking for Noah.'

'Shit. She didn't follow you here, did she?'

'Definitely not. I checked.'

'Good. This is the last thing she wants to see.'

'Do you know how to use it? I had training on it a while ago.'

'No need. I've used them before.' Mallory unlocked the machine and, peeling off the protective strips, placed the pads on Noah's chest. She turned on the machine and waited. A computer voice told them a shock was needed.

'Stand back, Tom.' Mallory pressed the button. There was no discernible movement in Noah's body and the machine informed her to continue CPR.

'What do you think?'

Mallory began on his chest again and looked up. 'I don't think it's going to work. This machine is for unresponsive patients with a problem with their heartbeat. It's not like you see in the films. If he's flatlined, it's game over. I just need to be sure we've done all we can until help arrives.'

Tom looked at his watch. 'In about seven hours.'

'If the weather hasn't changed, we are looking at about that time.' Mallory carried on with the CPR. After five minutes, she shook her head.

'We're going to need to leave him here. Cover him with some towels from the linen store. I'll go and tell his wife. We'll need to decide about Julia too.'

'Then what?' She saw Tom's face had a sheen of fear. 'Are you feeling all right?'

'Oh, I'm fine. I've had three tins of peaches today and I definitely checked the seal.'

But it's not just food, she wanted to tell him, but she needed all of Tom's confidence over the last few hours.

'Look, I'm going to go back to the shore. I managed to get a very weak signal there earlier when I was rescuing the Gregory family. I'm worried that as they only know about Grace's death, getting to us isn't a priority. I know Alex will be desperate to come but he needs to bring the police. I'm going to make the journey right now.'

'In the dark?'

'It's all I can do. I don't want them to wait until light. The wind is calmer already. I need people over here. Even if it's in a helicopter.'

'But what happened? It can't have been the food, I was so careful.' Tom wrung his hands. 'I'm never going to get a job as a chef ever again.'

Mallory bent over the wine bottle and sniffed it. 'I opened the bottle of wine and checked the cork. I doubt it was tampered with at dinner.'

'When then?'

Mallory looked around. Noah must had returned to his room briefly to pick up his swimming trunks. Unless he'd carried the wine around with him from the dining room, which Mallory thought unlikely given Charlotte's disapproval, what was much more likely was that he'd brought the wine to the spa and decided to finish the bottle while enjoying the pool and spa. That was enough time for Bryony to strike.

'He was careless,' said Mallory, 'but his is going to be the last death, I promise.' In her sopping clothes, she helped Tom cover Noah's body and locked the room.

52

Mallory knew she looked a fright but, given Charlotte was looking for her husband, she could not leave breaking the news of Noah's death until she'd changed into dry clothes. Charlotte was in the room with her door open, pushing a jumper into an expensive-looking holdall.

'Going somewhere?'

Charlotte jumped and clutched her chest. 'God, you frightened me. You said help was coming in the morning. I can't sleep so I might as well make myself useful.'

She was wearing a cashmere tracksuit, which clung to her thin frame.

'Can I come in? I need to speak to you.'

'What is it?' Charlotte's tone was irritable. When Mallory didn't answer, she stopped what she was doing. 'What's the matter? Is it Julia?'

'It's Noah.' Mallory closed the door behind her.

'Noah?' Whatever she'd been expecting it wasn't this. 'What's happened?'

'I'm afraid we've found Noah dead in the hot tub.'

'Dead?' Charlotte's expression changed from irritated to stupefied, her eyes glassy. She sat on the bed with a thud and Mallory took the clean glass from the table and filled it with water from the bathroom tap.

'Drink this.'

Charlotte gulped at the water. 'Dead?'

'I'm afraid so. I'm not sure how he died.' This at least was partially true. 'I'm so sorry, but I think it's best we leave his body where we found it.'

Charlotte rose. 'Can I at least see him?'

'I can't allow that, I'm sorry but it's best you don't see him until the police get here.'

'You think it's connected to the other girl who died?' Charlotte finished her water and placed the glass carefully on the table.

'Yes, I think it is. Can you tell me what happened after dinner?'

Charlotte let out a puff of air. 'I came back to the room first. Noah arrived a bit later. He's been in a funny mood all evening. He couldn't settle and obviously had a lot on his mind.'

'How long was he here?'

'Barely five minutes. He grabbed a towel, changed into his trunks, put on a dressing gown and left.'

'Did he have his bottle of wine with him?'

Charlotte frowned. 'I didn't see any wine.'

She'd been right. Noah must have left his drink by the hot tub while he came up for his shorts. 'Does he usually have a swim after a big meal?'

Charlotte kept her eyes on the carry bag. 'I suppose it was out of character for him. Only…'

'Only?'

'I got the impression he was enjoying some kind of subterfuge. He had that schoolboy's suppressed grin that he always adopts when intrigue is in the air. By intrigue, I mean a sexual dalliance.'

'He was unfaithful to you?'

'Always. I know his type too. Women like me. Tall and bony. It was inevitable he'd be attracted to her.'

'Who?'

'Mona.' Charlotte looked surprised. 'Who else?'

'You think he was due to meet her?'

'I think so. He doesn't get excited about much except women.'

Mallory looked at the holdall that Charlotte didn't seem able to take her eyes off. 'How exactly did you and Noah meet?'

Charlotte winced. 'Noah and I met in court.'

Mallory held her breath. Had she got it all wrong and was this Bryony? 'And when was this?'

'The autumn of 2014. I was being prosecuted for shoplifting.' Mallory exhaled, her head spinning. She grasped the bedpost and tried to focus her thoughts.

'And he defended you?'

'Good God, no. I'd be too small fish for Noah and, in any case, he'd never have married one of his clients. No, we met in a corridor when I spilled my coffee on the floor. He helped me mop up. Noah can – I mean could – be chivalrous when he wanted to be.'

'A shoplifting charge?'

Charlotte nodded, her expression miserable. Her eyes dropped to the holdall again. 'Would you mind if I had a look in there?' asked Mallory.

Charlotte shrugged and took a step back, leaving Mallory to open the bag. Underneath a cashmere jumper were three silver necklaces in their boxes and an intricate ring. All sold in the boutique near the top of the path.

'How did you get into the shop?'

'I took a bunch of keys from the office behind reception. I found them on a hook. I was sure that one of them would fit. They were nothing like the keys to the hotel room so I assumed they were for outside.'

'When was this?'

'Friday evening after dinner.'

'Do you still have them?'

Charlotte shook her head. 'I put them back at lunch-time on Saturday.'

In time for Bryony to pick them up and open Grace's door.

'You're clearly a natural. Tell me, does the name Bryony Clive mean anything to you?' Mallory asked.

'She was one of Noah's early cases. He told me about it once. I think she creeped him out to be honest. You don't think…'

Mallory shrugged, a wave of weariness washing over her. 'I don't think anything. Are you going to tell Julia about her father's death or would you like me to do it?'

Mallory shrank from the look of relief on Charlotte's face. 'Will you do it? She hates me. She calls me the klepto.'

And that, thought Mallory grimly, is what you are, but at least you're not The Birthday Girl.

53

Julia wasn't in her room and Mallory had a pretty good idea where she'd be. It was less than an hour since she'd told Elsa to help Julia with her research and, sure enough, in the sitting room, the two girls were peering at the photograph of Margaret Taylor and her Companions. Elsa had her finger on the glass and together they were studying each sister in turn.

'How are you getting on?'

Mallory's question startled the pair. They took in Mallory's wet clothes and rat-tailed hair and huddled slightly together.

'We can't work out who is Julia's great aunt,' said Elsa. 'Her name's Davina Cowell.'

'Have you looked behind the picture,' said Mallory, lifting the photo. 'There might be a list of names on the back.' She was putting off the inevitable but even a few minutes respite from the horror around her was helping. Together the three of them looked at the dull brown hessian backing.

'No names,' said Julia.

'Put it back on the wall,' said Elsa. 'Let's continue looking at the women. I spotted Alys's relative here, didn't I?'

Mallory nodded. 'You did.'

Together the girls pored over the faces. 'I can't see any family resemblance,' said Julia, finally.

It was pointless, Mallory felt like telling her. You've been duped. Either Davina Cowell isn't your aunt or she was never a nun of that name on the island. Bryony made it up to pique your interest and get your father here. Nothing more.

'Don't worry about that now,' said Mallory. 'I need to have a word with you about your father. Elsa, would you mind staying?'

Julia was white with shock as Mallory broke the news. She shook off Elsa's arm around her shoulder and ran down the corridor.

'I'll make sure she's OK,' Mallory told Elsa.

'Another death?' Elsa's eyes brimmed with tears. 'And Stella too.'

'Tom told you?'

'Yes, but I guessed.' Elsa fixed her eyes on Mallory. 'Is that it? Has everyone died who's going to?'

It was an odd turn of phrase but Mallory knew exactly what she meant. Elsa had proved her resilience and she deserved a truthful answer. 'I don't know. I'm going to the cabin to change out of my wet clothes and then I'm going to try to ring for urgent assistance. I'll stay out there all night if I must until my call connects. There's a chance I might get a signal by the harbour.'

'It doesn't usually work.'

'I know, but I need to try anyway. It's urgent. Go and sit with Tom and wait for me to get back.'

Mallory shrugged on her coat and went to Charlotte's room. The woman's eyes were ringed with red.

'You need to sit with Julia. I've told her the news. I know you don't get on but she's upset. Please.'

Charlotte hesitated.

'I need to ensure her safety,' Mallory said. 'I don't think either of you are at immediate risk. Sit with her and don't open the door unless it's to me or the police. And please, drink only water from the tap. Keep Julia away from any alcohol.'

Charlotte nodded, drawing her cardigan closer. Mallory stayed until she heard Julia open the door and let her stepmother in.

Feeling guilty about the responsibility she'd left with Elsa, she went to check on the girl. She was sitting on Tom's camp bed. Although they moved apart slightly at Mallory's appearance, an air of conspiratorial comfort surrounded them.

'Are you all right, Elsa?' The girl nodded and Mallory looked at Tom who again refused to meet her eye. Tom must be a little younger than her, late twenties perhaps. Elsa was just eighteen. In other circumstances she'd have spoken to Elsa, warned her about getting over friendly with work colleagues, but now it was the least of her worries.

'Are you OK? I'm going to my cabin now. I'll be back as soon as I can.'

Tom glanced at Elsa. 'She's safe here.'

'Are you sure about that?' asked Elsa. 'How do you know?'

'Listen.' Mallory stopped and grasped the girl by the shoulders. 'I can't be a hundred per cent about anyone. But I know who the killer is and what she does. She poisons people. Partly for pleasure and partly for revenge.'

'I don't feel brilliant, Mallory,' said Elsa.

No, she thought. Neither do I. There was a feeling of weightlessness, as if she were floating around in space.

She squeezed Elsa again. 'It'll be all right. Listen, I need to get to the shore and let them know the urgency of getting help. If I don't come back, lock all the doors and just wait. Rescue is just hours away. OK?'

'OK, but I think I might have a plan—'

Mallory groaned. 'No plans. OK? Stay in the kitchen with Tom.'

Elsa didn't answer, her expression determined.

54

Mona was in reception, dark smudges staining the skin under her blue eyes. She was sitting in one of the chairs, her feet resting on the glass table and a copy of *Vogue* on her lap. She looked up at Mallory, her gaze a challenge and a puzzle. Mallory fought the instinct to recoil from the woman.

'Can't sleep?' asked Mallory.

'No. You?'

'The same but I'm going to try. I'm off to change my clothes. I got a bit wet mopping up in the kitchen.'

Mona made no comment. Either she was the killer and knew Mallory was lying or she was innocent and unaware of the extent of the trouble they were in.

'Let me know if you need anything.'

'I might stand outside under the cover of the porch. I'm feeling a little cooped up. The weather isn't as blowy, I can hear it dying down.'

On cue, a gust rattled the broken window, shaking the wooden board Tom had nailed over the glass.

'Don't go far,' said Mallory as she pulled on her water-proof jacket, feeling Mona's eyes on her. To emphasise her point, she pulled the door shut with a thud. Don't follow me. Whether Mona was innocent or guilty, Mallory wasn't going to speak to her until she'd had time to do some thinking. She kept her head down as she pushed ahead in the steady rain. Once she'd got dry and changed her dressing, she'd try to get to the shoreline as she'd planned. Alex would be desperately trying to get a boat together, she was sure, but he couldn't know the extent of the carnage that was going to greet him. She needed to both warn him and hurry him along.

Although it had only been a day since she'd left the cabin, it felt like a lifetime. There was a strange stagnant feel to the room, the space airless despite the excess of wind outside. Mallory peeled off her jeans, grimacing as she inspected her wound. At last she had her ointment and she grabbed a handful of the gloop, smearing it over the injury and covering it with a fresh bandage. Hunting around for her warmest clothes, she pulled on her walking trousers and layered a sweatshirt onto two vests. Her feet were pale and wrinkled from exposure to the damp. She'd probably have ended up with trench foot if she hadn't changed out of her sopping socks.

She checked her charge on the phone and saw it was around forty per cent. Easily enough to make a call if she could find a signal. She found a torch and steeled herself for the walk to the harbour. *Have courage, Mallory*. After everything she'd been through – Joe's infidelity, Toby's indifference, Icebox Pete's serrated knife – she would not fail at this hurdle. As she was checking everything, a wave of nausea swept over her. She refused to panic. She'd had very little sleep and was feeling the effects of first the coffee and then the burning laurel. It was exhaustion, not poison. As she willed herself to get up, her walkie talkie sprung to life, making her jump.

'Hello.' There was a sense of déjà vu as she waited for the message.

'It's Tom.'

'Are you OK?'

'I'm fine but you'd better come back. It's Michael. I was doing a reccy on the downstairs rooms and I saw his door open. He's not looking good.'

'Fuck.' Mallory hurried back towards the hotel ignoring the wind and the rain plastering her face and through the empty reception. The door to room five was open and she saw Michael on the floor with Tom kneeling next to him. Mallory pushed the chef away.

'What's happened?'

Michael turned his face towards her. 'Sorry about this.'

'I told you to be careful,' Mallory said, lifting his head.

'I have been. I've been very, very careful.' Michael swallowed, the action painful for him and she grabbed a glass from the side of the bed.

'Let me get you some water. Listen outside, the wind has gone down a little. It's Sunday already. Help will arrive soon.'

'It's not soon enough. Can you get me some salt water so I can use it as an emetic?'

Mallory turned to Tom. 'Boil some water from the tap and add a couple of tablespoons of salt from the packet you used tonight.'

'Right.'

After Tom had left, Michael lifted his hand and grasped at her coat. 'Has something else happened? Tom is soaking wet.'

'Noah is dead. He has a connection to Bryony – he was a lawyer on her defence team. He was poisoned and it must be stronger than the stuff given to you because it stopped his heart completely.'

'Digitalis, maybe,' murmured Michael. 'It's what Bryony used at the tea party in 1996.'

'I've told Charlotte and Julia. It wasn't easy but one thing became clear. I know Bryony can't be Charlotte.'

'I'm sure I know who Bryony is.'

Mallory lay down on the floor next to him and resisted the temptation to wipe her hand across his face.

'Who? Who is Bryony?'

'I've seen Mona outside. I've got a better view than anyone else because I'm in a downstairs room.' He paused. 'Every morning and evening, at the same time, and I mean exactly the same time, I see Mona go outside with a brown case.'

'What times?'

'Seven a.m. in the mornings and six p.m. in the evening. I hadn't noticed how regular her movements were before, but I've started to write them down. Having a fixed routine would be consistent with Bryony's personality. She's used to rigid timetables – that lifestyle rubs off on ex-offenders.'

'It's her painting kit in the bag. I've seen the same case in her room.'

'She doesn't stay outside long enough to paint. She's outside half an hour at most.'

'Why didn't you tell me this before?'

'Because, like you, I thought Mona was doing her watercolours but I've been watching her.'

'Mona?' Mallory stared at Michael. 'But you had dinner with her this evening. What made you agree to that if you thought she was a poisoner?'

'I wanted to question her about her movements.'

'Jesus, and now look at you. We don't even know what you've been poisoned with.'

'It doesn't matter. It's not caustic so I have to bring it up and hang on until I get to hospital.'

Mallory thought of the prone body of Noah. 'You stay in your room. I'll get Tom to help you to bed once you've had the emetic.'

'It's worse than we thought,' said Michael. 'Every guest who's come through the hotel while she's been resident here might have been subject to her attentions. How long has she been staying here?'

'She'd been here a week when I arrived.' Mallory was thinking furiously. 'But I think you're wrong about other guests who've stayed in the hotel. All her plans have been geared towards this weekend.'

'No.' Michael's voice was little louder than a croak. 'Remember chapter six. Bryony was obsessed with poison. They discovered she'd been putting minute doses in her own family's meals. While Mona has been here, she's been trying out her poisons. The lethal doses have been reserved for her enemies.' Michael paused. 'What's the matter?'

Mallory gave a gasp of pain as her leg went into spasms. 'Don't worry. My leg is in agony. I thought it was getting better but now it feels worse. I'm also feeling sick.'

He grasped her arm, his fingers digging deep into her skin. 'Worse? How?'

'The wound has never healed properly. It's been an open sore ever since the stabbing but the stresses of this job mean I've put more pressure on it than I'd have liked.'

'But you said it was worse?'

'It's gone a strange colour, as if the skin is starting to die. I need to get it looked at when I get to the shore.'

'Do you cover it up with a sterile pad?'

Mallory stared at him. 'Of course I do. I put ointment on it first and then a dry pad.'

'Take it off.'

'What?'

'There are three main ways you can be poisoned. You eat it, inhale it or it's absorbed through the skin. You're being poisoned through your dressing or ointment.'

'Shit.' Mallory scrambled at her trouser leg, pulling it up and ripping off her dressing.

'Where do you keep the cream?'

'In my cabin.'

'Mona probably poisoned it when you were at work. Do you keep it locked?'

'When I'm sleeping, yes. Not always during the evenings. There's nothing to steal in there.'

'Then Mona's paid you a visit.' Michael mopped his brow. He was beginning to develop the ripe scent of the sick. 'Go to the shower and wash your leg. Put the water on as hot as you can stand it. Then use a towel to pat it dry. Please, Mallory, be quick.'

Mallory's head swam as she climbed to her feet. In the bathroom, she stripped off her trousers and angled the shower head over her leg. She closed her eyes and leant into the pain. When she could stand it no more, she used a clean towel to press into the wound and limped back to Michael.

'What poison do you think it is?'

'I don't know. Didn't Catherine De Medici kill one of her rivals with infected gloves? Any poison can be made into an ointment and smeared onto material. How do you feel?'

'Like shit, but not like I'm going to expire.'

'Same here, and it's no coincidence. Bryony was an expert in poisons. She knows what kills and what merely makes you sick. Alys had an underlying issue, remember.

She has nothing against us so we're merely part of the theatre.'

'There was never any chance that Grace, Stella or Noah would survive,' said Mallory. 'For them, it was personal.'

'The problem is that we can't be a hundred per cent sure she doesn't have someone else in her sights.'

At the thought of the poison seeping through her body, Mallory felt a surge of fury. As she stood, Tom came into the room, wiping his mouth.

'I've tested the drink myself.'

'Good. Take Michael to the bathroom and then put him to bed. I'm going to find Mona.'

55

Julia was playing music in her room, the sound of the heavy beat seeping from under her door. It matched the thud in Mallory's head. In ordinary circumstances, she'd have knocked and asked Julia to turn it down but anything that helped the girl get through the night was fine with her. She suspected few of the other guests were sleeping – the calm dawn only hours away. Mallory pressed her ear against the door and heard muted voices. Charlotte was talking to her stepdaughter, giving comfort however poor their relationship was while Julia sobbed with terrible heaves. The sound steeled Mallory's resolve. The girl had lost her father. Whatever Noah's shortcomings had been, he didn't deserve to die like that.

At Mona's room, she tapped quietly on the door and braced herself for the confrontation, but her knock remained unanswered. Digging into her pocket, Mallory once more used her master key to open a guest bedroom door. She stepped inside the empty room, noticing that the space was immaculate. Mona was extraordinarily tidy, giving a glimpse of what her cell must have been like in prison. It possibly was why Mona had chosen a long-term stay in one room. The effect of a well-appointed, luxurious cell.

Mallory opened the wardrobe and ran her hands along the long dresses and cardigans that were Mona's style.

The items were closely packed together. Like most hotel rooms, guests weren't given a huge amount of wardrobe space. Mona's scent wafted off some of the items, her signature floral perfume. Another clue Mallory had missed – the love of nature even in her choice of scent. Mallory looked around. There were no signs of packing.

Mallory sat on the bed and thought. As a child, Bryony hadn't made any attempt to hide her crimes and despite the empty room, the absence of evidence of flight suggested Mona would once again brazen out her capture. Mallory rubbed her face. Something wasn't sitting well with her reasoning, and she had a fair idea why. The poison coursing through her was muddling her head, making clarity difficult. Think. As an eleven-year-old, Bryony had been willing to admit her actions even if she'd been unclear what incarceration had meant. Her talent suggested she had thrived in the reform school system, nurtured perhaps by a supportive art teacher. A creative profession was one of the few careers where a criminal conviction might not cause any long-lasting damage. As Mona, Bryony had been self-employed and had avoided any detection.

If Stella had been right, there was a child involved somewhere. Mona was rake thin and hardly maternal. Yet she appeared fascinated by Edith. The scar of having a child removed might just account for Mona's thirst for revenge. Mallory remembered when Joe had told her about his last affair. That had been bad enough, although it was simply another infidelity among so many. It was the fact that this other woman was carrying Joe's child that had spurred Mallory to rage. For a moment, as he'd told her without an ounce of regret, knowing it would spell the end of their marriage, she'd wanted to kill them all. Joe, the other women and, yes, the child. No one ever spoke about that, did they? No one discussed that you could be a cop *and* a potential murderer.

Mallory shook away the thoughts. Mona was no potential murderer but a convicted killer who had surely struck again and again in the Cloister. But where was her poison? Mallory thought she knew every room in this hotel and had seen no chemistry workshop. Mallory's gaze fell on the old leather case that Michael had also spotted. Mallory opened the case and looked at the watercolours. Some were in a palette but there were also bottles of varying viscous liquids. Mallory picked one up and sniffed it.

'What are you doing?'

Mallory jumped and faced the woman, trying to hide the terror that the sight of her induced. Mona's curly red hair was like Medusa's, wild snake-like curls sprung from her head in damp spirals.

'I'm looking through your paints.'

'And that's enough explanation? I think I deserve a little more. I am entitled to my privacy.'

'Are you?' Mallory swallowed, the roof of her mouth parched. 'Perhaps you lost any rights when you came here under false pretences.'

A sweep of emotions crossed Mona's face. 'I see. And what, may I ask, are you intending to do about it?'

Mallory stared at the woman. 'Do about it? I'm doing nothing. My job is to keep everyone safe. The police will be here and they will want to talk to you.'

'OK.' Mona picked up a towel and began to rub her hair. 'I just went out for a walk to see if the weather had calmed. I can't sleep knowing we'll be rescued soon. Can I ask what you're doing with my case?'

'I'm wondering where you kept your poison and I think this is a good a place as any. Do you want to tell me what's in each of these bottles?'

The towel slid out of Mona's hands onto the floor. 'Poison?' She looked at the pot of red liquid in Mallory's hand. 'What are you talking about?'

Mallory's world spun and shifted. She felt her strength ebb as she stumbled over to a chair, collapsing into its depths.

'Are you Bryony Clive?'

'Bryony Clive.' Mona stopped aghast. 'Who— you mean The Birthday Girl? Of course I'm not.'

Mallory shook her head, trying to think. 'You're not?' She gazed up into Mona's face but only saw embarrassment and confusion. Bryony had been proud of her crimes and Mona's reaction wasn't fitting. Mallory tried to stand but her leg wouldn't hold beneath her.

'I don't know whether to laugh or cry. I've done lots of things in my life but I've never killed anyone. Are you OK?'

'No, I'm not.' Mallory was beginning to shiver. 'When I said you were here under false pretences, why didn't you deny it.'

Mona put her hands in the air, a gesture of defeat. 'Let's forget it.'

'I don't think so.'

Mona sighed. 'OK, OK. I'm not just here illustrating my book. Painting is a side-line for me. I'd never make enough money to earn a living.' Mona paused. 'I'm an environmental scientist. I work for an organisation who wanted to buy the Cloister to make the island a centre of nature study. Negotiations were at an advanced state, we had Cardiff University on board, until Alex, with his city money, came in and outbid us.'

'Bloody hell.' Mallory rubbed her mouth, aware it was becoming increasingly difficult to swallow.

Mona sat on the bed. 'I am here under false pretences, you're right. We haven't given up on Eldey. We're hoping to show that excess tourism to the island is having an effect on the wildlife. I'm taking samples and I send them off for analysis. Look.'

Mona crossed the room and lifted her paints out of the bag. Underneath, in a concealed compartment, was a test tube rack and vials of chemicals.

'These haven't been touched by anyone else?'

'I promise you, no one has got near my bag. I negotiated a deal with Alex to get the room at a reduced rate. He liked the thought of having a sort of artist in residence. I take samples of soil, foliage and so on and do an initial processing here. Then I send samples to my company for full analysis. I cross over to the post office on the mainland every few days.'

'Shit – was it you I saw outside my cabin on the night of Grace's death?'

'Probably. As part of the study, I take samples at the same time of the day, early morning and late evening. However, I'd been asked to do some extra leaf analysis and I took a risk going out in the storm. The thing is, while I was out there, I also saw someone else. I saw—'

'Beth Gregory.'

'How did you know?'

'It doesn't matter.' Mallory was sick to her stomach. She had gathered all her reserves for this confrontation with Mona and she had made a fatal miscalculation based on Michael's hypothesis. She would need to track Beth down and face a foe all the more frightening, one in the guise of a washed-out young mother. There was one final question she needed to ask Mona.

'Stella thought she saw you looking at Edith. It made us wonder if you'd had a child.'

Mona made a face. 'I wish. My biological clock is ticking. I need to stop making stupid relationship decisions, and I include Alex in that, and settle down.'

On shaking legs, Mallory finally heaved herself up. 'I have to go. Just one final question. What was it with you and Noah Vass?'

'Noah? Nothing at all. Why do you ask?'

'He seemed to have a thing about you. I wondered if you knew each other already.'

Mona shrugged, a woman who knew the powers of her own attraction. 'He had his eyes on every female in this place. It was him who was watching me through the glass when I was swimming, I'm sure.'

'I saw the bedsheets.'

'Oh, that.' Mona laughed. 'Alex and I have become close quite quickly. Unfortunately, he's going to be furious when he realises who I really am.'

56

BRYONY/BETH: THE BIRTHDAY GIRL

She had precious little time left. Her strength was leaving her and she had the final part of her plan to put into action. It had split her poisoned heart to leave Edith, but her child would be fine. The anonymity order would stand even once her activities on Eldey became public knowledge. The press wouldn't like it, of course. They'd hated her from the start and she'd had to count her lucky stars that they'd named her The Birthday Girl when the nickname could have been much, much worse. She couldn't believe they'd sent her to that crummy detention centre. She'd had an idea she'd go to reform school, which would have been fine. A nice library to continue her research and hopefully access to a garden. That's all she needed. You could make a poison out of many innocuous flowers and shrubs. Instead, the centre had been surrounded by patchy asphalt with a brick wall encircling the perimeter. When she realised the staff were watching her carefully, she'd changed her plans.

Her GCSE in chemistry had been hidden amongst the handful of other qualifications. There had been a bit of bother when it came to A levels but she managed to convince the institution's director she was interested in science. By the time she'd been accepted on the Open

University degree she was in an adult prison and authorities had more dangerous inmates to worry about.

Her only job on release had been with a prison charity. A waste of her talents but it had brought her Scott, whose mother was a director on the board of the organisation. Even she had blanched at her son marrying the infamous Bryony Clive, but Beth had maintained her façade, produced a grandchild and, when the press came sniffing around again, secured a whole-life order protecting them all. What not a single person in authority nor her family had realised was that Bryony had old scores to settle. She might maintain the façade of a happy family life. Why not? She had served her sentence, and marrying and producing a child had given her an air of normality. Reformed Bryony. But outside was no better than within. It had taken her a few years to understand this but her future held no joy. Her obsession was reeling out of control once more and even Edith was beginning to suffer from her mother's warped passion. That was the trouble with poison. A little bit goes a long way. It was time to bring everything to a close on her terms. After she had exacted her revenge.

Beth regarded the boat. She'd need to be quick as her strength was seeping out of her. She dragged it slowly. Mallory – oh so clever Mallory – had done her best to incapacitate the vessel. However, all she needed to do was get it onto the sea. After that, what happened, happened.

She was glad it was over. Glad she'd done what she'd done – she'd never have settled into family life. She'd never met anyone as clever as herself, no, not even Mallory, and she knew now she never would. Her final act would be to step into that void and experience what her school friends had suffered. The ultimate triumph.

57

'Please help us, Beth's gone.'

Scott Gregory's skin was the colour of a bleached pebble. He carried Edith in his arms and Mallory noticed the child was alert once more as she concentrated on chewing the edge of a blanket.

'Do you have any idea where she might be? I need to find her urgently,' she asked.

Scott's expression changed to one of acute misery, his mouth settling into a thin line. 'She's gone outside. She's taken her coat and boots. I thought she might be heading to the mausoleum on the other side of the island. She told me she was desperate to see it and it would be just like Beth to do whatever she wants.'

'The mausoleum? OK.' Mallory swallowed at the thought of returning to that place.

'But…' Scott pulled Edith into his chest and she let off a wail of protest. 'She might have gone back to the boat-house. You interrupted us, and Beth doesn't like unfinished business.'

Mallory took a step back at his words. 'Then that's where I'll go first. If she's not there, I'll carry on to the crypt.' She paused taking in the father and child. 'How long have you known?'

'Known what?' Even his response was half-hearted. The game was up.

'Known that she's Bryony Clive.'

Scott shrugged and turned his face away from her.

'You married her knowing she was a killer.'

'She served her sentence. She never made any effort to hide what she'd done with me. She told me on our third date and I knew she was an ex-felon through my mother's charity. She wanted it to be out in the open. She was terrified the newspapers would track her down. They were always trying. People wanted to write a book, an article, a radio drama. She's been given protection but what's anonymity these days where anything can be put on the web? It was only when Edith was born that we began to feel safe. A judge put a whole-life order to protect us all, but especially our child. We began to feel less hunted.'

'I honestly don't think you know your wife at all.' Bryony turned Beth had simply been biding her time. 'Beth is obsessed by poisons. You must have heard about the case beyond what she discussed with you – she was infamous. Haven't you been afraid?'

Scott was defiant, his face in high colour. 'I've never been afraid of my wife.'

'But look what she's done here.'

'You can't prove anything.'

Mallory, aware that sweat was pouring from her skin, grabbed Scott's arm and dug her fingers in hard. 'I bloody well can and the police will be able to prove plenty too. Why's she decided to settle scores suddenly? She got Grace, Stella and Noah to the island under false pretences. Why go to all that trouble?'

'Beth has a long memory.'

'I bet she has. But why now?'

'There's a new book coming out by that woman, Anna Kirby. She's been putting out feelers, trying to track down Beth, who got wind of her enquiries.'

'But Beth's identity was hidden by law. You said things got easier after Edith's birth. You'd have been protected from any exposure.' Mallory was overcome by a spasm of pain. She had to get down to the boathouse.

'Anna, or Stella, which was her real name, didn't want to expose Beth, she wanted to work with her. But Beth had never forgiven her for the original book. It was all lies and sensational claims. Beth asked me to look after Edith while she met Stella. She told me she wanted to reason with her.'

'We know how Beth reasons with people. What about Grace?' She saw his confusion. 'The girl who died on Saturday night.'

'I know nothing about what happened to her.'

'You sure?' Mallory stared hard at him. His answer would make a difference to whether he'd be given his freedom to bring up Edith or would be prosecuted alongside Beth for enabling the killings. 'And Noah?'

Scott opened his mouth. 'What about him?'

Mallory turned. Scott would find out soon enough about the body count of Beth's revenge plans. 'I have to find her. If you're lucky, you might find a lawyer who will prove you knew nothing about your wife's intentions. But tell me, how do you think Beth would react if you did something to upset her?'

Scott didn't answer but Mallory heard Edith say, 'Where's Mama?'

Mallory forced herself to look at the child. 'I'm going to find Mama now for you.' The eyes that looked up at her were identical to Beth's. A series of images flashed through Mallory's brain. Elsa pointing at Bridget Marsh in the photo and noticing her likeness to Alys. Elsa again in front of the photo looking for Julia's relative using the same method. She realised with a sudden clarity how Grace had spotted Beth as Bryony. It wasn't Beth who'd looked like her childhood friend, but her daughter. It was Edith she'd been looking at when she'd remembered the tragic birthday tea.

–

The dry clothes she'd donned were soaking within minutes as Mallory battled the dying storm. She'd found a pair of gloves in her jacket and even the meagre warmth on her hands made her feel better. The rain cooled her fever a little. Her mind felt a little less woolly although her eyesight was beginning to blur at the edges. Mallory shook her head, clearing water from her face, and ploughed across the grass. She no longer cared who was looking at her from the window – her foe was no longer hidden behind her. She would get to Beth and lock her in the boathouse until help came. Alys, Grace, Stella and Noah. They all deserved justice whatever their personality flaws. She remembered this from her policing days. How she would have liked Shan next to her, urging her to keep going. She conjured a mental image of her colleague and tramped on. As she got to the top of a path she saw another figure, too small to be Beth, rush across the lawn.

'Go on,' screamed Elsa. 'Don't worry about me.'

'Get back inside,' Mallory shouted.

Her words fell on deaf ears as Elsa plunged on. 'I'll be fine,' the girl shouted back. 'I'm getting help.'

Mallory pushed on to the path, taking care on the treacherous cobbles. Although blowy, she was steadier on her feet than during her last trip. The lull was coming and the pitch black was turning the murky grey of a September morning. As she neared the bottom of the path, Mallory could see a light in the emerging dawn moving away from the boathouse down the shingle towards the sea. Mallory picked up her pace, the light rain pitting her face. She was hobbling, her numb leg slip-sliding underneath her as she concentrated on the light. It was only as she neared that she realised the glow was placed beyond the sweep of the beach. Beth had launched the boat and was trying to start the engine, desperately tugging at the motor to get it started.

'You won't get anywhere,' Mallory shouted across the water. 'I've drained the engine.'

Beth ignored her, still pulling at the chain until, giving up, she lifted an oar and began to row. Her movements carried her further from the shore – she was heading east and the swell pushed the boat up and down in the murk. Mallory focused on the waves – in the distance there would soon be a glimmer of yellow from the rising sun.

'It's over, Bryony,' shouted Mallory, but Beth pulled harder on the oars, battling the swell of the tide.

'Shit.' Mallory zipped up her jacket. Thank God she'd put on her windcheater rather than the puffa jacket she sometimes used. The thick down would have been useless in the water, pulling her into the sea's depths.

She moved forward to wade into the water, conscious of the danger Beth, the sea, and her weak body presented. I want to survive this and see Toby again, thought Mallory. I was mad to come here.

'Go back,' Beth shouted. 'Leave me alone.' Her voice had an odd note to it. A crack that Mallory hadn't noticed before.

'You know I can't do that.' The Arctic-cold water was up to her neck. The days of freezing showers had given her some resilience but this was something else. There was only one thing for it. She took a plunge and dived in keeping her head above water and pushing through the swell with a front crawl. Beth should have been able to get away from her. Mallory would be no match for a strong rower, but she saw she was gaining on the boat. Beth had, unaccountably, stopped rowing.

'Go back.'

Mallory plunged ahead until she reached the orange boat and grasped at a handle. She heard Beth drop the oars. 'What's that noise?'

Mallory forced herself to listen above the slap of the waves to a sound that was tolling out across the bay. A bell. Someone was ringing the bell tower – a call for help across the waves. Elsa, thank you, she offered up to her colleague. 'It's the cloister bell. It's calling for help. It'll soon be over, Beth. Beth?'

Above her had gone quiet and as she hung on to the ropes, she was aware of a dangerous warmth seeping through her. She had no strength to get herself onto the boat and it would be here, after everything, in these waters, that she'd die.

58

Exhausted, Mallory clung on to the dinghy. The swell pushed her body up from the sea like a mermaid before sucking her back into its inky blackness. She could hear Beth, or Bryony, trying again to start the motor. The engine spluttered but failed to catch and it wasn't a blessing. Once Beth realised the futility of trying to start the boat, she would turn her attention to Mallory and that would be the end. Mallory, never a strong swimmer, could not let go of the grips and attempt to get back to shore. The poison in her surgical pad had seeped through her body and weakened her already low defences.

In the distance, she could hear Elsa continuing to toll the cloister bell as if it were her own life rather than Mallory's that depended on help arriving.

'Hold on, Mallory. Hold on.' Elsa's surprisingly loud voice rose across the bay, mingling with the screeches of the gulls. It caught Beth's attention too.

'Why did you come after me?' she asked Mallory, turning away from the inert engine. 'If you'd stayed on the shore, you'd have got rid of me. You'd have done your best. No one would have judged you. Why carry on chasing me?'

'Once a cop, always a cop. Sorry.'

Mallory's teeth were chattering, and she was losing all feeling in her fingers despite her leather gloves. Through sea-watery eyes, Mallory saw that Beth was clutching her chest as she tried to speak. It was as if she too was having life sucked out of her. The feeling Mallory had experienced on the beach hadn't been an illusion. The girl was losing some of her frightening potency.

'You should have just let me go. I'm not – not sure – how much strength I have left.' On her hands and knees, Beth slowly crawled towards Mallory.

'What have you been poisoning us with, Beth?'

Beth stopped and lay on her front, her breathing laboured. Despite her exhaustion, she sounded triumphant. 'Cherry laurel has a number of uses. The berries infused in coffee make the drinker very sick, depending on how much has been ingested. Laurel leaves when burned in concentrated amounts produce hydrogen cyanide, which is lethal in high doses. Cyanide mixed with sodium hydroxide creates sodium cyanide. It's the same stuff Nazi war criminals used to kill themselves.'

Mallory saw that Beth was proud of her knowledge of chemistry. 'Which is what you used to kill Grace.'

'Of course.'

'And Noah?'

'Well, Noah was on his guard, wasn't he? I had some digitalis with me for old times' sake.'

So Michael had been right. Noah's heart had stopped and her ministrations with the defibrillator had been in vain.

Still on her stomach, Beth crawled forward, her pale face glowing with elation. 'And for the finale, *Conium maculatum*,' she whispered in Mallory's ear. 'It was always going to be my poison of choice.'

'For me?' Mallory asked her.

'No, for me. Hemlock. Do you know I killed myself on Thursday?'

Mallory blinked to bring the spectre in front of her into focus. The salt in her eyes helped, the sting counteracting the dangerous heaviness in her head. 'What do you mean?'

'Hemlock takes forty-eight hours to do its worst damage. It gradually reduces your ability to breathe, especially if you keep taking minute amounts. Very soon, it shall stop my lungs altogether. It's the poison of Socrates. The preferred choice of the intelligent and brave. He stayed lucid until the very end, as will I.'

'Use the paddles,' Mallory coughed as a wave splashed her face. 'We can row back to the beach and save ourselves. There must be an antidote for hemlock.'

'On no. This is the end for me. I don't want to be saved and I don't want to go back to prison. The end is as I planned.'

'This isn't like you, please. You were happy to serve your time before. Why end it differently this time?'

'Because everything's the same whether you're in prison or out. There is no freedom.'

'Please help me then,' said Mallory. 'I have a son.'

'And I have a daughter.' Beth's face was next to Mallory's once more.

Mallory felt two arms pull at her shoulders. Beth's strength was leaving her but even being lifted half a foot out of the water allowed Mallory to lift her knee onto the boat's edge. 'Pull my body too.'

Beth reached over and grasping Mallory's trousers, dragged her over the edge into the dinghy. Mallory screamed as she hit the deck, her wounded leg in agony.

'Mallory! What's she doing to you?' she heard Elsa shout over the radio.

Mallory winced as bile rose in her throat. 'Thank you,' she said to Beth.

'No need to thank me. You will tell everyone that I wasn't sorry. That this was my plan all along.'

'What did you put in my cream?' she asked Beth. 'Will I die in forty-eight hours too?'

'It was poison from the berries. Not enough to kill you. I just wanted to slow you down. Your wound will heal and Michael's too. Tell him next time to check his shaving brush.' Her breathing had become a rattle as Beth lay down in the boat next to Mallory, her face turned upwards towards the slate-grey sky. 'What was it like?'

'What do you mean?' Mallory looked around for a blanket to put over them. Their bodies were open to the elements and they would die soon from exposure if the poison didn't get them first.

'How did you feel when the poison was working?'

'I felt terrible.' Mallory moved her head and saw a flash of disappointment on Beth's face. She wanted the specifics, Mallory saw. The agonies and sweats in gruesome detail. Mallory would not feed her obsession. 'Aren't you at all sorry for any of the deaths? Grace had watched you kill her friends. Didn't she deserve to live?'

'It was a scientific experiment. That's what you need to understand.'

'Why Eldey? Why settle old scores now?'

'Eldey because of Bridget Marsh. It's always been an island of women and it was just too perfect when I got an email advertising this place. I remember it from my childhood holidays on the mainland opposite Eldey. I wanted to visit but my mother was having none of it. "Shrivelled up nuns," she'd called them. There were only about five residents left by then but I was so desperate to visit. I read Stella's book, you know. She said she never forgot the girls lying on the ground at the tea party. Of course she didn't. And you'll never forget what happened here.'

Mallory could feel the wind on her cheeks. All her energy had disappeared. It felt like the end of time and also the beginning. 'Why now, Beth?'

Bryony Clive who'd become Beth Gregory closed her eyes. 'I just told you, I can't help it. There's no reason. I just wanted to see some of the players from that time again. The people who contributed to my downfall. Noah made his reputation in my case, Stella her fortune, Grace had a life I'd been deprived of. I heard about this place and thought, why not?'

'You sent Beth an invite for a competition win and Stella received an anonymous tip-off that she could find you here. You were sure they'd come.'

'I was sure. Noah was more unpredictable. I remember his arrogance from the trial. I did wonder at maybe getting to him through his wife, but Julia seemed an easier bet.'

Cruel to bring a child into her scheming. 'There was never any relative who was an Eldey nun?'

'Of course not.'

'But what about the weather?'

Beth shrugged. 'I was always going to get caught. The weather just made things a little more fun.'

'You weren't actually trying to escape at the boathouse then?'

'It was Scott's dumb idea. I went along with it for a bit of distraction.' Beth winced and put out her hand. 'I can't help myself. I'm not sorry.'

Beth heaved as the air in her lungs gave out. It reminded Mallory of Stella's last gasps although Beth had ensured a more peaceful passing for herself. She watched Beth struggle to take in the sea air, her body desperately clinging to life in its final seconds.

'Help is coming,' said Mallory, but Beth's gaze lost all awareness.

With a final breath, she died, as did Bryony Clive. In due course, Mallory would mourn the passing of the adult Beth who she'd stood next to at the window, watching the storm pass across the island not realising that inside the woman, Bryony Clive had never gone away. She would not mourn the passing of Bryony. Prison had only blunted the edge of her obsession, not eradicated it. The final act of her mania had been to drink the poison of Socrates and see if she too remained lucid until her death. As always, Bryony had been right.

'Mallory,' said Elsa over the radio. 'Are you OK? The boats are coming. I can see them now.' Elsa continued to toll the bells even though the help she was calling for was responding to the peals.

Mallory lifted her head and rolled over so she could see the lights of the town. Two boats were making their way towards them. The lifeboat had been launched and was slicing through the waves towards her dinghy while Owen's tug was heading straight towards the landing stage. You can stop ringing the bell, she wanted to shout at Elsa but there was an inevitability about the heavy clang that fitted the drama of the moment as she rose and fell in the boat next to Beth's body. It tolls for me, she thought, before her tired body blacked out.

59

Mallory knew she was still on Eldey before she opened her eyes. Her ears were assailed by the thrum of the sea. Not the violent booms that had shaken the building at the height of the storm but the steady ebb and flow of the waves hitting rock and shingle. There was also the lingering smell of seaweed and beeswax, the latter testament to Elsa's cleaning. It was far removed from the antiseptic odour of the hospital room that she'd endured after her accident. She lay still as her tired brain brought into focus a jumble of memories – the bodies of Alys, Grace, Stella, Noah and finally Beth, the smell of the rubber dingy she'd desperately clung on to, the sound of the bell tolling. She gathered her courage. The storm had passed and whatever she faced, she wouldn't be cut off from the rest of the world. The last thing she had seen, before everything went dark, was help arriving by boat. She turned her head and forced her eyes open, frowning as a face swam in front of her blurred gaze.

'Toby.' She reached out and grasped her son's hand. 'You made it. Your dad left a message to say you were on your way.'

'He's furious. I left without telling him.'

'I know.' And it was all her fault, according to Joe, but criticising her ex in front of their son would be a mistake. 'Why did you decide to come here?' The poison that Beth had smeared into her ointment was still doing its work. Mallory rubbed her head, trying to make sense of it.

'After I spoke to you, it was on the news that there was flooding in South Wales. I checked on the internet and it said no boats were going to Eldey. When I tried to call you back, the phone was down. I wanted to check you were OK.'

And have an adventure, thought Mallory. Behind the concern, she could see a spark of excitement. Perhaps that was what Toby had needed all along – a bit of independence – instead of two anxious parents hovering over him.

'How did you get here?' she asked in a whisper, conscious her throat was red raw.

'By train, idiot. How else?'

Mallory felt pinpricks of tears behind her eyes. 'But—'

'You sounded so scared when we spoke. I'd never heard you like that before. I took some money I'd stashed away and came to stay with you. I've got a plan – I'm going to ask the hotel for a job. School sucks, London sucks. Only, when I got to the harbour, the place was wild. It was like a scene out of *Titanic*. They directed me to Owen who was waiting for a lull to get to you.'

'Owen? Thank God you found him.'

'He couldn't sit still. He'd heard something about the first lady who died from your boss, Alex. I've met him too.'

Mallory pushed herself up. 'What were you thinking of? And, no, you can't have a job here.'

'What were *you* thinking of? You've been like Miss Marple.'

Mallory groaned. 'I feel as old as Miss Marple. Why am I still on the island?'

'We're waiting for an ambulance boat. Michael, the man with the stick, said it was too dangerous to put you in the tug, you might get hypothermia. It was more important to warm you up first.'

'How is he? And for God's sake, don't let him hear you calling him the man with the stick.'

'He looks ill, to be honest. He said he'd wait for your boat. He won't leave the island until he knows you're safe, Mum.'

Mallory wondered if that was a note of sly amusement in his voice; her son teasing her about her love life.

'You were the first to arrive?' asked Mallory. 'When I was lying on the dinghy, I saw boats in the distance.'

'Owen brought me and Alex over in his boat. The lifeboat got to you first. Mum,' Toby paused. 'Have you any idea how many dead people there are on the island?'

Mallory's head began to pound. 'Um, four. Grace, Stella, Noah and Bryony, I mean Beth.'

'The Birthday Girl.' Toby's eyes were round. 'Four dead people on a small island. That's sick. You'll be famous.'

'Five dead people including Alys. Don't forget her too.' Mallory looked at Toby. He was the son of two coppers. The apple hadn't fallen far from the tree. She could feel his excitement.

'If only my life was always this exciting.'

She felt him squeeze her hand. 'Can I stay with you for a bit? Please. I've already mentioned it to Alex and he said it was OK as long as you said yes.'

Mallory swung her legs around, her head still thudding, and gently tested one foot on the floor. 'You need to go back to school.'

'Holidays, then. I could come for vacations, couldn't I? Did you know there's a crypt at the other end of the island?'

A wave of nausea swept over Mallory. 'I know,' she said.

'So, what about it? A job in the holidays?'

He was as persistent as his father. 'Maybe. I'm not sure I'll be able to stay. I need to see what the permanent damage is to my leg. Anyway, guests might be in short supply once the news is out.'

'The news *is* out. You've been on BBC news and it's all over the internet. I was listening to it in the kitchen with Tom.'

'Tom, is it? You have got to know everyone. What did they say?'

'That four bodies have been found on the island in a story reminiscent of an Agatha Christie novel.'

'Oh no, poor Alex.'

'What do you mean? Alex says the website's had more bookings this morning than in the last week. Everyone's desperate to come.'

'It's true.' Mallory saw Alex standing in the doorway. 'As Elsa already knew, it appears that everyone loves a murder.'

'Alex,' Mallory's voice dropped to a whisper as Toby left the room to check for the boat. 'It's horrific what those people went through. Beth was a monster. You can't trade on that.'

'The Birthday Girl meets her nemesis on Eldey island. I'm not going to promote it but we're going to need the bookings to make up revenue. The forensic team are likely to be here for days. They want to talk to you, of course.'

Mallory groaned. 'Can you help me up?'

'I'm not sure that's a good idea. Can't you wait for the ambulance?'

'No. How's Elsa?'

'On the mainland. She was a bit wet after ringing the bell but was more concerned about you. Once she knew you were OK, she was happy to leave the island. I wanted her home with her family. I've got a horrible feeling she might not be coming back, which is a shame as she was a good worker.'

'With the heart of a lion.' Mallory sat back on the bed, her head spinning.

'Tom went with her. In fact, everyone's left except Michael. He wouldn't go while you were still ill.' Alex looked at Mallory. 'Will you be coming back?'

'I think I've a son who's fallen under Eldey's spell.'

'There's a holiday job here if he wants it. He's too young to be here by himself. There are strict employment rules for under sixteens.'

'We'll see.'

There was a knock on the door. A man in a pale cream mackintosh came into the room. Stocky with a head of curly brown hair. He pointed towards the door with his thumb.

'Out.' Toby and Alex obliged without a word.

'DI Harri Evans, I presume.' Mallory swallowed, trying to fight down the nausea.

The corners of his mouth rose as if to smile but he thought better of it. 'Quite a mess here. When you've been checked over by the hospital, you and I need to have a chat.'

'Suits me. I'm waiting for the ambulance, I believe.'

'Change of plan. The closed launch is here. There's an ambulance on the quayside waiting for you.'

'What about Michael?'

'Doctor Hutton? He's coming with you. We think he's not as well as he's making out to be. He'll join you on the boat.'

'It's over though, isn't it?'

'I suppose so. I wish to God she hadn't chosen my patch for her games.'

'She knew the island from her childhood holidays. There's something potent about the legend of Bridget Marsh. You know it?'

This time he smiled. 'One of my mam's favourite stories. Reckon it's not the first time Eldey has had a killer. You know, you could put me out of a job if you carry on like this. Four murders and you clear them up within forty-eight hours.'

Mallory groaned. 'Not quick enough.'

'Seriously though, you staying around for a bit?'

Mallory looked up at him, surprised. 'You mean on Eldey?'

'Well, not specifically Eldey, but us detectives at Dyfed Powys are chronically understaffed. We've always got a bit of consultancy work. It's all the rage.'

'I… I'm not sure, Harri.'

'Well, no need for you to make a decision now but—' he tapped his jacket pocket '—I've got your number. Ready to go?'

Toby materialised to help her down to the mooring. She was put in the golf trolley – for the first time since her arrival, she was happy to be helped into the buggy. Toby climbed in beside her. In his hand he held a sandwich. 'I found some stuff in the kitchen,' he told her.

Mallory took it out of his hand and threw it onto the lawn.

'I thought you wanted me to eat more.'

'The birds can have it,' she said as they bumped down the hill towards a covered police craft waiting for her.

'The ambulance is already at the harbour. We'll have you across in a jiffy.' Mallory allowed a policeman to help her onto the boat while Toby's long legs hopped over the side. From the top she could see Michael standing next to the bell tower.

'I've sent the cart back up for him and we'll be off,' said the copper. 'CID are with the bodies. They'll want to talk to you later.'

Mallory watched as Michael turned to greet the cart.

'He seems nice, Mum,' said Toby, giving her a side-eyed glance.

'He is nice. But my priority is getting better and being with you.' Mallory leant back and closed her eyes.

Toby shrugged, trying to hide his pleasure. 'He could visit.'

'He could,' agreed Mallory.

She kept her eyes shut as she felt the boat rock as Michael climbed aboard.

'How are you, Mallory?' he asked.

'I feel terrible.' She felt him put his hand in hers and give it a squeeze as the motor on the boat gave a roar. As they sped off, she opened her eyes and looked not at Michael or her son but at the disappearing façade of the Cloister as it receded into the distance. Near the bell, she saw the figure of DI Harri Evans watching them leave. He raised his hand briefly at the cruiser and turned back to the hotel. Harri, she suspected, wasn't a man to take no for an answer. She wondered when the first call asking for help would come.

She gave the island a final look. Eldey. The island of the devout and not so devout. And now with another layer to add to its history.

AUTHOR'S NOTE

Dear Reader

I spent my childhood in South Wales and one of my earliest memories is going on a school trip to the atmospheric and slightly frightening Caldey Island. I was entranced by the place but in terror of the community of religious brothers who lived in the monastery there. There was something so completely other about the island and I've always wanted to incorporate this wonderful place into my fiction. Before writing *The Birthday Girl*, I read a book about Graham Young, known as the teacup poisoner. Graham had a fascination with poisons all his life and it got me thinking how someone with this obsession would act if they had the chance to take revenge on the people who brought them to justice.

The Birthday Girl is the first book in my new Pembrokeshire based series featuring former Met detective Mallory Dawson. Using Caldey as my inspiration, I created the fictional island of Eldey where a former convent has been converted into a luxury boutique hotel. I have a passion for old churches and other historic buildings. My mother, Enfys, grew up inside what was then called the Welsh Folk Museum at St Fagans as my grandfather, Garfield, was employed as one of the first stonemasons there. I consider my obsession with old buildings to be in my blood!

I loved writing the book and I hope you enjoyed reading it. You can find out more about me at www.crimepieces.com, on Twitter @sarahrward1 or on Facebook @sarahwardcrime.

Best wishes

Sarah

ACKNOWLEDGEMENTS

I always wanted to set a book in Wales, where I spent part of my childhood, and revisiting Pembrokeshire for this novel has been a delight. Thank you to my editor Siân Heap at Canelo for her enthusiasm for the book and forthcoming series, and to my agent Kirsty McLachlan at Morgan Green Creatives for continuing to champion my work.

Tony Butler is a keen-eyed early reader of my novels and I'm always grateful for his and his wife Judith's support. Crime writer Julie-Ann Corrigan saw an early draft of the opening of the novel and gave me excellent feedback. Thanks too to other supportive colleagues including those in the Crime Writers Association and to the still-meeting Covid coffee club members: Vicky Dawson, Ettie Williams and Joanne Williams. Thanks to the Royal Literary Fund for providing, through the Fellowship scheme, time for me to write and to the readers who chat on my Saturday morning Facebook posts. We have a lovely community talking about books, if you want to join in at: https://www.facebook.com/SarahWardCrime

Love and thanks, as ever, to my husband Andy. Also to Dad for continuing to send my books far and wide to his friends and relatives, and to Adrian, Amelie, Ed, Katie, Jacob and Luke. Thanks too to my family in Wales who gave me a warm welcome when I dropped by on my research trips. Anita and Anwen, Heulwen and Steve, Eryl and Eynon, Annette, Lynwen and Hywel and especially my cousin and family history co-conspirator Gareth, to whom this book is dedicated.

Do you love crime fiction and are always on the lookout for brilliant authors?

Canelo Crime is home to some of the most exciting novels around. Thousands of readers are already enjoying our compulsive stories. Are you ready to find your new favourite writer?

Find out more and sign up to our newsletter at canelocrime.com